eleanor & park

also by rainbow rowell

attachments

eleanor & park

rainbow rowell

 st. martin's griffin ❧ new york

ELEANOR & PARK. Copyright © 2013 by Rainbow Rowell. All rights reserved. Printed in the United States of America. For information, address St. Martin's Press, 175 Fifth Avenue, New York, N.Y. 10010.

www.stmartins.com

Design by Anna Gorovoy

Library of Congress Cataloging-in-Publication Data

Rowell, Rainbow.
    Eleanor & Park / Rainbow Rowell. — 1st ed.
        p. cm.
    ISBN 978-1-250-05399-2 (International Edition)
    [1. Love—Fiction.   2. Dating (Social customs)—Fiction.   3. High schools—Fiction.   4. Schools—Fiction.]   I. Title.   II. Title: Eleanor and Park.
    PZ7.R79613Ele 2013
    [Fic]—dc23

                                                                    2012042136

St. Martin's Griffin books may be purchased for educational, business, or promotional use. For information on bulk purchases, please contact Macmillan Corporate and Premium Sales Department at 1-800-221-7945, extension 5442, or write specialmarkets@macmillan.com.

International Edition: October 2013

20 19

For Forest, Jade, Haven, and Jerry—
and everyone else in the back of the truck

He'd stopped trying to bring her back.

She only came back when she felt like it, in dreams and lies and broken-down déjà vu.

Like, he'd be driving to work, and he'd see a girl with red hair standing on the corner—and he'd swear, for half a choking moment, that it was her.

Then he'd see that the girl's hair was more blond than red.

And that she was holding a cigarette . . . And wearing a Sex Pistols T-shirt.

Eleanor hated the Sex Pistols.

Eleanor . . .

Standing behind him until he turned his head. Lying next to him just before he woke up. Making everyone else seem drabber and flatter and never good enough.

Eleanor ruining everything.

Eleanor, gone.

He'd stopped trying to bring her back.

august 1986

1

park

XTC was no good for drowning out the morons at the back of the bus.

Park pressed his headphones into his ears.

Tomorrow he was going to bring Skinny Puppy or the Misfits. Or maybe he'd make a special bus tape with as much screaming and wailing on it as possible.

He could get back to New Wave in November, after he got his driver's license. His parents had already said Park could have his mom's Impala, and he'd been saving up for a new tape deck. Once he started driving to school, he could listen to whatever he wanted or nothing at all, *and* he'd get to sleep in an extra twenty minutes.

"That doesn't exist!" somebody shouted behind him.

"It so fucking does!" Steve shouted back. "Drunken Monkey style, man, it's a real fucking thing. You can kill somebody with it. . . ."

"You're full of shit."

"*You're* full of shit," Steve said. "Park! Hey, Park."

Park heard him, but didn't answer. Sometimes, if you ignored Steve for a minute, he moved on to someone else. Knowing that was 80 percent of surviving with Steve as your neighbor. The other 20 percent was just keeping your head down. . . .

Which Park had momentarily forgotten. A ball of paper hit him in the back of the head.

"Those were my Human Growth and Development notes, dicklick," Tina said.

"I'm sorry, baby," Steve said. "I'll teach you all about human growth and development—what do you need to know?"

"Teach her Drunken Monkey style," somebody said.

"*Park!*" Steve shouted.

Park pulled down his headphones and turned to the back of the bus. Steve was holding court in the last seat. Even sitting, his head practically touched the roof. Steve always looked like he was surrounded by doll furniture. He'd looked like a grown man since the seventh grade, and that was before he grew a full beard. Slightly before.

Sometimes Park wondered if Steve was with Tina because she made him look even more like a monster. Most of the girls from the Flats were small, but Tina couldn't be five feet. Massive hair included.

Once, back in middle school, some guy had tried to give Steve shit about how he better not get Tina pregnant because if he did, his giant babies would kill her. "They'll bust out of her stomach like in *Aliens*," the guy said. Steve broke his little finger on the guy's face.

When Park's dad heard, he said, "Somebody needs to teach that Murphy kid how to make a fist." But Park hoped nobody would. The guy who Steve hit couldn't open his eyes for a week.

Park tossed Tina her balled-up homework. She caught it.

"Park," Steve said, "tell Mikey about Drunken Monkey karate."

"I don't know anything about it." Park shrugged.

"But it exists, right?"

"I guess I've heard of it."

"There," Steve said. He looked for something to throw at Mikey, but couldn't find anything. He pointed instead. "I fucking told you."

"What the fuck does Sheridan know about kung fu?" Mikey said.

"Are you retarded?" Steve said. "His mom's Chinese."

Mikey looked at Park carefully. Park smiled and narrowed his eyes. "Yeah, I guess I see it," Mikey said. "I always thought you were Mexican."

"Shit, Mikey," Steve said, "you're such a fucking racist."

"She's not Chinese," Tina said. "She's Korean."

"Who is?" Steve asked.

"Park's mom."

Park's mom had been cutting Tina's hair since grade school. They both had the exact same hairstyle: long spiral perms with tall feathered bangs.

"She's fucking hot is what she is," Steve said, cracking himself up. "No offense, Park."

Park managed another smile and slunk back into his seat, putting his headphones back on and cranking up the volume. He could still hear Steve and Mikey, four seats behind him.

"But what's the fucking point?" Mikey asked.

"Dude, would you want to fight a drunk monkey? They're fucking huge. Like *Every Which Way But Loose,* man. Imagine that bastard losing his shit on you."

Park noticed the new girl at about the same time everybody else did. She was standing at the front of the bus, next to the first available seat.

There was a kid sitting there by himself, a freshman. He put his bag down on the seat beside him, then looked the other way. All down the aisle, anybody who was sitting alone moved to the edge of their seats. Park heard Tina snicker; she lived for this stuff.

The new girl took a deep breath and stepped farther down the aisle. Nobody would look at her. Park tried not to, but it was kind of a train wreck/eclipse situation.

The girl just looked like exactly the sort of person this would happen to.

Not just new—but big and awkward. With crazy hair, bright red on top of curly. And she was dressed like . . . like she *wanted* people to look at her. Or maybe like she didn't get what a mess she was. She had on a plaid shirt, a man's shirt, with half a dozen weird necklaces hanging around her neck and scarves wrapped around her wrists. She reminded Park of a scarecrow or one of the trouble dolls his mom kept on her dresser. Like something that wouldn't survive in the wild.

The bus stopped again, and a bunch more kids got on. They pushed past the girl, knocking into her, and dropped into their own seats.

That was the thing—everybody on the bus already had a seat. They'd all claimed one on the first day of school. People like Park, who were lucky enough to have a whole seat to themselves, weren't going to give that up now. Especially not for someone like this.

Park looked back up at the girl. She was just standing there.

"Hey, you," the bus driver yelled, "sit down!"

The girl started moving toward the back of the bus. Right into the belly of the beast. *God,* Park thought, *stop. Turn around.* He could feel Steve and Mikey licking their chops as she got closer. He tried again to look away.

Then the girl spotted an empty seat just across from Park. Her face lit with relief, and she hurried toward it.

"Hey," Tina said sharply.

The girl kept moving.

"Hey," Tina said, *"Bozo."*

Steve started laughing. His friends fell in a few seconds behind him.

"You can't sit there," Tina said. "That's Mikayla's seat."

The girl stopped and looked up at Tina, then looked back at the empty seat.

"Sit down," the driver bellowed from the front.

"I have to sit somewhere," the girl said to Tina in a firm, calm voice.

"Not my problem," Tina snapped. The bus lurched, and the girl rocked back to keep from falling. Park tried to turn the volume up on his Walkman, but it was already all the way up. He looked back at the girl; it looked like she was starting to cry.

Before he'd even decided to do it, Park scooted toward the window.

"Sit down," he said. It came out angrily. The girl turned to him, like she couldn't tell whether he was another jerk or what. "Jesus-fuck," Park said softly, nodding to the space next to him, "just *sit down*."

The girl sat down. She didn't say anything—thank God, she didn't thank him—and she left six inches of space on the seat between them.

Park turned toward the Plexiglas window and waited for a world of suck to hit the fan.

2

eleanor

Eleanor considered her options:

1. She could walk home from school. Pros: exercise, color in her cheeks, time to herself. Cons: She didn't know her new address yet, or even the general direction to start walking.
2. She could call her mom and ask for a ride. Pros: lots. Cons: Her mom didn't have a phone. Or a car.
3. She could call her dad. Ha.
4. She could call her grandma. Just to say hi.

She was sitting on the concrete steps at the front of the school, staring out at the row of yellow buses. Her bus was right there. No. 666.
Even if Eleanor could avoid the bus today, even if her fairy god-

mother showed up with a pumpkin carriage, she'd still have to find a way to get back to school tomorrow morning.

And it's not like the devil-kids on the bus were going to wake up on the other side of their beds tomorrow. Seriously. It wouldn't surprise Eleanor if they unhinged their jaws the next time she saw them. That girl in the back with the blond hair and the acid-washed jacket? You could practically see the horns hidden in her bangs. And her boyfriend was possibly a member of the Nephilim.

That girl—all of them—hated Eleanor before they'd even laid eyes on her. Like they'd been hired to kill her in a past life.

Eleanor couldn't tell if the Asian kid who finally let her sit down was one of them, or whether he was just really stupid. (But not *stupid*-stupid—he was in two of Eleanor's honors classes.)

Her mom had insisted that the new school put Eleanor in honors classes. She'd freaked when she saw how bad Eleanor's grades were from last year in the ninth grade. "This can't be a surprise to you, Mrs. Douglas," the counselor said. *Ha,* Eleanor thought, *you'd be surprised what could be a surprise at this point.*

Whatever. Eleanor could stare at the clouds just as easily in honors classes. There were just as many windows.

If she ever even came back to this school.

If she ever even got home.

Eleanor couldn't tell her mom about the bus situation anyway, because her mom had already said that Eleanor didn't have to ride the bus. Last night, when she was helping Eleanor unpack . . .

"Richie said he'll take you," her mom said. "It's on his way to work."

"Is he going to make me ride in the back of his truck?"

"He's trying to make peace, Eleanor. You promised that you'd try, too."

"It's easier for me to make peace from a distance."

"I told him you were ready to be part of this family."

"I'm *already* part of this family. I'm like a charter member."

"Eleanor," her mom said. "Please."

"I'll just ride the bus," Eleanor had said. "It's not a big deal. I'll meet people."

Ha, Eleanor thought now. *Giant, dramatic ha.*

Her bus was going to leave soon. A few of the other buses were already pulling away. Somebody ran down the steps next to Eleanor and accidentally kicked her bag. She pulled it out of the way and started to say sorry—but it was that stupid Asian kid, and he frowned when he saw that it was her. She frowned right back at him, and he ran ahead.

Oh, fine, Eleanor thought. *The children of hell shan't go hungry on my watch.*

3

park

She didn't talk to him on the ride home.

Park had spent all day trying to think of how to get away from the new girl. He'd have to switch seats. That was the only answer. But switch to what seat? He didn't want to force himself on somebody else. And even the act of switching seats would catch Steve's attention.

Park had expected Steve to start in on him as soon as he let the girl sit down, but Steve went right back to talking about kung fu again. Park, by the way, knew plenty about kung fu. Because his dad was obsessed with martial arts, not because his mom was Korean. Park and his little brother, Josh, had been taking taekwondo since they could walk.

Switch seats, *how* . . .

He could probably find a seat up front with the freshmen, but that would be a spectacular show of weakness. And he almost hated to think about leaving the weird new girl at the back of the bus by herself.

He hated himself for thinking like this.

If his dad knew he was thinking like this, he'd call Park a pussy. Out loud, for once. If his grandma knew, she'd smack him on the back of the head. *Where are your manners?* she'd say. *Is that any way to treat somebody who's down on her luck?*

But Park didn't have any luck—or status—to spare on that dumb redhead. He had just enough to keep himself out of trouble. And he knew it was crappy, but he was kind of grateful that people like that girl existed. Because people like Steve and Mikey and Tina existed, too, and they needed to be fed. If it wasn't that redhead, it was going to be somebody else. And if it wasn't somebody else, it was going to be Park.

Steve had let it go this morning, but he wouldn't keep letting it go. . . .

Park could hear his grandma again, *Seriously, son, you're giving yourself a stomachache because you did something nice while other people were watching?*

It wasn't even that nice, Park thought. He'd let the girl sit down, but he'd sworn at her. When she showed up in his English class that afternoon, it felt like she was there to haunt him. . . .

"Eleanor," Mr. Stessman said. "What a powerful name. It's a queen's name, you know."

"It's the name of the fat Chipette," somebody behind Park whispered. Somebody else laughed.

Mr. Stessman gestured to an empty desk up front.

"We're reading poetry today, Eleanor," he said. "Dickinson. Perhaps you'd like to get us started."

He opened her book to the right page and pointed. "Go ahead," he said, "clear and loud. I'll tell you when to stop."

The new girl looked at Mr. Stessman like she hoped he was kidding. When it was clear that he wasn't—he almost never was—she started to read.

"I had been hungry all the years," she read. A few kids laughed. Jesus, Park thought, only Mr. Stessman would make a chubby girl read a poem about eating on her first day of class.

"Carry on, Eleanor," Mr. Stessman said.

She started over, which Park thought was a terrible idea.

"I had been hungry all the years," she said, louder this time.

My noon had come, to dine,
I, trembling, drew the table near,
And touched the curious wine.
T'was this on tables I had seen,
When turning, hungry, lone,
I looked in windows, for the wealth
I could not hope to own.

Mr. Stessman didn't stop her, so she read the whole poem in that cool, defiant voice. The same voice she'd used on Tina.

"That was wonderful," Mr. Stessman said when she was done. He was beaming. "Just wonderful. I hope you'll stay with us, Eleanor, at least until we do *Medea*. That's a voice that arrives on a chariot drawn by dragons."

When the girl showed up in history, Mr. Sanderhoff didn't make a scene. But he did say, "Ah. Queen Eleanor of Aquitaine," when she handed him her paperwork. She sat down a few rows ahead of Park and, as far as he could tell, spent the whole period staring at the sun.

Park couldn't think of a way to get rid of her on the bus. Or a way to get rid of himself. So he put his headphones on before the girl sat down and turned the volume all the way up.

Thank God she didn't try to talk to him.

4

eleanor

She got home that afternoon before all the little kids, which was good because she wasn't ready to see them again. It had been such a freak show when she walked in last night. . . .

Eleanor had spent so much time thinking about what it would be like to finally come home and how much she missed everybody—she thought they'd throw her a ticker tape parade. She thought it would be a big hugfest.

But when Eleanor walked in the house, it was like her siblings didn't recognize her.

Ben just glanced at her, and Maisie—Maisie was sitting on Richie's lap. Which would have made Eleanor throw right up if she hadn't just promised her mom that she'd be on her best behavior for the rest of her life.

Only Mouse ran to hug Eleanor. She picked him up gratefully. He was five now, and heavy.

"Hey, Mouse," she said. They'd called him that since he was a baby; she couldn't remember why. He reminded her more of a big, sloppy puppy—always excited, always trying to jump into your lap.

"Look, Dad, it's Eleanor," Mouse said, jumping down. "Do you know Eleanor?"

Richie pretended not to hear. Maisie watched and sucked her thumb. Eleanor hadn't seen her do that in years. She was eight now, but with her thumb in her mouth, she looked just like a baby.

The baby wouldn't remember Eleanor at all. He'd be two. . . . There he was, sitting on the floor with Ben. Ben was eleven. He stared at the wall behind the TV.

Their mom carried the duffel bag with Eleanor's stuff into a bedroom off the living room, and Eleanor followed her. The room was tiny, just big enough for a dresser and some bunk beds. Mouse ran into the room after them. "You get the top bunk," he said, "and Ben has to sleep on the floor with me. Mom already told us, and Ben started to cry."

"Don't worry about that," their mom said softly. "We all just have to readjust."

There wasn't room in this room to readjust. (Which Eleanor decided not to mention.) She went to bed as soon as she could, so she wouldn't have to go back out to the living room.

When she woke up in the middle of the night, all three of her brothers were asleep on the floor. There was no way to get up without stepping on one of them, and she didn't even know where the bathroom was. . . .

She found it. There were only five rooms in the house, and the bathroom just barely counted. It was attached to the kitchen—like literally attached, without a door. This house was designed by cave trolls, Eleanor thought. Somebody, probably her mom, had hung a flowered sheet between the refrigerator and the toilet.

When she got home from school, Eleanor let herself in with her new key. The house was possibly even more depressing in daylight—dingy and bare—but at least Eleanor had the place, and her mom, to herself.

It was weird to come home and see her mom, just standing in the kitchen, like . . . like normal. She was making soup, chopping onions. Eleanor felt like crying.

"How was school?" her mom asked.

"Fine," Eleanor said.

"Did you have a good first day?"

"Sure. I mean, yeah, it was just school."

"Will you have a lot of catching up to do?"

"I don't think so."

Her mom wiped her hands on the back of her jeans and tucked her hair behind her ears, and Eleanor was struck, for the ten-thousandth time, by how beautiful she was.

When Eleanor was a little girl, she'd thought her mom looked like a queen, like the star of some fairy tale.

Not a princess—princesses are just pretty. Eleanor's mother was beautiful. She was tall and stately, with broad shoulders and an elegant waist. All her bones seemed more purposeful than other people's. Like they weren't just there to hold her up; they were there to make a point.

She had a strong nose and a sharp chin, and her cheekbones were high and thick. You'd look at Eleanor's mom and think she must be carved into the prow of a Viking ship somewhere or maybe painted on the side of a plane. . . .

Eleanor looked a lot like her.

But not enough.

Eleanor looked like her mother through a fish tank. Rounder and softer. Slurred. Where her mother was statuesque, Eleanor was heavy. Where her mother was finely drawn, Eleanor was smudged.

After five kids, her mother had breasts and hips like a woman in a cigarette ad. At sixteen, Eleanor was already built like she ran a medieval pub.

She had too much of everything and too little height to hide it. Her breasts started just below her chin, her hips were . . . a parody. Even her mom's hair, long and wavy and auburn, was a more legitimate version of Eleanor's bright red curls.

Eleanor put her hand to her head self-consciously.

"I have something to show you," her mom said, covering the soup, "but I didn't want to do it in front of the little kids. Here, come on."

Eleanor followed her into the kids' bedroom. Her mom opened the closet and took out a stack of towels and a laundry basket full of socks.

"I couldn't bring all your things when we moved," she said. "Obviously we don't have as much room here as we had in the old house. . . ." She reached into the closet and pulled out a black plastic garbage bag. "But I packed as much as I could."

She handed Eleanor the bag and said, "I'm sorry about the rest."

Eleanor had assumed that Richie threw all her stuff in the trash a year ago, ten seconds after he'd kicked her out. She took the bag in her arms. "It's okay," she said. "Thanks."

Her mom reached out and touched Eleanor's shoulder, just for a second. "The little kids will be home in twenty minutes or so," she said, "and we'll eat dinner around four thirty. I like to have everything settled before Richie comes home."

Eleanor nodded. She opened the bag as soon as her mom left the room. She wanted to see what was still hers. . . .

The first thing she recognized were the paper dolls. They were loose in the bag and wrinkled; a few were marked with crayons. It had been years since Eleanor had played with them, but she was still happy to see them there. She pressed them flat and laid them in a pile.

Under the dolls were books, a dozen or so, that her mother must have grabbed at random; she wouldn't have known which were Eleanor's favorites. Eleanor was glad to see *Garp* and *Watership Down*. It sucked that *Oliver's Story* had made the cut, but *Love Story* hadn't. And *Little Men* was there, but not *Little Women* or *Jo's Boys*.

There were a bunch more papers in the bag. Eleanor had a file cabinet in her old room, and it looked like her mom had grabbed most of the folders. Eleanor tried to get everything into a neat stack, all the report cards and school pictures and letters from pen pals.

She wondered where the rest of the stuff from the old house had ended up. Not just her stuff, but everybody's. Like the furniture and the toys, and all of her mom's plants and paintings. Her grandma's

Danish wedding plates . . . The little red UFF DA! horse that always used to hang above the sink.

Maybe it was packed away somewhere. Maybe her mom was hoping the cave-troll house was just temporary.

Eleanor was still hoping that Richie was just temporary.

At the bottom of the black trash bag was a box. Her heart jumped a little when she saw it. Her uncle in Minnesota used to send her family a Fruit of the Month Club membership every Christmas, and Eleanor and her brothers and sister would always fight over the boxes that the fruit came in. It was stupid, but they were good boxes—solid, with nice lids. This one was a grapefruit box, soft from wear at the edges.

Eleanor opened it carefully. Nothing inside had been touched. There was her stationery, her colored pencils, and her Prismacolor markers (another Christmas present from her uncle). There was a stack of promotional cards from the mall that still smelled like expensive perfumes. And there was her Walkman. Untouched. Un-batteried, too, but nevertheless, there. And where there was a Walkman, there was the possibility of music.

Eleanor let her head fall over the box. It smelled like Chanel No. 5 and pencil shavings. She sighed.

There wasn't anything to do with her recovered belongings once she'd sorted through them. There wasn't even room in the dresser for Eleanor's clothes. So she set aside the box and the books, and carefully put everything else back in the garbage bag. Then she pushed the bag back as far as she could on the highest shelf in the closet, behind the towels and a humidifier.

She climbed onto her bunk and found a scraggly old cat napping there. "Shoo," Eleanor said, shoving him. The cat leapt to the floor and out the bedroom door.

5

park

Mr. Stessman was making them all memorize a poem, whatever poem they wanted. Well, whatever poem they picked.

"You're going to forget everything else I teach you," Mr. Stessman said, petting his mustache. "Everything. Maybe you'll remember that Beowulf fought a monster. Maybe you'll remember that 'To be or not to be' is *Hamlet*, not *Macbeth*. . . .

"But everything else? Forget about it."

He was slowly walking up and down each aisle. Mr. Stessman loved this kind of stuff—theater in the round. He stopped next to Park's desk and leaned in casually with his hand on the back of Park's chair. Park stopped drawing and sat up straight. He couldn't draw, anyway.

"So, you're going to memorize a poem," Mr. Stessman continued, pausing a moment to smile down at Park like Gene Wilder in the chocolate factory.

"Brains love poetry. It's sticky stuff. You're going to memorize this poem, and five years from now, we're going to see each other at the Village Inn, and you'll say, 'Mr. Stessman, I still remember "The Road Not Taken"'! Listen . . . *Two roads diverged in a yellow wood . . .*'

He moved on to the next desk. Park relaxed.

"Nobody gets to pick 'The Road Not Taken,' by the way, I'm sick to death of it. And no Shel Silverstein. He's grand, but you've graduated. We're all adults here. Choose an adult poem. . . .

"Choose a *romantic* poem, that's my advice. You'll get the most use out of it."

He walked by the new girl's desk, but she didn't turn away from the window.

"Of course, it's up to you. You may choose 'A Dream Deferred'— Eleanor?" She turned blankly. Mr. Stessman leaned in. "You may choose it, Eleanor. It's poignant and it's truth. But how often will you get to roll that one out?

"No. Choose a poem that speaks to you. Choose a poem that will help you speak to someone else."

Park planned to choose a poem that rhymed, so it would be easier to memorize. He liked Mr. Stessman, he really did—but he wished he'd dial it back a few notches. Whenever he worked the room like this, Park got embarrassed for him.

"We meet tomorrow in the library," Mr. Stessman said, back at his desk. "Tomorrow, we're gathering rosebuds."

The bell rang. On cue.

6

eleanor

"Watch it, Raghead." Tina pushed roughly past Eleanor and climbed onto the bus.

She had everybody else in their gym class calling Eleanor Bozo, but Tina had already moved on to Raghead and Bloody Mary. "Cuz it looks like your whole head is on the rag," she'd explained today in the locker room.

It made sense that Tina was in Eleanor's gym class—because gym was an extension of hell, and Tina was definitely a demon. A weird, miniature demon. Like a toy demon. Or a teacup. And she had a whole gang of lesser demons, all dressed in matching gym suits.

Actually, everyone wore matching gym suits.

At Eleanor's old school, she'd thought it had sucked that they had to wear gym *shorts*. (Eleanor hated her legs even more than she hated the rest of her body.) But at North, they had to wear gym *suits*. Polyester Onesies. The bottom was red, and the top was red and white striped, and it all zipped up the front.

"Red isn't your color, Bozo," Tina had said the first time Eleanor suited up. The other girls all laughed, even the black girls who hated Tina. Laughing at Eleanor was Dr. King's mountain.

After Tina pushed past her, Eleanor took her time getting on the bus—but she still got to her seat before that stupid Asian kid. Which meant she'd have to get up to let him have his spot by the window. Which would be awkward. It was all awkward. Every time the bus hit a pothole, Eleanor practically fell in the guy's lap.

Maybe somebody else on the bus would drop out or die or something and she'd be able to move away from him.

At least he didn't ever talk to her. Or look at her.

At least she didn't *think* he did; Eleanor never looked at him.

Sometimes she looked at his shoes. He had cool shoes. And sometimes she looked to see what he was reading. . . .

Always comic books.

Eleanor never brought anything to read on the bus. She didn't want Tina, or anybody else, to catch her with her head down.

park

It felt wrong to sit next to somebody every day and not talk to her. Even if she was weird. (Jesus, was she weird. Today she was dressed like a Christmas tree, with all this stuff pinned to her clothes, shapes cut out of fabric, ribbon. . . .) The ride home couldn't go fast enough. Park couldn't wait to get away from her, away from everybody.

"Dude, where's your dobok?"

He was trying to eat dinner alone in his room, but his little brother wouldn't let him. Josh stood in the doorway, already dressed for taekwondo and inhaling a chicken leg.

"Dad's going to be here, like, now," Josh said through the drumstick, "and he's gonna shit if you're not ready."

Their mom came up behind Josh and thumped him on the head. "Don't cuss, dirty mouth." She had to reach up to do it. Josh was his father's son; he was already at least seven inches taller than their mom—and three inches taller than Park.

Which sucked.

Park pushed Josh out the door and slammed it. So far, Park's strategy for maintaining his status as older brother despite their growing size differential was to pretend he could still kick Josh's ass.

He *could* still beat him at taekwondo—but only because Josh got impatient with any sport where his size wasn't an obvious advantage. The high school football coach had already started coming to Josh's Pee Wee games.

Park changed into his dobok, wondering if he was going to have to start wearing Josh's hand-me-downs pretty soon. Maybe he could take a Sharpie to all Josh's Husker football T-shirts and make them say Hüsker Dü. Or maybe it wouldn't even be an issue—Park might never get any taller than five foot four. He might never grow out of the clothes he had now.

He put on his Chuck Taylors and took his dinner into the kitchen, eating over the counter. His mom was trying to get gravy out of Josh's white jacket with a washcloth.

"Mindy?"

That's how Park's dad came home every night, like the dad in a sitcom. *(Lucy?)* And his mom would call out from wherever she was, *In here!*

Except she said it, *In hee-ya!* Because she was apparently never going to stop sounding like she just got here yesterday from Korea. Sometimes Park thought she kept the accent on purpose, because his dad liked it. But his mom tried so hard to fit in in every other way. . . . If she could sound like she grew up right around the corner, she would.

His dad barreled into the kitchen and scooped his mom into his arms. They did this every night, too. Full-on make-out sessions, no matter who was around. It was like watching Paul Bunyan make out with one of those *It's a Small World* dolls.

Park grabbed his brother's sleeve. "Come on, let's go." They could wait in the Impala. Their dad would be out in a minute, as soon as he'd changed into his giant dobok.

eleanor

She still couldn't get used to eating dinner so early.

When did this all start? In the old house, they'd all eaten together, even Richie. Eleanor wasn't complaining about not having to eat with Richie. . . . But now it was like their mom wanted them all out of the way before he came home.

She even made him a totally different dinner. The kids would get grilled cheese, and Richie would get steak. Eleanor wasn't complaining about the grilled cheese either—it was a nice break from bean soup, and beans and rice, and *huevos y frijoles*. . . .

After dinner, Eleanor usually disappeared into her room to read, but the little kids always went outside. What were they going to do when it got cold—and when it started getting dark early? Would they all hide in the bedroom? It was crazy. Diary-of-Anne-Frank crazy.

Eleanor climbed up onto her bunk bed and got out her stationery box. That dumb gray cat was sleeping in her bed again. She pushed him off.

She opened the grapefruit box and flipped through her stationery. She kept meaning to write letters to her friends from her old school. She hadn't gotten to say good-bye to anybody when she left. Her mom had shown up out of the blue and pulled Eleanor out of class, all "Get your things, you're coming home."

Her mom had been so happy.

And Eleanor had been so happy.

They went straight to North to get Eleanor registered, then stopped at Burger King on the way to the new house. Her mom kept squeezing Eleanor's hand. . . . Eleanor had pretended not to notice the bruises on her mom's wrist.

The bedroom door opened, and her little sister walked in, carrying the cat.

"Mom wants you to leave the door open," Maisie said, "for the breeze." Every window in the house was open, but there didn't seem to be any breeze. With the door open, Eleanor could just see Richie sitting on the couch. She scooted down the bed until she couldn't.

"What are you doing?" Maisie asked.

"Writing a letter."

"To who?"

"I don't know yet."

"Can I come up?"

"No." For the moment, all Eleanor could think about was keeping her box safe. She didn't want Maisie to see the colored pencils and clean paper. Plus, part of her still wanted to punish Maisie for sitting in Richie's lap.

That never would have happened before.

Before Richie kicked Eleanor out, all the kids were allied against him. Maybe Eleanor had hated him the most, and the most openly—but they were all on her side, Ben and Maisie, even Mouse. Mouse used to steal Richie's cigarettes and hide them. And Mouse was the one they'd send to knock on their mom's door when they heard bedsprings. . . .

When it was worse than bedsprings, when it was shouting or crying, they'd huddle together, all five of them, on Eleanor's bed. (They'd all had their own beds in the old house.)

Maisie sat at Eleanor's right hand then. When Mouse cried, when Ben's face went blank and dreamy, Maisie and Eleanor would lock eyes.

"I hate him," Eleanor would say.

"I hate him so much, I wish he was dead," Maisie would answer.

"I hope he falls off a ladder at work."

"I hope he gets hit by truck."

"A garbage truck."

"Yeah," Maisie would say, gritting her teeth, "and all the garbage will fall on his dead body."

"And then a bus will run him over."

"Yeah."

"I hope I'm on it."

Maisie put the cat back on Eleanor's bed. "It likes to sleep up there," she said.

"Do you call him Dad, too?" Eleanor asked.

"He is our dad now," Maisie said.

Eleanor woke up in the middle of the night. Richie had fallen asleep in the living room with the TV on. She didn't breathe on the way to the bathroom and was too scared to flush the toilet. When she got back to her room, she closed the door. Fuck the breeze.

7

park

"I'm going to ask Kim out," Cal said.

"Don't ask Kim out," Park said.

"Why not?" They were sitting in the library, and they were supposed to be looking for poems. Cal had already picked out something short about a girl named Julia and the "liquefaction of her clothes." ("Crass," Park said. "It can't be crass," Cal argued. "It's three hundred years old.")

"Because she's Kim," Park said. "You can't ask her out. Look at her."

Kim was sitting at the next table over with two other preppy girls.

"Look at her," Cal said, "she's a Betty."

"Jesus," Park said. "You sound so stupid."

"What? That's a thing. A Betty is a thing."

"But you got it from *Thrasher* or something, right?"

"That's how people learn new words, Park"—Cal tapped a book of poetry—"reading."

"You're trying too hard."

"She's a Betty," Cal said, nodding at Kim and getting a Slim Jim out of his backpack.

Park looked at Kim again. She had bobbed blond hair and hard, curled bangs, and she was the only kid in school with a Swatch. Kim was one of those people who never wrinkled. . . . She wouldn't make eye contact with Cal. She'd be afraid he'd leave a stain.

"This is my year," Cal said. "I'm getting a girlfriend."

"But probably not Kim."

"Why not Kim? You think I need to aim lower?"

Park looked up him. Cal wasn't a bad-looking guy. He had kind of a tall Barney Rubble thing going on. . . . He already had pieces of Slim Jim caught in his front teeth.

"Aim elsewhere," Park said.

"Screw that," Cal said, "I'm starting at the top. And I'm getting you a girl, too."

"Thanks, but no thanks," Park said.

"Double-dating," Cal said.

"No."

"In the Impala."

"Don't get your hopes up." Park's dad had decided to be a fascist about Park's driver's license; he'd announced last night that Park had to learn to drive a stick first. Park opened another book of poetry. It was all about war. He closed it.

"Now there's a girl who might want a piece of you," Cal said. "Looks like *somebody's* got jungle fever."

"That isn't even the right kind of racist," Park said, looking up. Cal was nodding toward the far corner of the library. The new girl was sitting there, staring right at them.

"She's kind of big," Cal said, "but the Impala is a spacious automobile."

"She's not looking at me. She's just staring, she does that. Watch." Park waved at the girl, but she didn't blink.

He'd made eye contact with her only once since her first day on the bus. It was last week, in history, and she'd practically gouged out his eyes with hers.

If you don't want people to look at you, Park had thought at the time, *don't wear fishing lures in your hair.* Her jewelry box must look like a junk drawer. Not that everything she wore was stupid. . . .

She had a pair of Vans he liked, with strawberries on them. And she had a green sharkskin blazer that Park would wear himself if he thought he could get away with it.

Did she think she was getting away with it?

Park braced himself every morning before she got on the bus, but you couldn't brace yourself enough for the sight of her.

"Do you know her?" Cal asked.

"No," Park said quickly. "She's on my bus. She's weird."

"Jungle fever is a thing," Cal said.

"For black people. If you like black people. And it's not a compliment, I don't think."

"Your people come from the jungle," Cal said, pointing at Park. *"Apocalypse Now,* anyone?"

"You should ask Kim out," Park said. "That's a really good idea."

eleanor

Eleanor wasn't going to fight over an E. E. Cummings book like it was the last Cabbage Patch Kid. She found an empty table in the African American literature section.

That was another fucked-up thing about this school—effed up, she corrected herself.

Most of the kids here were black, but most of the kids in her honors classes were white. They got bused in from west Omaha. And the white kids from the Flats, dishonor students, got bused in from the other direction.

Eleanor wished she had more honors classes. She wished there was honors gym. . . .

Like they'd ever let her into honors gym. Eleanor would get put in remedial gym first. With all the other fat girls who couldn't do sit-ups.

Anyway. Honor students—black, white, or Asia Minor—tended to be nicer. Maybe they were just as mean on the inside, but they were scared of getting in trouble. Or maybe they were just as mean on the inside, but they'd been trained to be polite—to give up their seats for old people and girls.

Eleanor had honors English, history, and geography, but she spent the rest of her day in Crazytown. Seriously, *Blackboard Jungle*. She should probably try harder in her smart classes so that she wouldn't get kicked out of them.

She started copying a poem called "Caged Bird" into her notebook. . . . Sweet. It rhymed.

8

park

She was reading his comics.

At first Park thought he was imagining it. He kept getting this feeling that she was looking at him, but whenever he looked over at her, her face was down.

He finally realized that she was staring at his lap. Not in a gross way. She was looking at his comics—he could see her eyes moving.

Park didn't know that anyone with red hair could have brown eyes. (He didn't know that anyone could have hair *that* red. Or skin that white.) The new girl's eyes were darker than his mom's, really dark, almost like holes in her face.

That made it sound bad, but it wasn't. It might even be the best thing about her. It kind of reminded Park of the way artists draw Jean

Grey sometimes when she's using her telepathy, with her eyes all blacked out and alien.

Today the girl was wearing a giant men's shirt with seashells all over it. The collar must have been really big, like disco-big, because she'd cut it, and it was fraying. She had a man's necktie wrapped around her ponytail like a big polyester ribbon. She looked ridiculous.

And she was looking at his comics.

Park felt like he should say something to her. He always felt like he should say *something* to her, even if it was just hello or excuse me. But he'd gone too long without saying anything since the first time he cursed at her, and now it was all just irrevocably weird. For *an hour* a day. Thirty minutes on the way to school, thirty minutes back.

Park didn't say anything. He just held his comics open wider and turned the pages more slowly.

eleanor

Her mom looked tired when Eleanor got home. Like more tired than usual. Hard and crumbling at the edges.

When the little kids stormed in after school, her mom lost her temper over something stupid—Ben and Mouse fighting over a toy—and she pushed them all out the back door, Eleanor included.

Eleanor was so startled to be outside that she stood on the back stoop for a second, staring down at Richie's Rottweiler. He'd named the dog Tonya after his ex-wife. She was supposed to be a real man-eater, Tonya—Tonya the dog—but Eleanor had never seen her more than half awake.

Eleanor tried knocking on the door. "Mom! Let me back in. I haven't even taken a bath yet."

She usually took her bath right after school, before Richie got home. It took a lot of the stress out of not having a bathroom door, especially since somebody'd torn down the sheet.

Her mom ignored her.

The little kids were already out on the playground. The new house was right next door to an elementary school—the school where Ben and Mouse and Maisie went—and the playground was just beyond their backyard.

Eleanor didn't know what else to do, so she walked out to where she could see Ben, by the swing set, and sat on one of the swings. It was finally jacket weather. Eleanor wished she had a jacket.

"What are you supposed to do when it gets too cold to play outside?" she asked Ben.

He was taking Matchbox cars out of his pockets and lining them up in the dirt. "Last year," he said, "Dad made us go to bed at seven thirty."

"God. You, too? Why do you guys call him that?" She tried not to sound angry.

Ben shrugged. "I guess because he's married to Mom."

"Yeah, but—" Eleanor ran her hands up and down the swing chains, then smelled them. "—we never used to call him that. Do you feel like he's your dad?"

"I don't know," Ben said flatly. "What's that supposed to feel like?"

She didn't answer him, so he went back to setting up his cars. He needed a haircut: his strawberry blond hair was curling almost to his collar. He was wearing an old T-shirt of Eleanor's and a pair of corduroy pants that their mom had cut off into shorts. He was almost too old for all this, for cars and parks—eleven. The other boys his age played basketball all night or hung out in groups at the edge of the playground. Eleanor hoped that Ben was a late bloomer. There was no room in that house to be a teenager.

"He likes it when we call him Dad," Ben said, still lining up the cars.

Eleanor looked out at the playground. Mouse was playing with a bunch of kids who had a soccer ball. Maisie must have taken the baby somewhere with her friends. . . .

It used to be Eleanor who was stuck with the baby all the time. She wouldn't even mind watching him now—it would give her something to do—but Maisie didn't want Eleanor's help.

"What was it like?" Ben asked.

"What was what like?"

"Living with those people."

The sun was about an inch above the horizon, and Eleanor looked hard at it.

"Okay," she said. Terrible. Lonely. Better than here.

"Were there other kids?"

"Yeah. Really little kids. Three of them."

"Did you have your own room?"

"Sort of." Technically, she hadn't had to share the Hickmans' living room with anyone else.

"Were they nice?" he asked.

"Yeah . . . yeah. They were nice. Not as nice as you."

The Hickmans had started out nice. But then they got tired.

Eleanor was only supposed to stay with them for a few days, maybe a week. Just until Richie cooled down and let her come home.

"It'll be like a slumber party," Mrs. Hickman said to Eleanor the first night she made up the couch. Mrs. Hickman—Tammy—knew Eleanor's mom from high school. There was a photo over their TV of the Hickmans' wedding. Eleanor's mom was the maid of honor—in a dark green dress, with a white flower in her hair.

At first, her mom would call Eleanor at the Hickmans' almost every day after school. After a few months, the calls stopped. It turned out that Richie hadn't paid the phone bill, and it got disconnected. But Eleanor didn't know that for a while.

"We should call the state," Mr. Hickman kept telling his wife. They thought Eleanor couldn't hear them, but their bedroom was right over the living room. "This can't go on, Tammy."

"Andy, it's not her fault."

"I'm not saying it's her fault, I'm just saying we didn't sign on for this."

"She's no trouble."

"She's not ours."

Eleanor tried to be even less trouble. She practiced being in a room without leaving any clues that she'd been there. She never turned on the TV or asked to use the phone. She never asked for seconds at dinner.

She never asked Tammy and Mr. Hickman for anything—and they'd never had a teenager, so it didn't occur to them that there might be anything she might need. She was glad that they didn't know her birthday. . . .

"We thought you were gone," Ben said, pushing a car into the dirt. He looked like somebody who didn't want to cry.

"Of ye of little faith," Eleanor said, kicking her swing into action.

She looked around again for Maisie and found her sitting over where the older boys were playing basketball. Eleanor recognized most of the boys from the bus. That stupid Asian kid was there, jumping higher than she would have guessed he could. He was wearing long black shorts and a T-shirt that said MADNESS.

"I'm out of here," Eleanor told Ben, stepping off the swing and pushing down the top of his head. "But not gone or anything. Don't get your panties in a bunch."

She walked back into the house and rushed through the kitchen before her mom could say anything. Richie was in the living room. Eleanor walked between him and the TV, eyes straight ahead. She wished she had a jacket.

9

park

He was going to tell her that she did a good job on her poem.

That would be a giant understatement, anyway. She was the only person in class who'd read her poem like it wasn't an assignment. She recited it like it was a living thing. Like something she was letting out. You couldn't look away from her as long as she was talking. (Even more than Park's usual not being able to look away from her.) When she was done, a lot of people clapped and Mr. Stessman hugged her. Which was totally against the Code of Conduct.

Hey. Nice job. In English. That's what Park was going to say.

Or maybe, *I'm in your English class. That poem you read was cool.*

Or, *You're in Mr. Stessman's class, right? Yeah, I thought so.*

Park picked up his comics after taekwondo Wednesday night, but he waited until Thursday morning to read them.

eleanor

That stupid Asian kid totally knew she was reading his comics. He even looked up at Eleanor sometimes before he turned the page, like he was *that polite.*

He definitely wasn't one of them, the bus demons. He didn't talk to anyone on the bus. (Especially not her.) But he was in with them somehow because, when Eleanor was sitting next to him, they all left her alone. Even Tina. It made Eleanor wish she could sit next to him all day long.

This morning, when she got on the bus, it kind of felt like he was waiting for her. He was holding a comic called *Watchmen,* and it looked so ugly that Eleanor decided not to bother eavesdropping. Or eavesreading. Whatever.

(She liked it best when he read the *X-Men,* even though she didn't get everything that was going on there; the *X-Men* were worse than *General Hospital.* It took Eleanor a couple weeks to figure out that Scott Summers and Cyclops were the same guy, and she still wasn't sure what was up with Phoenix.)

But Eleanor didn't have anything else to do, so her eyes wandered over to the ugly comic. . . . And then she was reading. And then they were at school. Which was totally weird because they weren't even halfway through with it.

And which totally sucked because it meant he would read the rest of the comic during school, and have something lame like *Rom* out on the way home.

Except he didn't.

When Eleanor got on the bus that afternoon, the Asian kid opened up *Watchmen* right where they'd left off.

They were still reading it when they got to Eleanor's stop—there was so much going on, they both stared at every frame for, like, entire minutes—and when she got up to leave, he handed it to her.

Eleanor was so surprised, she tried to hand it back, but he'd already turned away. She shoved the comic between her books like it was something secret, then got off the bus.

She read it three more times that night, lying on the top bunk, petting the scrubby old cat. Then she put it in her grapefruit box overnight, so that nothing would happen to it.

park

What if she didn't give it back?

What if he didn't get to finish the first issue of *Watchmen* because he'd lent it to a girl who hadn't asked for it and probably didn't even know who Alan Moore was.

If she didn't give it back, they were even. That would cancel out the whole Jesus-fuck-sit-down scenario.

Jesus . . . No, it wouldn't.

What if she *did* give it back? What was he supposed to say then? Thanks?

eleanor

When she got to their seat, he was looking out the window. She handed him the comic, and he took it.

10

eleanor

The *next* morning, when Eleanor got on the bus, there was a stack of comics on her seat.

She picked them up and sat down. He was already reading.

Eleanor put the comics between her books and stared at the window. For some reason, she didn't want to read in front of him. It would be like letting him watch her eat. It would be like . . . admitting something.

But she thought about the comics all day, and as soon she got home, she climbed onto her bed and got them out. They were all the same title—*Swamp Thing*.

Eleanor ate dinner sitting cross-legged on her bed, extra careful not to spill anything on the books because every issue was in pristine condition; there wasn't so much as a bent corner. (Stupid, perfect Asian kid.)

That night, after her brothers and sister fell asleep, Eleanor turned the light back on so she could read. They were the loudest sleepers ever. Ben talked in his sleep, and Maisie and the baby both snored. Mouse wet the bed—which didn't make noise, but still disturbed the general peace. The light didn't seem to bother them, though.

Eleanor was only distantly conscious of Richie watching TV in the next room, and she practically fell off the bed when he jerked the bedroom door open. He looked like he expected to catch some middle-of-the-night high jinks, but when he saw that it was just Eleanor and that she was just reading, he grunted and told her to turn out the light so the little kids could sleep.

After he shut the door, Eleanor got up and turned off the light. (She could just about get out of bed without stepping on somebody now, which was lucky for them because she was the first one up every morning.)

She might have gotten away with leaving the light on, but it wasn't worth the risk. She didn't want to have to look at Richie again.

He looked exactly like a rat. Like the human being version of a rat. Like the villain in a Don Bluth movie. Who knew what her mom saw in him; Eleanor's dad was messed-up-looking, too.

Every *once* in a while—when Richie managed to take a bath, put on decent clothes, and stay sober all on the same day—Eleanor could *sort of* see why her mom might have thought he was handsome. Thank the Lord that didn't happen very often. When it did, Eleanor felt like going to the bathroom and sticking a finger down her throat.

Anyway. Whatever. She could still read. There was enough light coming in from the window.

park

She read stuff as fast as he could give it to her. And when she handed it back to him the next morning, she always acted as if she were handing him something fragile. Something precious. You wouldn't even know that she touched the comics except for the smell.

Every book Park lent her came back smelling like perfume. Not like the perfume his mom wore. (Imari.) And not like the new girl; she smelled like vanilla.

But she made his comics smell like roses. A whole field of them.

She'd read all his Alan Moore in less than three weeks. Now he was giving her X-comics five at a time, and he could tell that she liked them because she wrote the characters' names on her books, in between band names and song lyrics.

They still didn't talk on the bus, but it had become a less confrontational silence. Almost friendly. (But not quite.)

Park would *have* to talk to her today—to tell her that he didn't have anything to give her. He'd overslept, then forgotten to grab the stack of comics he set out for her the night before. He hadn't even had time to eat breakfast or brush his teeth, which made him self-conscious, knowing he was going to be sitting so close to her.

But when she got on the bus and handed him yesterday's comics, all Park did was shrug. She looked away. They both looked down.

She was wearing that ugly necktie again. Today it was tied around her wrist. Her arms and wrists were scattered with freckles, layers of them in different shades of gold and pink, even on the back of her hands. Little boy hands, his mom would call them, with short-short nails and ragged cuticles.

She stared down at the books in her lap. Maybe she thought he was mad at her. He stared at her books, too—covered in ink and art nouveau doodles.

"So," he said, before he knew what to say next. "You like the Smiths?" He was careful not to blow his morning breath on her.

She looked up, surprised. Maybe confused. He pointed at her book, where she'd written *How Soon Is Now?* in tall green letters.

"I don't know," she said. "I've never heard them."

"So you just want people to *think* you like the Smiths?" He couldn't help but sound disdainful.

"Yeah," she said, looking around the bus. "I'm trying to impress the locals."

He didn't know if she could help but sound like a smart-ass, but she sure wasn't trying. The air soured between them. Park shifted against the wall. She looked across the aisle to stare out the window.

When he got to English, he tried to catch her eye, but she looked away. He felt like she was trying so hard to ignore him that she wouldn't even participate in class.

Mr. Stessman kept trying to draw her out—she was his new favorite target whenever things got sleepy in class. Today they were supposed to be discussing *Romeo and Juliet,* but nobody wanted to talk.

"You don't seem troubled by their deaths, Miss Douglas."

"I'm sorry?" she said. She narrowed her eyes at him.

"It doesn't strike you as sad?" Mr. Stessman asked. "Two young lovers lay dead. *Never was a story of more woe.* Doesn't that get to you?"

"I guess not," she said.

"Are you so cold? So cool?" He was standing over her desk, pretending to plead with her.

"No . . ." she said. "I just don't think it's a tragedy."

"It's *the* tragedy," Mr. Stessman said.

She rolled her eyes. She was wearing two or three necklaces, old fake pearls, like Park's grandmother wore to church, and she twisted them while she talked. "But he's so obviously making fun of them," she said.

"Who is?"

"Shakespeare."

"Do tell. . . ."

She rolled her eyes again. She knew Mr. Stessman's game by now. "Romeo and Juliet are just two rich kids who've always gotten every little thing they want. And now, they *think* they want each other."

"They're in love . . ." Mr. Stessman said, clutching his heart.

"They don't even know each other," she said.

"It was love at first sight."

"It was 'Oh my God, he's so cute' at first sight. If Shakespeare wanted you to believe they were in love, he wouldn't tell you in almost the very first scene that Romeo was hung up on Rosaline. . . . It's Shakespeare making fun of love," she said.

"Then why has it survived?"

"I don't know, because Shakespeare is a really good writer?"

"No!" Mr. Stessman said. "Someone else, someone with a heart. Mr. Sheridan, what beats in your chest? Tell us, why has *Romeo and Juliet* survived four hundred years?"

Park hated talking in class. Eleanor frowned at him, then looked away. He felt himself blush.

"Because . . ." he said quietly, looking at his desk, "because people want to remember what it's like to be young? And in love?"

Mr. Stessman leaned back against the blackboard and rubbed his beard.

"Is that right?" Park asked.

"Oh, it's definitely right," Mr. Stessman said. "I don't know if that's why *Romeo and Juliet* has become the most beloved play of all time. But, yes, Mr. Sheridan. Truer words never spoken."

She didn't acknowledge Park in history class, but she never did.

When he got on the bus that afternoon, she was already there. She got up to let him have his place by the window, and then she surprised him by talking. Quietly. Almost under her breath. But talking.

"It's more like a wish list," she said.

"What?"

"They're songs I'd like to hear. Or bands I'd like to hear. Stuff that looks interesting."

"If you've never heard the Smiths, how do you even know about them?"

"I don't know," she said defensively. "My friends, my old friends . . . magazines. I don't know. Around."

"Why don't you just listen to them?"

She looked at him like he was officially an idiot. "It's not like they play the Smiths on Sweet 98."

And then, when Park didn't say anything, she rolled her inky brown eyes into the back of her head. *"God,"* she said.

They didn't talk any more all the way home.

That night, while he did his homework, Park made a tape with all his favorite Smiths songs, plus a few songs by Echo & the Bunnymen, and Joy Division.

He put the tape and five more X-comics into his backpack before he went to bed.

11

eleanor

"Why are you so quiet?" Eleanor's mother asked. Eleanor was taking a bath, and her mom was making fifteen-bean soup. "That leaves three beans for each us," Ben had cracked to Eleanor earlier.

"I'm not quiet. I'm taking a bath."

"Usually you sing in the bathtub."

"I do *not*," Eleanor said.

"You do. You usually sing 'Rocky Raccoon.'"

"*God*. Well, thanks for telling me, I won't anymore. God."

Eleanor got dressed quickly and tried to squeeze past her mother. Her mom grabbed her by the wrists. "I like to hear you sing," she said. She reached for a bottle on the counter behind Eleanor and rubbed a drop of vanilla behind each of the girl's ears. Eleanor raised her shoulders like it tickled.

"Why do you always do that? I smell like a Strawberry Shortcake doll."

"I do it," her mom said, "because it's cheaper than perfume, but it smells just as good." Then she rubbed some vanilla behind her own ears and laughed.

Eleanor laughed with her, and stood there for a few seconds, smiling. Her mom was wearing soft old jeans and a T-shirt, and her hair was pulled back in a smooth ponytail. She looked almost like she used to. There was a picture of her—at one of Maisie's birthday parties, scooping ice cream cones—with a ponytail just like that.

"Are you okay?" her mom asked.

"Yeah . . ." Eleanor said, "yeah, I'm just tired. I'm going to do my homework and go to bed." Her mom seemed to know that something was off, but she didn't push. She used to make Eleanor tell her everything. *What's going on up there?* she'd say, knocking on the top of Eleanor's head. *Are you making yourself crazy?* Her mom hadn't said anything like that since Eleanor moved home. She seemed to realize that she'd lost her right to knock.

Eleanor climbed up onto her bunk and pushed the cat to the end. She didn't have anything to read. Nothing new, anyway. Was he done bringing her comics? Why had he even started? She ran her fingers over the embarrassing song titles—"This Charming Man" and "How Soon Is Now?"—on her math book. She wanted to scribble them out, but he'd probably notice and lord it over her.

Eleanor really was tired; that wasn't a lie. She'd been staying up, reading, almost every night. She fell asleep that night right after dinner.

She woke up to shouting. Richie shouting. Eleanor couldn't tell what he was saying.

Underneath the shouting, her mother was crying. She sounded like she'd been crying for a long time—she must be completely out of her head if she was letting them hear her cry like that.

Eleanor could tell that everyone else in the room was already awake. She hung off the bunk until she could see the little kids take shape in the dark. All four of them were sitting together in a clump of blankets on the floor. Maisie was holding the baby, rocking him almost frantically. Eleanor slid off the bed soundlessly and huddled with them. Mouse immediately climbed into her lap. He was shaking and wet, and he wrapped his arms and legs around Eleanor like a monkey. Their mother shrieked, two rooms away, and they all five jumped together.

If this had happened two summers ago, Eleanor would have run and banged on the door herself. She would have yelled at Richie to stop. She would have called 911 at the very, very, very least. But now that seemed like something a child would do, or a fool. Now, all she could think about was what they were going to do if the baby actually started to cry. Thank God he didn't. Even he seemed to realize that trying to make this stop would only ever make it worse.

When her alarm went off the next morning, Eleanor couldn't remember having fallen to sleep. She couldn't remember when the crying had stopped.

A horrible thought came to her, and she got up, stumbling over the kids and the blankets. She opened the bedroom door and smelled bacon.

Which meant that her mother was alive.

And that her stepdad was probably still eating breakfast.

Eleanor took a deep breath. She smelled like pee. *God*. The cleanest clothes she had were the ones she wore yesterday, which Tina would surely point out, because it was a goddamn gym day on top of everything else.

She grabbed her clothes and stepped purposefully out into the living room, determined not to make eye contact with Richie if he was there. He was. (*That demon. That bastard.*) Her mother was standing at the stove, standing more still than usual. You couldn't not notice the bruise on the side of her face. Or the hickey under her chin. (*That fuck, that fuck, that fuck.*)

"Mom," Eleanor whispered urgently, "I have to clean off."

Her mother's eyes slowly focused on her. "What?"

Eleanor gestured at her clothes, which probably just looked wrinkled. "I slept on the floor with Mouse."

Her mother glanced nervously into the living room; Richie would punish Mouse if he knew. "Okay, okay," she said, pushing Eleanor into the bathroom. "Give me your clothes, I'll watch the door. And don't let him smell it. I don't need it this morning."

As if Eleanor were the one who'd peed all over everything.

She washed off the top half of her body, then the bottom, so that she wouldn't ever be totally naked. Then she walked back through the living room, wearing yesterday's clothes, trying really hard not to smell like pee.

Her books were in her bedroom, but Eleanor didn't want to open the door and let out any more acrid air—so she just left.

She got to the bus stop fifteen minutes early. She still felt rumpled and panicked, and thanks to the bacon, her stomach was growling.

12

park

When Park got on the bus, he'd set the comics and Smiths tape on the seat next to him, so they'd just be waiting for her. So he wouldn't have to say anything.

When she got on the bus a few minutes later, Park could tell that something was wrong. She got on like she was lost and ended up there. She was wearing the same thing she'd worn yesterday—which wasn't *that* weird, she was always wearing a different version of the same thing—but today was different. Her neck and wrists were bare, and her hair was a mess—a pile, an all-over glob of red curls.

She stopped at their seat and looked down at the pile of stuff he'd left for her. (Where were her schoolbooks?) Then she picked everything up, careful as ever, and sat down.

Park wanted to look at her face, but he couldn't. He stared at her

wrists instead. She picked up the cassette. He'd written HOW SOON IS
NOW AND MORE on the thin white sticker.

She held it out to him. "Thank you . . ." she said. Now *that* was
something he'd never heard her say before. "But I can't."

He didn't take it.

"It's for you, take it," he whispered. He looked up from her hands
to her dropped chin.

"No," she said, "I mean, thank you, but . . . I can't." She tried again
to give him the tape, but he still wouldn't take it. Why did she have to
make every little thing so hard?

"I don't want it," he said.

She clenched her teeth and glared. She really must hate him.

"No," she said, practically loud enough for other people to hear. "I
mean, I *can't*. I don't have any way to listen to it. *God,* just take it back."

He took it. She covered her face. The kid in the seat across from
them, a twerpy senior who was actually named Junior, was watching.

Park frowned at Junior until he turned away. Then Park turned
back to the girl. . . .

He took his Walkman out of the pocket of his trench coat and
popped out his Dead Kennedys tape. He slid the new tape in, pressed
Play, then—carefully—put the headphones over her hair. He was so
careful, he didn't even touch her.

He could hear the swampy guitar start and then the first line of the
song: *"I am the son . . . and the heir . . ."*

She lifted her head a little but didn't look at him. She didn't move
her hands away from her face.

When they got to school, she took the headphones off and gave
them back to him.

They got off the bus together and stayed together. Which was weird.
Usually, they broke away from each other as soon as they hit the sidewalk. That's what seemed weird now, Park thought; they walked the
same way every day, her locker was just down the hall from his—how
had they managed to go their separate ways every morning?

Park stopped for a minute when they got to her locker. He didn't
step close to her, but he stopped. She stopped, too.

"Well," he said, looking down the hall, "now you've heard the Smiths."

And she . . .

Eleanor laughed.

eleanor

She should have just taken the tape.

She didn't need to be telling everybody what she had and didn't have. She didn't need to be telling weird Asian kids anything.

Weird Asian kid.

She was pretty sure he was Asian. It was hard to tell. He had green eyes. And skin the color of sunshine through honey.

Maybe he was Filipino. Was that in Asia? Probably. Asia's out-of-control huge.

Eleanor had only known one Asian person in her life—Paul, who was in her math class at her old school. Paul was Chinese. His parents had moved to Omaha to get away from the Chinese government. (Which seemed like an extreme choice. Like they'd looked at the globe and said, "Yup. That's as far away as possible.")

Paul was the one who'd taught Eleanor to say *Asian* and not *oriental*. "Oriental's for food," he'd said.

"Whatever, La Choy Boy," she'd said back.

Eleanor couldn't figure out what an Asian person was doing in the Flats anyway. Everybody else here was seriously white. Like, white by choice. Eleanor had never even heard the N-word said out loud until she moved here, but the kids on her bus used it like it was the only way to indicate that somebody was black. Like there was no other word or phrase that would work.

Eleanor stayed away from the N-word, even in her head. It was bad enough that, thanks to Richie's influence, she went around mentally calling everyone she met a "motherfucker." (Irony.)

There were three or four other Asian kids at their school. Cousins. One of them had written an essay about being a refugee from Laos.

And then there was Ol' Green Eyes.

Whom she was apparently going to tell her whole life story to. Maybe on the way home, she'd tell him that she didn't have a phone or a washing machine or a toothbrush.

That last thing, she was thinking about telling her counselor. Mrs. Dunne had sat Eleanor down on her first day of school and given a little speech about how Eleanor could tell her *anything*. All through the speech, she kept squeezing the fattest part of Eleanor's arm.

If Eleanor told Mrs. Dunne *everything*—about Richie, her mom, everything—Eleanor didn't know what would happen.

But if she told Mrs. Dunne about the toothbrush . . . maybe Mrs. Dunne would just get her one. And then Eleanor could stop sneaking into the bathroom after lunch to rub her teeth with salt. (She'd seen that in a Western once. It probably didn't even work.)

The bell rang—10:12.

Just two more periods until English. She wondered if he'd talk to her in class. Maybe that's what they did now.

She could still hear that voice in her head—not his—the singer's. From the Smiths. You could hear his accent, even when he was singing. He sounded like he was crying out.

I am the sun . . .
And the air . . .

Eleanor didn't notice at first how un-horrible everyone was being in gym. (Her head was still on the bus.) They were playing volleyball today, and once Tina said, "Your serve, bitch," but that was it, and that was practically jocular, all things Tina-considered.

When Eleanor got to the locker room, she realized why Tina had been so low-key; she was just waiting. Tina and her friends—and the black girls, too, everybody wanted a piece of this—were standing at the end of Eleanor's row, waiting for her to walk to her locker.

It was covered with Kotex pads. A whole box, it looked like.

At first Eleanor thought the pads were actually bloody, but when she got closer, she could see that it was just red Magic Marker. Some-body had written RAGHEAD and BIG RED on a few of the pads, but they were the expensive kind, so the ink was already starting to absorb.

If Eleanor's clothes weren't in that locker, if she were wearing any-thing other than this gym suit, she would have just walked away.

Instead she walked past the girls, with her chin as high as she could manage, and methodically peeled the pads off her locker. There were even some inside, stuck to her clothes.

Eleanor cried a little bit, she couldn't help it, but she kept her back to everybody so there wouldn't be a show. It was all over in a few minutes anyway because nobody wanted to be late to lunch. Most of the girls still had to change and redo their hair.

After everyone else walked away, two black girls stayed. They walked over to Eleanor and started pulling pads off the wall. "Ain't no thing," one of the girls whispered, crumpling a pad into a ball. Her name was DeNice, and she looked too young to be in the tenth grade. She was small, and she wore her hair in two braided pigtails.

Eleanor shook her head, but didn't say anything.

"Those girls are trifling," DeNice said. "They're so insignificant, God can hardly see them."

"Hmm-hmm," the other girl agreed. Eleanor was pretty sure her name was Beebi. Beebi was what Eleanor's mom would call "a big girl." Much bigger than Eleanor. Beebi's gym suit was even a different color from everybody else's, like they'd had to special-order it for her. Which made Eleanor feel bad about feeling so bad about her own body . . . and which also made her wonder why she was the official fat girl in the class.

They threw the pads in the trash and pushed them under some wet paper towels so that nobody would find them.

If DeNice and Beebi wouldn't have been standing there, Eleanor might have kept some of the pads, the ones that didn't have any writ-ing on them, because, God, what a waste.

She was late to lunch, then late to English. And if she didn't know already that she liked that stupid, effing Asian kid, she knew it now.

Because even after everything that had happened in the last

forty-five minutes—and everything that had happened in the last twenty-four hours—all Eleanor could think about was seeing Park.

park

When they got back on the bus, she took his Walkman without arguing. And without making him put it on for her. At the stop before hers, she handed it back.

"You can borrow it," he said quietly. "Listen to the rest of the tape."

"I don't want to break it," she said.

"You're not going to break it."

"I don't want to use up the batteries."

"I don't care about the batteries."

She looked up at him then, in the eye, maybe for the first time ever. Her hair looked even crazier than it had this morning—more frizzy than curly, like she was working on a big red Afro. But her eyes were dead serious, cold sober. Any cliché you've ever heard used to describe Clint Eastwood, those were Eleanor's eyes.

"Really," she said. "You don't care."

"They're just batteries," he said.

She emptied the batteries and the tape from Park's Walkman, handed it back to him, then got off the bus without looking back.

God, she was weird.

eleanor

The batteries started to die at 1 A.M., but Eleanor kept listening for another hour until the voices slowed to a stop.

13

eleanor

She remembered her books today, and she was wearing fresh clothes. She'd had to wash her jeans out in the bathtub last night, so they were still kind of damp. . . . But altogether, Eleanor felt a thousand times better than she had yesterday. Even her hair was halfway cooperating. She'd clumped it up into a bun and wrapped it with a rubber band. It was going to hurt like crazy trying to tear the rubber band out, but at least it was staying for now.

Best of all, she had Park's songs in her head—and in her chest, somehow.

There was something about the music on that tape. It felt different. Like, it set her lungs and her stomach on edge. There was something exciting about it, and something nervous. It made Eleanor feel like everything, like the *world,* wasn't what she'd thought it was. And that was a good thing. That was the greatest thing.

When she got on the bus that morning, she immediately lifted her head to find Park. He was looking up, too, like he was waiting for her. She couldn't help it, she grinned. Just for a second.

As soon as she sat down, Eleanor slunk low in the seat, so the back-of-the-bus ruffians wouldn't be able to see from the top of her head how happy she felt.

She could feel Park sitting next to her, even though he was at least six inches away.

She handed him the comics, then tugged nervously at the green ribbon wound round her wrist. She couldn't think of what to say. She started to worry that maybe she wouldn't say anything, that she wouldn't even thank him. . . .

Park's hands were perfectly still in his lap. And perfectly perfect. Honey colored with clean, pink fingernails. Everything about him was strong and slender. Every time he moved, he had a reason.

They were almost to school when he broke the silence. "Did you listen?"

She nodded, letting her eyes climb as high as his shoulders.

"Did you like it?" he asked.

She rolled her eyes. "Oh my God. It was . . . just, like—" She spread out all her fingers. "—so awesome."

"Are you being sarcastic? I can't tell."

She looked up at his face, even though she knew how that was going to feel, like someone was hooking her insides out through her chest. "No. It was awesome. I didn't want to stop listening. That one song— is it 'Love Will Tear Us Apart'?"

"Yeah, Joy Division."

"Oh my God, that's the best beginning to a song ever."

He imitated the guitar and the drums.

"Yeah, yeah, yeah," she said. "I just wanted to listen to those three seconds over and over."

"You could have." His eyes were smiling, his mouth only sort of.

"I didn't want to waste the batteries," she said.

He shook his head, like she was dumb.

"Plus," she said, "I love the rest of it just as much, like the high part, the melody, the *dahhh, dah-de-dah-dah, de-dahh, de dahhh.*"

He nodded.

"And his voice at the end," she said, "when he goes just a little bit too high . . . And then the *very* end, where it sounds like the drums are fighting it, like they don't want the song to be over . . ."

Park made drum noises with his mouth: *"Ch-ch-ch, ch-ch-ch."*

"I just want to break that song into pieces," she said, "and love them all to death."

That made him laugh. "What about the Smiths?" he asked.

"I didn't know who was who," she said.

"I'll write it down for you."

"I liked it all."

"Good," he said.

"I loved it."

He smiled, but turned away to look out the window. She looked down.

They were pulling into the parking lot. Eleanor didn't want this new talking thing—like, *really* talking, back and forth and smiling at each other—to stop.

"And . . ." she said quickly, "I love the *X-Men*. But I hate Cyclops."

He whipped his head back. "You can't hate Cyclops. He's team cap-tain."

"He's boring. He's worse than Batman."

"What? You hate Batman?"

"God. So boring. I can't even make myself read it. Whenever you bring *Batman,* I catch myself listening to Steve, or staring out the window, wishing I was in hypersleep." The bus came to a stop.

"Huh," he said, standing up. He said it really judgmentally.

"What?"

"Now I know what you're thinking when you stare out the window."

"No, you don't," she said. "I mix it up."

Everybody else was pushing down the aisle past them. Eleanor stood up, too.

"I'm bringing you *The Dark Knight Returns,*" he said.

"What's that?"

"Only the least boring Batman story ever."

"The least boring Batman story ever, huh? Does Batman raise *both* eyebrows?"

He laughed again. His face completely changed when he laughed. He didn't have dimples, exactly, but the sides of his face folded in on themselves, and his eyes almost disappeared.

"Just wait," he said.

park

That morning, in English, Park noticed that Eleanor's hair came to a soft red point on the back of her neck.

eleanor

That afternoon, in history, Eleanor noticed that Park chewed on his pencil when he was thinking. And that the girl sitting behind him—what's her name, Kim, with the giant breasts and the orange Esprit bag—obviously had a crush on him.

park

That night, Park made a tape with the Joy Division song on it, over and over again.

He emptied all his handheld video games and Josh's remote control cars, and called his grandma to tell her that all he wanted for his birthday in November was AA batteries.

14

eleanor

"I know she doesn't think I'm going to jump over that thing," DeNice said.

DeNice and the other girl, the big girl, Beebi, talked to Eleanor now in gym. (Because being assaulted with maxi pads is a great way to win friends and influence people.)

Today in class, their gym teacher, Mrs. Burt, had shown them how to swing over a thousand-year-old gymnastics horse. She said that next time, everybody had to try.

"She has got another thing coming," DeNice said after class, in the locker room. "Do I look like Mary Lou Retton?"

Beebi giggled. "Better tell her you didn't eat your Wheaties."

Actually, Eleanor thought, DeNice did kind of look like a gymnast. With her little-girl bangs and braids. She looked way too young to be in high school, and her clothes just made it worse. Puffed-sleeve shirts, overalls, matching ponytail balls . . . She wore her gym suit baggy, like a romper.

Eleanor wasn't scared of the horse, but she didn't want to have to run down the mats with the whole class watching her. She didn't want to run, period. It made her breasts feel like they were going to detach from her body.

"I'm going to tell Mrs. Burt that my mom doesn't want me to do anything that might rupture my hymen," Eleanor said. "For religious reasons."

"For real?" Beebi asked.

"No," Eleanor said, giggling. "Well. Actually . . ."

"You're nasty," DeNice said, hitching up her overalls.

Eleanor put her T-shirt on over her head, then wriggled out of her gym suit, using the shirt as cover.

"Are you coming?" DeNice asked.

"Well, I'm probably not going to start skipping class now just because of gymnastics," Eleanor said, hopping to pull up her jeans.

"No, are you coming to lunch?"

"Oh," Eleanor said, looking up. They were waiting for her at the end of the lockers. "Yeah."

"Then hurry up, Miss Jackson."

She sat with DeNice and Beebi at their usual table by the windows. During passing period, Eleanor saw Park walk by.

park

"Why can't you get your driver's license by homecoming?" Cal asked.

Mr. Stessman had them in small groups. They were supposed to be comparing Juliet to Ophelia.

"Because I can't bend time and space," Park said. Eleanor was sitting across the room by the windows. She was paired up with a guy named Eric, a basketball player. He was talking, and Eleanor was frowning at him.

"If you had your car," Cal said, "we could ask Kim."

"You can ask Kim," Park said.

Eric was one of those tall guys who always walked with his shoulders about a foot behind his hips. Constantly doing the limbo. Like he was afraid to hit his head on every doorjamb.

"She wants to go with a group," Cal said. "Plus I think she likes you."

"What? I don't want to go to homecoming with Kim. I don't even like her. I mean, you know . . . *You* like her."

"I know. That's why the plan works. We all go to homecoming together. She figures out you don't like her, she's miserable, and guess who's standing right there, asking her to slow dance?"

"I don't want to make Kim miserable."

"It's her or me, man."

Eric said something else, and Eleanor frowned again. Then she looked over at Park—and stopped frowning. Park smiled.

"One minute," Mr. Stessman said.

"Crap," Cal said. "What have we got? . . . Ophelia was bonkers, right? And Juliet was what, a sixth-grader?"

eleanor

"So Psylocke is another girl telepath?"

"Uh-huh," Park said.

Every morning when Eleanor got on the bus, she worried that Park wouldn't take off his headphones. That he would stop talking to her as suddenly as he'd started . . . And if that happened—if she got on the bus one day and he didn't look up—she didn't want him to see how devastated it would make her.

So far, it hadn't happened.

So far, they hadn't *stopped* talking. Like, literally. They talked every second they were sitting next to each other. And almost every conversation started with the words "What do you think—?"

What did Eleanor think about that U2 album? She loved it.

What did Park think of *Miami Vice*? He thought it was boring.

"Yes," they said when they agreed with each other. Back and forth—"Yes," "Yes," "Yes!"

"*I know.*"

"*Exactly.*"

"*Right?*"

They agreed about everything important and argued about everything else. And that was good, too, because whenever they argued, Eleanor could always crack Park up.

"Why do the X-Men need another girl telepath?" she asked.

"This one has purple hair."

"It's all so sexist."

Park's eyes got wide. Well, sort of wide. Sometimes she wondered if the shape of his eyes affected how he saw things. That was probably the most racist question of all time.

"The X-Men aren't sexist," he said, shaking his head. "They're a metaphor for acceptance; they've sworn to protect a world that hates and fears them."

"Yeah," she said, "but—"

"There's no *but*," he said, laughing.

"*But,*" Eleanor insisted, "the girls are all so stereotypically girly and passive. Half of them just think really hard. Like *that's* their superpower, *thinking*. And Shadowcat's power is even worse—she disappears."

"She becomes intangible," Park said. "That's different."

"It's still something you could do in the middle of a tea party," Eleanor said.

"Not if you were holding hot tea. Plus, you're forgetting Storm."

"I'm not forgetting Storm. She controls the weather with her head; it's still just thinking. Which is about all she *could* do in those boots."

"She has a cool Mohawk . . ." Park said.

"Irrelevant," Eleanor answered.

Park leaned his head back against the seat, smiling, and looked at the ceiling. "The X-Men aren't sexist."

"Are you trying to think of an empowered X-Woman?" Eleanor

asked. "How about Dazzler? She's a living disco ball. Or the White Queen? She thinks really hard while wearing spotless white lingerie."

"What kind of power would *you* want?" he asked, changing the subject. He turned his face toward her, laying his cheek against the top of the seat. Still smiling.

"I'd want to fly," Eleanor said, looking away from him. "I know it's not very useful, but . . . it's *flying*."

"Yes," he said.

park

"Damn, Park, are you going on a ninja mission?"

"Ninjas wear black, Steve."

"What?"

Park should have gone inside to change after taekwondo, but his dad said he had to be back by nine, and that gave him less than an hour to show Eleanor.

Steve was outside working on his Camaro. He didn't have his license yet either, but he was getting ready.

"Going to see your girlfriend?" he called to Park.

"What?"

"Sneaking out to see your girlfriend? Bloody Mary?"

"She's not my girlfriend," Park said, then swallowed.

"Sneaking out ninja-style," Steve said.

Park shook his head and broke into a run. Well, she wasn't, he thought to himself, cutting through the alley.

He didn't know where Eleanor lived, exactly. He knew where she got on the bus, and he knew that she lived next to the school. . . .

It must be this one, he thought. He stopped at a small white house. There were a few broken toys in the yard, and a giant Rottweiler was asleep on the porch.

Park walked toward the house slowly. The dog lifted its head and watched him for a second, then settled back to sleep. It didn't move, even when Park climbed the steps and knocked on the door.

The guy who answered looked too young to be Eleanor's dad. Park was pretty sure he'd seen this guy around the neighborhood before. He didn't know whom he'd expected to come to the door. Somebody more exotic. Somebody more like her.

The guy didn't even say anything. Just stood at the door and waited.

"Is Eleanor home?" Park asked.

"Who wants to know?" He had a nose like a knife, and he looked straight down it at Park.

"We go to school together," Park said.

The guy looked at Park for another second, then closed the door. Park wasn't sure what to do. He waited for a few minutes; then right as he was thinking about leaving, Eleanor opened the door just enough to slide through.

Her eyes were round with alarm. In the dark like this, it didn't even look like she had irises.

As soon as he saw her, he knew it had been a mistake to come here—he felt like he should have known that even sooner. He'd been so caught up in showing her . . .

"Hey," he said.

"Hi."

"I . . ."

". . . came to challenge me in hand-to-hand combat?"

Park reached into the front of his dobok and pulled out the second issue of *Watchmen*. Her face lit up; she was so pale, so luminous under the streetlight, that wasn't just an expression.

"Have you read it?" she asked.

He shook his head. "I thought we could . . . together."

Eleanor glanced back at the house, then stepped quickly off the porch. He followed her down the steps, across the gravel driveway, to the back stoop of the elementary school. There was a big safety light over the door. Eleanor sat on the top step, and he sat next to her.

It took twice as long to read *Watchmen* as it did any other comic, and it took even longer tonight because it was so strange to be sitting together somewhere other than on the bus. To even see each other outside of school. Eleanor's hair was wet and hanging in long, dark curls around her face.

When they got to the last page, all Park wanted to do was sit and talk about it. (All he really wanted to do was sit and talk to Eleanor.)

But she was already standing up and looking back at her house. "I've got to go," she said.

"Oh," he said. "Okay. I guess I do, too."

She left him sitting on the elementary school steps. She was disappearing inside the house before he could think about saying good-bye.

eleanor

When she walked back into the house, the living room was dark, but the TV was on. Eleanor could see Richie sitting on the couch and her mom standing in the doorway of the kitchen.

It was just a few steps to her room. . . .

"Is that your boyfriend?" Richie asked before she made it. He didn't look up from the TV.

"No," she said. "He's just a boy from school."

"What did he want?"

"To talk to me about an assignment."

She waited in her bedroom doorway. Then, when Richie didn't say anything more, she stepped inside, shutting the door behind her.

"I know what you're up to," he said, raising his voice, just as the door closed. "Nothing but a bitch in heat."

Eleanor let his words hit her full-on. Took them right in the chin.

She climbed into bed and clenched her eyes and jaw and fists— held everything clenched until she could breathe without screaming.

Until this moment, she'd kept Park in a place in her head that she thought Richie couldn't get to. Completely separate from this house and everything that happened here. (It was a pretty awesome place. Like the only part of her head fit for praying.)

But now Richie was in there, just pissing all over everything. Making everything she felt feel as rank and rotten as him.

Now she couldn't think about Park—

About the way he looked in the dark, dressed in white, like a superhero.

About the way he smelled, like sweat and bar soap.

About the way he smiled when he liked something, with his lips just turned up at the corners . . .

Without feeling Richie leer.

She kicked the cat out of the bed, just to be mean. He squawked, but jumped right back up.

"Eleanor," Maisie whispered from the bottom bunk, "was that your boyfriend?"

Eleanor crushed her teeth together. "No," she whispered back viciously. "He's just a boy."

15

eleanor

Her mother stood in the bedroom the next morning while Eleanor got ready. "Here," she whispered, taking the hairbrush and drawing Eleanor's hair into a ponytail without brushing out the curl. "Eleanor . . ." she said.

"I know why you're in here," Eleanor said, pulling away. "I don't want to talk about it."

"Just listen."

"No. *I know*. He won't come back, okay? I didn't invite him, but I'll tell him, and he won't come back."

"Okay, well . . . good," her mom said, folding her arms, still whispering. "It's just that you're so young."

"No," Eleanor said, "that's not what it is. But it doesn't even matter. He won't come back, okay? It isn't even like that, anyway."

Her mom left the room. Richie was still in the house. Eleanor ran out the front door when she heard him turn on the bathroom sink.

It's not even like that, she thought as she walked to the bus stop. And thinking it made her want to cry, because she knew it was true.

And wanting to cry just made her angry.

Because if she was going to cry about something, it was going to be the fact that her life was complete shit—not because some cool, cute guy didn't like her *like that.*

Especially when just being Park's friend was pretty much the best thing that had ever happened to her.

She must have looked ticked off when she got on the bus because Park didn't say hi when she sat down.

Eleanor looked into the aisle.

After a few seconds, he reached over and pulled at the old silk scarf she'd tied around her wrist. "I'm sorry," he said.

"For what?" She even sounded angry. God, she was a jerk.

"I don't know," he said. "I feel like maybe I got you in trouble last night. . . ."

He pulled on the scarf again, so she looked at him. She tried not to look mad—but she'd rather look mad than look like she'd spent all night thinking about how beautiful his lips were.

"Was that your dad?" he asked.

She jerked her head back. "*No.* No, that was my . . . mother's husband. He's not really *my* anything. My problem, I guess."

"Did you get in trouble?"

"Sort of." She really didn't want to talk to Park about Richie. She'd just about scraped all the Richie off the Park place in her head.

"I'm sorry," he said again.

"It's okay," she said. "It wasn't your fault. Anyway, thanks for bringing *Watchmen.* I'm glad I got to read it."

"It was cool, huh?"

"Oh, *yeah.* Kind of brutal. I mean that part with the Comedian . . ."

"Yeah . . . sorry."

"No, I didn't mean that. I mean . . . I think I need to reread it."

"I read it again twice last night. You can take it tonight."

"Yeah? Thanks."

He was still holding the end of her scarf, rubbing the silk idly between his thumb and fingers. She watched his hand.

If he were to look up at her now, he'd know exactly how stupid she was. She could feel her face go soft and gummy. If Park were to look up at her now, he'd know everything.

He didn't look up. He wound the scarf around his fingers until her hand was hanging in the space between them.

Then he slid the silk and his fingers into her open palm.

And Eleanor disintegrated.

park

Holding Eleanor's hand was like holding a butterfly. Or a heartbeat. Like holding something complete, and completely alive.

As soon as he touched her, he wondered how he'd gone this long without doing it. He rubbed his thumb through her palm and up her fingers, and was aware of her every breath.

Park had held hands with girls before. Girls at Skateland. A girl at the ninth-grade dance last year. (They'd kissed while they waited for her dad to pick them up.) He'd even held Tina's hand, back when they "went" together in the sixth grade.

And always before, it had been fine. Not much different from holding Josh's hand when they were little kids crossing the street. Or holding his grandma's hand when she took him to church. Maybe a little sweatier, a little more awkward.

When he'd kissed that girl last year, with his mouth dry and his eyes mostly open, Park had wondered if maybe there was something wrong with him.

He'd even wondered—seriously, while he was kissing her, he'd wondered this—whether he might be gay. Except he didn't feel like kissing any guys either. And if he thought about She-Hulk or Storm (instead of this girl, Dawn) the kissing got a lot better.

Maybe I'm not attracted to real girls, he'd thought at the time. *Maybe I'm some sort of perverted cartoon-sexual.*

Or maybe, he thought now, he just didn't recognize all those other girls. The way a computer drive will spit out a disk if it doesn't recognize the formatting.

When he touched Eleanor's hand, he recognized her. He knew.

eleanor

Disintegrated.

Like something had gone wrong beaming her onto the Starship *Enterprise.*

If you've ever wondered what that feels like, it's a lot like melting— but more violent.

Even in a million different pieces, Eleanor could still feel Park holding her hand. Could still feel his thumb exploring her palm. She sat completely still because she didn't have any other option. She tried to remember what kind of animals paralyzed their prey before they ate them. . . .

Maybe Park had paralyzed her with his ninja magic, his Vulcan handhold, and now he was going to eat her.

That would be awesome.

park

They broke apart when the bus stopped. A flood of reality rushed through Park, and he looked around nervously to see if anyone had been watching them. Then he looked nervously at Eleanor to see if she'd noticed him looking.

She was still staring at the floor, even as she picked up her books and stood in the aisle.

If someone had been watching, what would they have seen? Park couldn't imagine what his face had looked like when he touched Eleanor. Like somebody taking the first drink in a Diet Pepsi commercial. Over-the-top bliss.

He stood behind her in the aisle. She was just about his height. Her hair was pulled up, and her neck was flushed and splotchy. He resisted the urge to lay his cheek against it.

He walked with her all the way to her locker, and leaned against the wall as she opened it. She didn't say anything, just shifted some books onto the shelf and took down a few others.

As the buzz of touching her faded, he was starting to realize that Eleanor hadn't actually done anything to touch him back. She hadn't bent her fingers around his. She hadn't even looked at him. She still hadn't looked at him. *Jesus.*

He knocked gently on her locker door.

"Hey," he said.

She shut the door. "Hey, what?"

"Okay?" he asked.

She nodded.

"I'll see you in English?" he asked.

She nodded and walked away.

Jesus.

eleanor

All through first and second and third hour, Eleanor rubbed her palm. Nothing happened.

How could it be possible that there were that many nerve endings all in one place?

And were they always there, or did they just flip on whenever they felt like it? Because, if they were always there, how did she manage to turn doorknobs without fainting?

Maybe this was why so many people said it felt better to drive a stick shift.

park

Jesus. Was it possible to rape somebody's hand?

Eleanor wouldn't look at Park during English and history. He went to her locker after school, but she wasn't there.

When he got on the bus, she was already sitting in their seat—but sitting in his spot, against the wall. He was too embarrassed to say anything. He sat down next to her and let his hands hang between his knees. . . .

Which meant she really had to reach for his wrist, to pull his hand into hers. She wrapped her fingers around his and touched his palm with her thumb.

Her fingers were trembling.

Park shifted in his seat and turned his back to the aisle.

"Okay?" she whispered.

He nodded, taking a deep breath. They both stared down at their hands.

Jesus.

16

eleanor

Saturdays were the worst.

On Sundays, Eleanor could think all day about how close it was to Monday. But Saturdays were ten years long.

She'd already finished her homework. Some creep had written *do i make you wet* on her geography book, so she spent a really long time covering it up with a black ink pen. She tried to turn it into some kind of flower.

She watched cartoons with the little kids until golf came on, then played double solitaire with Maisie until they were both bored stupid.

Later, she'd listen to music. She'd saved the last two batteries Park had given her so that she could listen to her tape player today when she missed him most. She had five tapes from him now—which meant, if her batteries lasted, she had 450 minutes to spend with Park in her head, holding his hand.

Maybe it was stupid, but that's what she did with him, even in her fantasies—even where anything was possible. As far as Eleanor was concerned, that just showed how wonderful it was to hold Park's hand.

(Besides they didn't *just* hold hands. Park touched her hands like they were something rare and precious, like her fingers were intimately connected to the rest of her body. Which, of course, they were. It was hard to explain. He made her feel like more than the sum of her parts.)

The only bad thing about their new bus routine was that it had seriously cut back on their conversations. She could hardly look at Park when he was touching her. And Park seemed to have a hard time finishing his sentences. (Which meant he liked her. *Ha*.)

Yesterday, on the way home from school, their bus had to take a fifteen-minute detour because of a busted sewer pipe. Steve had started cussing about how he needed to get to his new job at the gas station. And Park had said, "Wow . . ."

"What?" Eleanor sat by the wall now, because it made her feel safer, less exposed. She could almost pretend that they had the bus to themselves.

"I can actually burst sewers with my mind," Park said.

"That's a very limited mutation," she said. "What do they call you?"

"They call me . . . um . . ." And then he'd started laughing and pulled at one of her curls. (That was a new, awesome development— the hair touching. Sometimes he'd come up behind her after school, and tug at her ponytail or tap the top of her bun.)

"I . . . don't know what they call me," he said.

"Maybe the Public Works," she said, laying her hand on top of his, finger to finger. Her fingertips came to his last knuckle. It might be the only part of her that was smaller than him.

"You're like a little girl," he said.

"What do you mean?"

"Your hands. They just look . . ." He took her hand in both of his. "I don't know . . . vulnerable."

"Pipemaster," she whispered.

"What?"

"That's your superhero name. No, wait—the Piper. Like, 'Time to pay the Piper!'"

He laughed and pulled at another curl.

That was the most talking they'd done in two weeks. She'd started to write him a letter—she'd started it a million times—but that seemed like such a seventh grade thing to do. What could she write?

Dear Park, I like you. You have really cute hair.

He did have really cute hair. Really, really. Short in the back, but kind of long and fanned out in the front. It was completely straight and almost completely black, which, on Park, seemed like a lifestyle choice. He always wore black, practically head to toe. Black punk rock T-shirts over black, thermal long-sleeved shirts. Black sneakers. Blue jeans. Almost all black, almost every day. (He did have one white T-shirt, but it said BLACK FLAG on the front in big black letters.)

Whenever Eleanor wore black, her mom said that she looked like she was going to a funeral—in a coffin. Anyway, her mom used to say stuff like that, back when she occasionally noticed what Eleanor was wearing. Eleanor had taken all the safety pins from her mom's sewing kit and used them to pin scraps of silk and velvet over the holes in her jeans, and her mom hadn't even mentioned it.

Park looked good in black. It made him look like he was drawn in charcoal. Thick, arched black eyebrows. Short black lashes. High, shining cheeks.

Dear Park, I like you so much. You have really beautiful cheeks.

The only thing she didn't like to think about, about Park, was what he could possibly see in her.

park

The pickup kept dying.

Park's dad wasn't saying anything, but Park knew he was getting pissed.

"Try again," his dad said. "Just listen to the engine, then shift."

That was an oversimplification if Park had ever heard one. Listen to the engine, depress the clutch, shift, gas, release, steer, check your mirrors, signal your turn, look twice for motorcycles. . . .

The crappy part was that he was pretty sure he could do it if his dad wasn't sitting there, fuming. Park could see himself doing it in his head just fine.

It was like this at taekwondo sometimes, too. Park could never master something new if his dad was the one teaching it.

Clutch, shift, gas.

The pickup died.

"You're thinking too much," his dad snapped.

Which is what his dad always said. When Park was a kid, he'd try to argue with him. "I can't *help* but think," Park would say during taekwondo. "I can't turn off my brain."

"If you fight like that, somebody's going to turn it off for you."

Clutch, shift, grind.

"Start it again. . . . Now, don't think, just shift. . . . I said, *don't think.*"

The truck died again. Park put his hands at ten and two and laid his head on the steering well, bracing himself. His dad was radiating frustration.

"Goddamn, Park, I don't know what to do with you. We've been working on this for a year. I taught your brother to drive in two weeks."

If his mom were here, she would have called foul at this. *You don't do that,* she'd say. *Two boys. Different.*

And his dad would grit his teeth.

"I guess Josh doesn't have any trouble not thinking," Park said.

"Call your brother stupid all you want," his dad said. "He can drive a manual transmission."

"But I'm only ever gonna get to drive the Impala," Park muttered into the dash, "and it's an automatic."

"That isn't the point," his dad half shouted. If Park's mom were here, she would have said, *Hey, mister, I don't think so. You go outside and yell at sky, you so angry.*

What did it say about Park that he wished his mom would follow him around defending him?

That he was a pussy.

That's what his dad thought. It's probably what he was thinking now. He was probably being so quiet because he was trying not to say it out loud.

"Try it again," his dad said.

"No, I'm done."

"You're done when I say you're done."

"No," Park said, "I'm done now."

"Well, I'm not driving us home. Try it again."

Park started the truck. It died. His dad slammed his giant hand against the glove box. Park opened the truck door and jumped to the ground. His dad shouted his name, but Park kept walking. They were only a couple miles from home.

If his dad drove by him on the way home, Park didn't notice. When he got back to his neighborhood, at dusk, Park turned down Eleanor's street instead of his own. There were two little reddish blond kids playing in her yard, even though it was kind of cold.

He couldn't see into the house. Maybe if he stood here long enough, she'd look out the window. Park just wanted to see her face. Her big brown eyes, her full pink lips. Her mouth kind of looked like the Joker's—depending on who was drawing him—really wide and curvy. Not psychotic, obviously . . . Park should never tell her this. It definitely didn't sound like a compliment.

Eleanor didn't look out the window. But the kids were staring at him, so Park walked home.

Saturdays were the worst.

17

eleanor

Mondays were the best.

Today, when she got on the bus, Park actually smiled at her. Like, smiled at her the whole time she was walking down the aisle.

Eleanor couldn't bring herself to smile directly back at him, not in front of everybody. But she couldn't help but smile, so she smiled at the floor and looked up every few seconds to see whether he was still looking at her.

He was.

Tina was looking at her, too, but Eleanor ignored her.

Park stood up when she got to their row, and as soon as she sat down, he took her hand and kissed it. It happened so fast, she didn't have time to die of ecstasy or embarrassment.

She let her face fall for just a few seconds against his shoulder, against the sleeve of his black trench coat. He squeezed her hand tight.

"I missed you," he whispered. She felt tears in her eyes and turned to the window.

They didn't say anything more all the way to school. Park walked with Eleanor to her locker, and they both stood there quietly, leaning against the wall almost until the bell rang. The hall was practically empty.

Then Park reached up and wrapped one of her red curls around his honey finger.

"Back to missing you," he said, letting it go.

She was late to homeroom and didn't hear Mr. Sarpy tell her that she had an office pass. He slammed it on her desk.

"Eleanor, wake up! You've got a pass from your counselor." God, he was a jerk—she was glad she didn't have him for a real class. As she walked to the office, she trailed her fingertips along the brick wall and hummed a song Park had given her.

She was so blissed out, she even smiled at Mrs. Dunne when she got to her office.

"Eleanor," she said, hugging her. Mrs. Dunne was big on hugging. She'd hugged Eleanor the very first time they met. "How are you?"

"I'm good."

"You *look* good," Mrs. Dunne said.

Eleanor looked down at her sweater (a very fat man had probably bought it to wear golfing in 1968) and at her holey jeans. God, how bad did she usually look? "Thanks, I guess."

"I've been talking to your teachers," Mrs. Dunne said. "Did you know you're getting A's in almost all your classes?"

Eleanor shrugged. She didn't have cable or a phone, and she felt like she was living underground in her own house. . . . There was plenty of time for homework.

"Well, you are," Mrs. Dunne said. "And I'm so *proud* of you."

Eleanor was glad there was a desk between them now. Mrs. Dunne looked like she had another hug coming on.

"But that's not why I called you down here. The reason you're here is because I got a telephone call for you this morning, before school started. A man called—he said that he was your dad—and that he was calling here because he didn't have your home number. . . ."

"I don't actually have a home number," Eleanor said.

"Ah," Mrs. Dunne said, "I see. Would your dad know that?"

"Probably not," Eleanor said. She was surprised he even knew what school she went to.

"Would you like to call him? You could use my office."

Would she like to call him? Why would he want to call her? Maybe something horrible (something *really* horrible) had happened. Maybe her grandma had died. God.

"Sure . . ." Eleanor said.

"You know," Mrs. Dunne said, "you can come use my phone whenever you need to." She stood up and sat on the edge of her desk, resting her hand on Eleanor's knee. Eleanor was *this close* to asking for a toothbrush, but she thought that would lead to a marathon of hugging and knee-rubbing.

"Thanks," Eleanor said instead.

"Okay," Mrs. Dunne said, beaming. "I'll be right back then. I'll just go freshen up my lipstick."

When Mrs. Dunne left, Eleanor dialed her dad's number. He answered after the third ring.

"Hey, Dad. It's Eleanor."

"Hey, baby, how are you?"

She thought for a second about telling him the truth. "Fine," she said.

"How's everybody?"

"Fine."

"You guys never call."

There was no use telling him that they didn't have a phone. Or pointing out that he never called them back when they did have a phone. Or even saying that maybe *he* should find a way to talk to *them*, him being the one with a phone and a car and a life of his own.

There was no use telling her dad anything. Eleanor had known that for so long, she couldn't even remember figuring it out.

"Hey, I've got a cool offer for you," he said. "I thought maybe you could come over on Friday night." Her dad had a voice like someone on TV, somebody who would try to sell you record compilations. Disco hits of the '70s or the latest Time–Life collection.

"Donna wants me to go to some wedding," he said, "and I told her you would probably watch Matt. Thought you might like some baby-sitting money."

"Who's Donna?"

"You know, Donna—Donna my fiancée. You guys met her the last time you were here."

That was almost a year ago. "Your neighbor?" Eleanor asked.

"Yeah, Donna. You can come over and spend the night. Watch Matt, eat pizza, talk on the phone . . . It will be the easiest ten bucks you ever made."

And actually, the first.

"Okay," Eleanor said. "Are you picking us up? Do you know where we live now?"

"I'll pick you up at school—just you this time. I don't want to give you a whole houseful of kids to watch. What time do they let you out of there?"

"Three."

"Cool. I'll see you Friday at three."

"All right."

"Well, all right. I love you, baby, study hard."

Mrs. Dunne was waiting in the doorway, with her arms open.

Fine, Eleanor thought as she walked down the hall. *Everything is fine. Everyone is fine.* She kissed the back of her hand, just to see how it felt on her lips.

park

"I'm not going to homecoming," Park said.

"Of course you're not going . . . to the *dance,*" Cal said. "I mean, it's way too late to rent a tux anyways."

They were early to English class. Cal sat two seats behind him, so Park kept having to look back over his shoulder to see if Eleanor had walked in yet.

"You're renting a tux?" Park asked.

"Uh, yeah," Cal said.

"Nobody rents a tux for homecoming."

"So who's going to look like the classiest guy there? Besides, what do you know—you're not even going—to the dance, that is. The football game, however? Different story."

"I don't even like football," Park said, looking back at the door.

"Could you stop being the worst friend in the world, for, like, five minutes?"

Park looked up at the clock. "Yes."

"Please," Cal said, "do me this one favor. There's a whole group of cool people going, and if you go, Kim will sit with us. You're a Kim magnet."

"Don't you see what a problem that is?"

"No. It's like I've found the perfect bait for my Kim trap."

"Stop saying her name like that."

"Why? She's not here yet, is she?"

Park glanced over his shoulder. "Can't you just like a girl who likes you back?"

"None of them like me back," Cal said. "I may as well like the one I really want. Come on, please. Come to the game on Friday—for me."

"I don't know . . ." Park said.

"Wow, what's up with her? She looks like she just killed somebody for fun."

Park whipped his head around. Eleanor. Smiling at him.

She had the kind of smile you see in toothpaste commercials, where you can see practically all of somebody's teeth. She should smile like that all the time, Park thought; it made her face cross over from weird to beautiful. He wanted to make her smile like that constantly.

Mr. Stessman pretended to fall against the chalkboard when he walked in. "Good God, Eleanor, stop. You're blinding me. Is that why you keep that smile locked away, because it's too powerful for mortal man?"

She looked down self-consciously and flattened her smile into a smirk.

"Psst," Cal said. Kim was sitting down between them. Cal locked his fingers together like he was begging. Park sighed and nodded his head.

eleanor

She waited for the phone call from her dad to go sour on her. (Conversations with her dad were like whiplash; they didn't always hurt right away.)

But it didn't. Nothing could bring Eleanor down. Nothing could drive Park's words from her head.

He *missed* her. . . .

Who knew what he missed. Her fatness. Her weirdness. The fact that she couldn't talk to him like a regular person. Whatever. Whatever perversion caused him to like her was his problem. But he did like her; she was sure of it.

At least for now.

For today.

He *liked* her. He missed her.

She was so distracted in gym class, she actually forgot not to try. They were playing basketball, and Eleanor caught the ball, colliding with one of Tina's friends, a jumpy, wiry girl named Annette. "Are you trying to start something?" Annette demanded, pushing forward— pushing the ball into Eleanor's chest. "Are you? Come on, then, let's go. Come on." Eleanor took a few steps back, out of bounds, and waited for Mrs. Burt to blow the whistle.

Annette stayed mad for the rest of the game, but Eleanor didn't let it get to her.

That feeling she used to have when she was sitting next to Park on the bus—that feeling that she was on base, that she was safe for the moment—she could summon it now. Like a force field. Like she was the Invisible Girl.

That would make Park Mr. Fantastic.

18

eleanor

Her mom wasn't going to let her babysit.

"He has *four* children," her mother said. She was rolling out dough for tortillas. "Did he forget that?"

Eleanor had stupidly told her mother about her dad's phone call in front of her brothers and sister—they'd all gotten really excited. And then Eleanor had to tell them that they weren't invited, that it was just babysitting, anyway, and that Dad wasn't even going to be there.

Mouse had started to cry, and Maisie got mad and stormed out. Ben asked Eleanor if she'd call Dad back to see if he could come along to help. "Tell him I babysit all the time," Ben said.

"Your father is a piece of work," her mother said. "Every time, he breaks your hearts. And every time, he expects me to pick up the pieces."

Pick up, sweep aside—same difference in her mom's world. Eleanor didn't argue.

"Please let me go," she said.

"Why do you want to go?" her mom asked. "Why do you even care about him? He's never cared about you."

God. Even if it was true, it still hurt to hear it that way.

"I *don't* care," Eleanor said. "I just need to get out of here. I haven't been anywhere but school in two months. Plus, he said he'd pay me."

"If he has extra money sitting around, maybe he should pay his child support."

"Mom . . . it's ten dollars. Please."

Her mother sighed. "Fine. I'll talk to Richie."

"No. *God.* Don't talk to Richie. He'll just say no. And anyway, he can't tell me that I can't see my father."

"Richie is the head of this household," her mom said. "Richie is the one who puts food on our table."

What food? Eleanor wanted to ask. *And, for that matter, what table?* They ate on the couch or on the floor or sitting on the back steps holding paper plates. Besides, Richie would say no just for the pleasure of saying it. It would make him feel like the king of Spain. Which was probably why her mom wanted to give him the chance.

"Mom." Eleanor put her face in her hand and leaned against the refrigerator. *"Please."*

"Oh, *fine,*" her mother said bitterly. "Fine. But if he gives you any money, you can split it with your brothers and sister. That's the least you can do."

They could have it all. All Eleanor wanted was the chance to talk to Park on the phone. To be able to talk to him without every inbred hellspawn in the Flats listening.

The next morning on the bus, while Park ran his finger along the inside of her bracelet, Eleanor asked him for his phone number.

He started laughing.

"Why is that funny?" she asked.

"Because," he said quietly. They said everything quietly, even though everyone else on the bus roared, even though you'd have to shout into a megaphone to be heard over all the cursing and idiocy. "I feel like you're hitting on me," he said.

"Maybe I shouldn't ask for your number," she said. "You've never asked for mine."

He looked up at her through his bangs. "I figured you weren't allowed to talk on the phone . . . after that time with your stepdad."

"I probably wouldn't be, if I had a phone." She usually tried not to tell Park things like that. Like, all the things she didn't have. She waited for him to react, but he didn't. He just ran his thumb along the veins in her wrist.

"Then why do you want my number?"

God, she thought, *never mind.* "You don't have to give it to me."

He rolled his eyes and got a pen out of his backpack, then reached over and took one of her books.

"No," she whispered, "don't. I don't want my mom to see it."

He frowned at her book. "I'd think you'd be more worried about her seeing *this.*"

Eleanor looked down. Crap. Whoever wrote that gross thing on her geography book had written on her history book, too.

suck me off it said in ugly blue letters.

She grabbed Park's pen and started scribbling it out.

"Why would you write that?" he asked. "Is that a song?"

"I didn't write it," she said. She could feel patches of red creep up her neck.

"Then who did?"

She gave him the meanest look she was capable of. (It was hard to look at him with anything other than gooey eyes.) "I don't know," she said.

"Why would *anyone* write that?"

"I don't *know.*" She pulled her books against her chest and wrapped her arms around them.

"Hey," he said.

Eleanor ignored him and looked out the window. She couldn't believe she'd let him see that on her book. It was one thing to let him see her crazy life a little bit at a time. . . . *So, yeah, I have a terrible stepdad, and I don't have a phone, and sometimes when we're out of dish soap, I wash my hair with flea and tick shampoo.* . . .

It was another thing to remind him that she was *that* girl. She may as well invite him to gym class. She might as well give him an alphabetical list of all the names they called her.

A—Ass, Fat
B—Bitch, Redheaded

He'd probably try to ask her *why* she was that girl.

"Hey," he said.

She shook her head.

It wouldn't do any good to tell him that she hadn't been *that* girl at her old school. Yeah, she'd been made fun of before. There were always mean boys—and there were always, always mean girls—but she'd had friends at her old school. She had people to eat lunch with and pass notes to. People used to pick her to be on their team in gym class just because they thought she was nice and funny.

"Eleanor . . ." he said.

But there was no one like Park at her old school.

There was no one like Park anywhere.

"What," she said to the window.

"How're you going to call me if you don't have my number?"

"Who said I was going to call you?" She hugged her books even closer.

He leaned against her, pressing his shoulder into hers. "Don't be mad at me," he said, sighing. "It makes me crazy."

"I'm never mad at you," she said.

"Right."

"I'm not."

"You must just be mad *near* me a lot."

She pushed her shoulder against his and smiled despite herself.

"I'm babysitting at my dad's house Friday night," she said, "and he said I could use the phone."

Park turned his face eagerly. It was painfully close to hers. She could kiss him—or head-butt him—before he'd ever have a chance to pull away. "Yeah?" he asked.

"Yeah."

"*Yeah,*" he said, smiling. "But you won't let me write down my number?"

"Tell me," she said. "I'll memorize it."

"Let me write it down."

"I'll memorize it to the tune of a song, so that I don't forget."

He started singing his number to the tune of "867-5309," which cracked her right up.

park

Park tried to remember the first time he saw her.

Because he could remember, on that day, seeing what everybody else saw. He could remember thinking that she was asking for it. . . .

That it was bad enough to have curly red hair. That it was bad enough to have a face shaped like a box of chocolates.

No, he hadn't thought exactly that. He'd thought . . .

That it was bad enough to have a million freckles and chubby baby cheeks.

God, she had adorable cheeks. Dimples on top of freckles, which shouldn't even be allowed, and round as crabapples. It was kind of amazing that more people didn't try to pinch her cheeks. His grandma was definitely going to pinch her when they met.

But Park hadn't thought that either, the first time he saw Eleanor on the bus. He remembered thinking that it was bad enough that she looked the way she did. . . .

Did she have to dress like that? And act like that? Did she have to try so hard to be different?

He remembered feeling embarrassed for her.

And now . . .

Now, he felt the fight rising up in his throat whenever he thought of people making fun of her.

When he thought of someone writing that ugly thing on her book . . . it made him feel like Bill Bixby just before he turned into the Hulk.

It had been so hard, on the bus, to pretend that it didn't bother him. He didn't want to make anything worse for her—he'd put his hands in his pockets and pressed them into fists, and held them that way all morning long.

All morning long, he'd wanted to punch something. Or kick something. Park had gym class right after lunch, and he ran so hard during drills, he'd started to retch up his fish sandwich.

Mr. Koenig, his gym teacher, made him leave class early and take a shower. "Hit the bricks, Sheridan. Now. This isn't *Chariots of* fuckin' *Fire*."

Park wished it was *only* righteous anger that he felt. He wished that he could feel defensive and protective of Eleanor without feeling . . . everything else.

Without feeling like they were making fun of him, too.

There were moments—not just today, moments every day since they'd met—when Eleanor made him self-conscious, when he saw people talking and he was sure they were talking about them. Raucous moments on the bus when he was sure that everyone was laughing at them.

And in those moments, Park thought about pulling back from her.

Not breaking up with her. That phrase didn't even seem to apply here. Just . . . easing away. Recovering the six inches between them.

He'd roll the thought over in his head until the next time he saw her.

In class, at her desk. On the bus, waiting for him. Reading alone in the cafeteria.

Whenever he saw Eleanor, he couldn't think about pulling away. He couldn't think about anything at all.

Except touching her.

Except doing whatever he could or had to, to make her happy.

———

"What do you mean you're not coming tonight?" Cal said.

They were in study hall, and Cal was eating a Snack Pack butterscotch pudding. Park tried to keep his voice down. "Something came up."

"Something?" Cal said, slamming his spoon into his pudding. "Like you being completely lame—is that what came up? Because that comes up a lot lately."

"No. *Something*. Like, a girl something."

Cal leaned in. "You've got a girl something?"

Park felt himself blush. "Sort of. Yeah. I can't really talk about it."

"But we had a plan," Cal said.

"You had a plan," Park said, "and it was terrible."

"Worst friend in the world," Cal said.

eleanor

She was so nervous, she couldn't even touch her lunch. She gave DeNice her creamed turkey and Beebi her fruit cocktail.

Park made her practice his phone number all the way home.

And then he wrote it on her book anyway. He hid it in song titles.

"Forever Young."

"That's a 4," he said. "Will you remember?"

"I won't have to," she said. "I already know your number by heart."

"And this is just a 5," he said, "because I can't think of any 5 songs, and this one"—*"Summer of '69"*—"With this one, remember the 6, but forget the 9."

"I hate that song."

"God, I know. . . . Hey, I can't think of any 2 songs."

" 'Two of Us,' " she said.

"Two of us?"

"It's a Beatles song."

"Oh . . . that's why I don't know it." He wrote it down.

"I know your number by heart," she said.

"I'm just afraid you're going to forget it," he said quietly. He pushed her hair out of her eyes with his pen.

"I'm not going to forget it," she said. Ever. She'd probably scream out Park's number on her deathbed. Or have it tattooed over her heart when he finally got sick of her. "I'm good with numbers."

"If you don't call me Friday night," he said, "because you can't remember my number . . ."

"How about this—I'll give you my dad's number, and if I haven't called you by nine, you can call me."

"That's an excellent idea," he said, "seriously."

"But you can't call it any other time."

"I feel like—" He started laughing and looked away.

"What?" she asked. She elbowed him.

"I feel like we have a date," he said. "Is that stupid?"

"No," she said.

"Even though we're together every day . . ."

"We're never really together," she said.

"It's like we have fifty chaperones."

"Hostile chaperones," Eleanor whispered.

"Yeah," Park said.

He put his pen in his pocket, then took her hand and held it to his chest for a minute.

It was the nicest thing she could imagine. It made her want to have his babies and give him both of her kidneys.

"A date," he said.

"Practically," she added.

19

eleanor

When she woke up that morning, she felt like it was her birthday—like she used to feel on her birthday, back when there was a shot in hell of ice cream.

Maybe her dad would have ice cream. . . . If he did, he'd probably throw it away before Eleanor got there. He was always dropping hints about her weight. Well, he used to, anyway. Maybe when he stopped caring about her altogether, he'd stopped caring about that, too.

Eleanor put on an old, striped men's shirt and had her mom tie one of her ties—like knot it, for real—around her neck.

Her mom actually kissed Eleanor good-bye at the door and told her to have fun, and to call the neighbors if things got weird with her dad.

Right, Eleanor thought, *I'll be sure to call you if Dad's fiancée calls me a bitch and then makes me use a bathroom without a door. Oh, wait . . .*

She was a little nervous. It had been a year, at least, since she'd seen her dad, and a while before that. He hadn't called at all when she lived with the Hickmans. Maybe he didn't know she was there. She never told him.

When Richie first started coming around, Ben used to get really angry and say he was going to move in with their dad—which was an empty effing promise, and everyone knew it. Even Mouse, who was just a toddler.

Their dad couldn't stand having them even for a few days. He used to pick them up from their mom's house, then drop them off at *his* mom's house, while he went off and did whatever it was that he did on the weekend. (Presumably, lots and lots of marijuana.)

Park cracked up when he saw Eleanor's tie. That was even better than making him smile.

"I didn't know we were getting dressed up," he said when she sat down next to him.

"I'm expecting you to take me someplace nice," she said softly.

"I will . . ." he said. He took the tie in both hands and straightened it. "Someday."

He was a lot more likely to say stuff like that on the way to school than he was on the way home. Sometimes she wondered if he was fully awake.

He turned practically sideways in his seat. "So you're leaving right after school?"

"Yeah."

"And you'll call me as soon as you get there. . . ."

"No, I'll call you as soon as the kid settles down. I really do have to babysit."

"I'm going to ask you a lot of personal questions," he said, leaning forward. "I have a list."

"I'm not afraid of your list."

"It's extremely long," he said, "and extremely personal."

"I hope you're not expecting *answers.* . . ."

He sat back in the seat and looked over at her. "I wish you'd go away," he whispered, "so that we could finally talk."

Eleanor stood on the front steps after school. She'd hoped to catch Park before he got on the bus, but she must have missed him.

She wasn't sure what kind of car to watch for; her dad was always buying classic cars, then selling them when money got tight.

She was starting to worry that he wasn't coming at all—he could've gone to the wrong high school or changed his mind—when he honked for her.

He pulled up in an old Karmann Ghia convertible. It looked like the car James Dean died in. Her dad's arm was hanging over the door, holding a cigarette. "Eleanor!"

She walked to the car and got in. There weren't any seat belts.

"Is that all you brought?" he asked, looking at her school bag.

"It's just one night." She shrugged.

"All right," he said, backing out of the parking space too fast. She'd forgotten what a crappy driver he was. He did everything too fast and one-handed.

Eleanor braced herself on the dashboard. It was cold out, and once they were driving, it got colder. "Can we put the top up?" she shouted.

"Haven't fixed it yet," her dad said, and laughed.

He still lived in the same duplex he'd lived in since her parents split up. It was solid and brick, and about a ten-minute drive from Eleanor's school.

When they got inside, he took a better look at her.

"Is that what all the cool kids are wearing these days?" he asked. She looked down at her giant white shirt, her fat paisley tie, and her half-dead purple corduroys.

"Yup," she said flatly. "This is pretty much our uniform."

Her dad's girlfriend—fiancée—Donna, didn't get off work until five, and after that, she had to pick her kid up from day care. In the meantime, Eleanor and her dad sat on the couch and watched ESPN.

He smoked cigarette after cigarette, and sipped Scotch out of a short glass. Every once in a while the phone would ring, and he'd have a long, laughy conversation with somebody about a car or a deal or a bet. You'd think that every single person who called was his best friend in the whole world. Her dad had baby blond hair and a round, boyish face. When he smiled, which was constantly, his whole face lit up like a billboard. If Eleanor paid too much attention, she hated him.

His duplex had changed since the last time she was here, and it was more than just the box of Fisher-Price toys in the living room and the makeup in the bathroom.

When they'd first started visiting him here—after the divorce, but before Richie—their dad's duplex had been a bare-bones bachelor pad. He didn't even have enough bowls for them all to have soup. He'd served Eleanor clam chowder once in a highball glass. And he had only two towels. "One wet," he'd said, "one dry."

Now Eleanor fixated on all the small luxuries strewn and tucked around the house. Packs of cigarettes, newspapers, magazines . . . Brand-name cereal and quilted toilet paper. His refrigerator was full of things you tossed into the cart without thinking about it just because they sounded good. Custard-style yogurt. Grapefruit juice. Little round cheeses individually wrapped in red wax.

She couldn't wait for her dad to leave so that she could start eating *everything*. There were stacks of Coca-Cola cans in the pantry. She was going to drink Coke like water all night—she might even wash her face with it. *And* she was going to order a pizza. Unless the pizza came out of her babysitting money. (That would be just like her dad. He'd take you to the cleaners with fine print.) Eleanor didn't care if eating all his food pissed him off or if it freaked out Donna. She might never see either of them again anyway.

Now she wished she *had* brought an overnight bag. She could have snuck home cans of Chef Boyardee and Campbell's chicken noodle soup for the little kids. She would have felt like Santa Claus when she came home. . . .

She didn't want to think about the little kids right now. Or Christmas.

She tried to turn the station to MTV, but her dad frowned at her. He was on the phone again.

"Can I listen to records?" she whispered.

He nodded.

She had an old mix tape in her pocket, and she was going to dub over it to make a tape for Park. But there was a whole packet of empty Maxell tapes sitting on her dad's stereo. Eleanor held a cassette up to her dad, and he nodded, flicking his cigarette into an ashtray shaped like a naked African woman.

Eleanor sat down in front of the crates full of record albums.

These used to be both of her parents' records, not just his. Her mom must not have wanted any of them. Or maybe her dad just took them without asking.

Her mom had loved this Bonnie Raitt album. Eleanor wondered if her dad ever listened to it.

She felt seven years old, flipping through their records.

Before she was allowed to take the albums out of their sleeves, Eleanor used to lay them out on the floor and stare at the artwork. When she was old enough, her dad taught her how to dust the records with a wood-handled velvet brush.

She could remember her mother lighting incense and putting on her favorite records—Judee Sill and Judy Collins and Crosby, Stills and Nash—while she cleaned the house.

She could remember her dad putting on records—Jimi Hendrix and Deep Purple and Jethro Tull—when his friends came over and stayed late into the night.

Eleanor could remember lying on her stomach on an old Persian rug, drinking grape juice out of a jelly jar, being extra quiet because her baby brother was asleep in the next room—and studying each record, one by one. Turning their names over and over in her mouth. Cream. Vanilla Fudge. Canned Heat.

The records smelled exactly like they always had. Like her dad's bedroom. Like Richie's coat. Like pot, Eleanor realized. Duh. She flipped through the records more matter-of-factly now, on a mission. Looking for *Rubber Soul* and *Revolver*.

Sometimes it seemed like she would never be able to give Park anything like what he'd given her. It was like he dumped all this treasure on her every morning without even thinking about it, without any sense of what it was worth.

She couldn't repay him. She couldn't even appropriately thank him. How can you thank someone for the Cure? Or the X-Men? Sometimes it felt like she'd always be in his debt.

And then she realized that Park didn't know about the Beatles.

park

Park went to the park to play basketball after school. Just to kill time. But he couldn't focus on the game—he kept looking up at the back of Eleanor's house.

When he got home, he called out to his mom. "Mom! I'm home!"

"Park," she called. "Out here! In the garage."

He grabbed a cherry Popsicle out of the freezer and headed out there. He smelled the permanent wave solution as soon as he opened the door.

Park's dad had converted their garage into a salon when Josh started kindergarten and their mom went to beauty school. She even had a little sign hanging by the side door. MINDY'S HAIR & NAILS.

Min-Dae, it said on her driver's license.

Everyone in the neighborhood who could afford a hair stylist came to Park's mom. On homecoming and prom weekends, she'd spend all day in the garage. Both Park and Josh were recruited from time to time to hold hot curling irons.

Today, his mom had Tina sitting in her chair. Tina's hair was wound tight in rollers, and Park's mom was squeezing something onto them with a plastic bottle. The smell burned his eyes.

"Hey, Mom," he said. "Hey, Tina."

"Hey, honey," his mom said. She pronounced it with two *n*'s.

Tina smiled broadly at him.

"Close eyes, Ti-na," his mom said. "Stay close."

"Hey, Mrs. Sheridan," Tina said, holding a white washcloth over her eyes, "have you met Park's girlfriend yet?"

His mom didn't look up from Tina's head. "Nooo," she said, clucking her tongue. "No girlfriend. Not Park."

"Uh-huh," Tina said. "Tell her, Park—her name is Eleanor, and she's new this year. We can't keep them apart on the bus."

Park stared at Tina. Shocked that she'd sell him out like this. Startled by her rosy take on bus life. Surprised that she was even paying attention to him, and to Eleanor. His mom looked over at Park, but not for long; Tina's hair was at a critical stage.

"I don't know about any girlfriend," his mom said.

"I'll bet you've seen her in the neighborhood," Tina said, assuring. "She has really pretty red hair. Naturally curly."

"Is that right?" his mom said.

"No," Park said, anger and everything else curdling in his stomach.

"You're such a guy, Park," Tina said from behind the washcloth. "I'm sure it's natural."

"No," he said, "she's not my girlfriend. I don't have a girlfriend," he said to his mom.

"Okay, okay," she said. "Too much girl talk for you. Too much girl talk, Ti-na. You go check on dinner now," she said to Park.

He backed out of the garage, still wanting to argue, feeling more denial twitching in his throat. He slammed the door, then went into the kitchen and slammed as much as he could in there. The oven. The cabinets. The trash.

"What the hell is wrong with you?" his dad said, walking into the kitchen.

Park froze. He could *not* get into trouble tonight.

"Nothing," he said. "Sorry. I'm sorry."

"Jesus, Park, take it out on the bag. . . ." There was an old-school punching bag in the garage, hanging way out of Park's reach.

"Mindy!" his dad shouted.

"Out here!"

Eleanor didn't call during dinner, which was good. That got on his dad's nerves.

But she didn't call after dinner either. Park walked around the house, picking things up randomly, then setting them down. Even though it didn't make sense, he worried that Eleanor wasn't calling because he'd betrayed her. That she'd know somehow, that she'd sense a disturbance in the Force.

The phone rang at seven fifteen, and his mom answered it. He could tell right away that it was his grandma.

Park tapped his fingers on a bookshelf. Why didn't his parents want call waiting? Everyone had call waiting. His *grandparents* had call waiting. And why couldn't his grandma just come over, if she wanted to talk? They lived right next door.

"No, I don't think so," his mother said. "*Sixty Minutes* always on Sunday. . . . Maybe you think of *Twenty-Twenty*? No? . . . John Stos-sel? No? . . . Geraldo Rivera? Di-anne Sawyer?"

Park gently banged his head against the living room wall.

"God damn it, Park," his dad snapped, "*what* is wrong with you?"

His dad and Josh were trying to watch *The A-Team*.

"Nothing," Park said, "nothing. I'm sorry. I'm just waiting for a phone call."

"Is your girlfriend calling?" Josh asked. "Park's dating Big Red."

"She's not . . ." Park caught himself shouting and clenched his fists. "If I ever hear you call her that again, I'll kill you. I'll literally kill you. I'll go to jail for the rest of my life, and it'll break Mom's heart, but I will. Kill. You."

His dad looked at Park like he always did, like he was trying to figure out what the fuck was wrong with him. "Park has a girlfriend?" he asked Josh. "Why do they call her Big Red?"

"I think it's because she has red hair and giant tits," Josh said.

"No way, dirty mouth," their mother said. She held her hand over the phone. "You"—she pointed at Josh—"in your room. *Now*."

"But Mom, *A-Team* is on."

"You heard your mother," their dad said. "You don't get to talk like that in this house."

"You talk like that," Josh said, dragging himself off the couch.

"I'm thirty-nine years old," their dad said, "and a decorated veteran. I'll say whatever the hell I want."

Their mother jabbed a long fingernail at his dad and covered the phone again. "I'll send you to your room, too."

"Honey, I wish you would," their dad said, throwing a throw pillow at her.

"Hugh Downs?" Park's mom said into the phone. The pillow fell on the floor and she picked it up. "No? . . . Okay, I'll keep thinking. Okay. Love you. Okay, bye-bye."

As soon as she hung up, the phone rang. Park sprang away from the wall. His dad grinned at him. His mom answered the phone.

"Hello?" she said. "Yes, one moment please." She looked at Park. "Telephone."

"Can I take it in my room?"

His mom nodded. His dad mouthed, *Big Red.*

Park ran into his room, then stopped to catch his breath before he picked up the phone. He couldn't. He picked it up anyway.

"I got it, Mom, thanks." He waited for the click. "Hello?"

"Hi," Eleanor said. He felt all the tension rush out of him. Without it, he could hardly stand up.

"Hi," he breathed.

She giggled.

"What?" he said.

"I don't know," she said. "Hi."

"I didn't think you were going to call."

"It isn't even seven thirty."

"Yeah, well . . . is your brother asleep?"

"He's not my brother," she said. "I mean, not yet. I guess my dad's engaged to his mom. But, no, he's not asleep. We're watching *Fraggle Rock*."

Park carefully picked up the phone and carried it to his bed. He sat down carefully. He didn't want her to hear anything. He didn't want her to know he had a twin-sized waterbed and a phone shaped like a Ferrari.

"What time is your dad coming home?" he asked.

"Late, I hope. They said they almost never get a babysitter."

"Cool."

She giggled again.

"What?" he asked.

"I don't know," she said, "I feel like you're whispering in my ear."

"I'm always whispering in your ear," he said, lying back on his pillows.

"Yeah, but it's usually about, like, Magneto or something." Her voice was higher on the phone, and richer, like he was listening to it on headphones.

"I'm not going to say anything tonight that I could say on the bus or during English class," he said.

"And I'm not going to say anything that I can't say in front of a three-year-old."

"Nice."

"I'm just kidding. He's in the other room, and he's totally ignoring me."

"So . . ." Park said.

"So . . ." she said, ". . . things we can't say on the bus."

"Things we can't say on the bus—go."

"I hate those people," she said.

He laughed, then thought of Tina and was glad that Eleanor couldn't see his face. "Me, too, sometimes. I mean, I guess I'm used to them. I've known most of them my whole life. Steve's my next-door neighbor."

"How did that happen?"

"What do you mean?" he asked.

"I mean, you don't seem like you're from there. . . ."

"Because I'm Korean?"

"You're Korean?"

"Half."

"I guess I don't really know what that means."

"Me neither," he said.

"What do you mean? Are you adopted?"

"No. My mom's from Korea. She just doesn't talk about it very much."

"How did she end up in the Flats?"

"My dad. He served in Korea, they fell in love, and he brought her back."

"Wow, really?"

"Yeah."

"That's pretty romantic."

Eleanor didn't know the half of it; his parents were probably making out right now. "I guess so," he said.

"That's not what I meant, though. I meant . . . that you're different from the other people in the neighborhood, you know?"

Of course he knew. They'd all been telling him so his whole life. When Tina liked Park instead of Steve in grade school, Steve had said, "I think she feels safe with you because you're like half-girl." Park hated football. He cried when his dad took him pheasant hunting. Nobody in the neighborhood could ever tell who he was dressed as on Halloween. ("I'm Doctor Who." "I'm Harpo Marx." "I'm Count Floyd.") And he kind of wanted his mom to give him blond highlights. Park *knew* he was different.

"No," he said. "I don't know."

"You . . ." she said, "you're so . . . cool."

eleanor

"Cool?" he said.

God. She couldn't believe she'd said that. Talk about uncool. Like the opposite of cool. Like, if you looked up *cool* in the dictionary, there'd be a photo of some cool person there saying, *What the eff is wrong with you, Eleanor?*

"I'm not cool," he said. "You're cool."

"Ha," she said. "I wish I were drinking milk, and I wish you were here, so that you could watch it shoot out my nose in response to that."

"Are you kidding me?" he said. "You're Dirty Harry."

"I'm dirty hairy?"

"Like Clint Eastwood, you know?"

"No."

"You don't care what anyone thinks about you," he said.

"That's crazy," she said. "I care what *everyone* thinks about me."

"I can't tell," he said. "You just seem like yourself, no matter what's happening around you. My grandmother would say you're comfortable in your own skin."

"Why would she say that?"

"Because that's how she talks."

"I'm *stuck* in my own skin," she said. "And why are we even talking about me? We were talking about you."

"I'd rather talk about you," he said. His voice a dropped a little. It was nice to hear just his voice and nothing else. (Nothing besides *Fraggle Rock* in the next room.) His voice was deeper than she'd ever realized, but sort of warm in the middle. He kind of reminded her of Peter Gabriel. Not singing, obviously. And not with a British accent.

"Where did *you* come from?" he asked.

"The future."

park

Eleanor had an answer for everything—but she still managed to evade most of Park's questions.

She wouldn't talk about her family or her house. She wouldn't talk about anything that happened before she moved to the neighborhood or anything that happened after she got off the bus.

When her sort-of stepbrother fell asleep around nine, she asked Park to call her back in fifteen minutes, so she could put the kid to bed.

Park ran to the bathroom and hoped that he wouldn't run into either of his parents. So far, they were leaving him alone.

He got back to his room. He checked the clock . . . eight more minutes. He put a tape in his stereo. He changed into pajama pants and a T-shirt.

He called her back.

"It so hasn't been fifteen minutes," she said.

"I couldn't wait. Do you want me to call you back?"

"No." Her voice was even softer now.

"Did he stay asleep?"

"Yeah," she said.

"Where are you now?"

"Like, where in the house?"

"Yeah, where."

"Why?" she asked, with something just gentler than disdain.

"Because I'm thinking about you," he said, exasperated.

"So?"

"Because I want to feel like I'm with you," he said. "Why do you make everything so hard?"

"Probably because I'm so cool . . ." she said.

"Ha."

"I'm lying on the floor in the living room," she said faintly. "In front of the stereo."

"In the dark? It sounds dark."

"In the dark, yeah."

He lay back on his bed again and covered his eyes with his arm. He could see her. In his head. He imagined green lights on a stereo. Street-lights through a window. He imagined her face glowing, the coolest light in the room.

"Is that U2?" he asked. He could hear "Bad" in the background.

"Yeah, I think it's my favorite song right now. I keep rewinding it, and playing it over and over again. It's nice not to have to worry about batteries."

"What's your favorite part?"

"Of the song?"

"Yeah."

"All of it," she said, "especially the chorus—I mean, I guess it's the chorus."

"I'm wide awake," he half sang.

"Yeah . . ." she said softly.

He kept singing then. Because he wasn't sure what to say next.

eleanor

"Eleanor?" Park said.

She didn't answer.

"Are you there?"

She was so out of it, she actually nodded her head. "Yes," she said out loud, catching herself.

"What are you thinking?"

"I'm thinking—I'm—I'm not thinking."

"Not thinking in a good way? Or a bad way?"

"I don't know," she said. She rolled over onto her stomach and pressed her face into the carpet. "Both."

He was quiet. She listened to him breathe. She wanted to ask him to hold the phone closer to his mouth.

"I miss you," she said.

"I'm right here."

"I wish you were here. Or that I was there. I wish that there was some chance of talking like this after tonight, or seeing each other. Like, *really* seeing each other. Of being alone, together."

"Why can't there be?" he asked.

She laughed. That's when she realized she was crying.

"Eleanor . . ."

"Stop. Don't say my name like that. It only makes it worse."

"Makes what worse?"

"Everything," she said.

He was quiet.

She sat up and wiped her nose on her sleeve.

"Do you have a nickname?" he asked. That was one of his tricks, whenever she was put off or irritated—changing the subject in the sweetest way possible.

"Yeah," she said, "Eleanor."

"Not Nora? Or Ella? Or . . . Lena, you could be Lena. Or Lenny or Elle . . ."

"Are you trying to give me a nickname?"

"No, I love your name. I don't want to cheat myself out of a single syllable."

"You're such a dork." She wiped her eyes.

"Eleanor . . . ," he said, "why can't we see each other?"

"God," she said, "don't. I'd almost stopped crying."

"Tell me. Talk to me."

"Because," she said, "because my stepdad would kill me."

"Why does he care?"

"He doesn't care. He just wants to kill me."

"Why?"

"Stop asking that," she said angrily. There was no stopping the tears now. "You always ask that. *Why.* Like there's an answer for everything. Not everybody has your life, you know, or your family. In your life, things happen for reasons. People make sense. But that's not *my* life. Nobody in my life makes sense. . . ."

"Not even me?" he asked.

"Ha. Especially not you."

"Why would you say that?" He sounded hurt. What did he have to be hurt about?

"Why, why, why . . ." she said.

"Yeah," he said, *"why.* Why are you always so mad at me?"

"I'm never mad at you." It came out a sob. He was so stupid.

"You are," he said. "You're mad at me right now. You always turn on me, just when we start to get somewhere."

"Get where?"

"Somewhere," he said. "With each other. Like, a few minutes ago, you said you missed me. And for maybe the first time ever, you didn't sound sarcastic or defensive or like you think I'm an idiot. And now you're yelling at me."

"I'm not yelling."

"You're mad," he said. "Why are you mad?"

She didn't want him to hear her cry. She held her breath. That made it worse.

"Eleanor . . ." he said.

Even worse.

"Stop *saying* that."

"What *can* I say, then? You can ask me why, you know. I promise I'll have answers."

He sounded frustrated with her, but not angry. She could only remember him sounding angry with her once. The first day she got on the bus.

"You can ask *me* why," he said again.

"Yeah?" She sniffed.

"Yeah."

"Okay." She looked down at the turntable, at her own reflection in the tinted acrylic lid. She looked like a fat-faced ghost. She closed her eyes. "Why do you even like me?"

park

He opened his eyes.

He sat up, stood up, started pacing around his small room. He went to stand by the window—the one that faced her house, even though it was a block away and she wasn't home—holding the base of the car phone against his stomach.

She'd asked him to explain something he couldn't even explain to himself.

"I don't like you," he said. "I need you."

He waited for her to cut him down. To say *Ha* or *God* or *You sound like a Bread song.*

But she was quiet.

He crawled back onto the bed, not caring whether she heard it swish. "You can ask me why I need you," he whispered. He didn't even have to whisper. On the phone, in the dark, he just had to move his lips and breathe. "But I don't know. I just know that I do. . . ."

"I miss you, Eleanor. I want to be with you all the time. You're the smartest girl I've ever met, and the funniest, and everything you do surprises me. And I wish I could say that those are the reasons I like you, because that would make me sound like a really evolved human being. . . .

"But I think it's got as much to do with your hair being red and your hands being soft . . . and the fact that you smell like homemade birthday cake."

He waited for her to say something. She didn't.

Someone knocked softly on his door.

"Just a second," he whispered into the phone. "Yeah?" he said.

His mom opened his door, just enough to push her head through. "Not too late," she said.

"Not too late," he said. She smiled and shut the door.

"I'm back," he said. "Are you there?"

"I'm here," Eleanor said.

"Say something."

"I don't know what to say."

"Say something, so that I don't feel so stupid."

"Don't feel stupid, Park," she said.

"Nice."

They were both quiet.

"Ask me why I like you," she finally said.

He felt himself smile. He felt like something warm had spilled in his heart. "Eleanor," he said, just because he liked saying it, "why do you like me?"

"I don't like you."

He waited. And waited . . .

Then he started to laugh. "You're kind of mean," he said.

"Don't laugh. It just encourages me."

He could hear that she was smiling, too. He could picture her. Smiling.

"I don't like you, Park," she said again. "I . . ." She stopped. "I can't do this."

"Why not?"

"It's embarrassing."

"So far, just for me."

"I'm afraid I'll say too much," she said.

"You can't."

"I'm afraid I'll tell you the truth."

"Eleanor . . ."

"Park."

"You don't like me . . ." he said, leading her, pressing the base of the phone into his lowest rib.

"I don't like you, Park," she said, sounding for a second like she actually meant it. "I . . ."—her voice nearly disappeared—"think I live for you."

He closed his eyes and pressed his head back into his pillow.

"I don't think I even breathe when we're not together," she whispered. "Which means, when I see you on Monday morning, it's been like sixty hours since I've taken a breath. That's probably why I'm so crabby, and why I snap at you. All I do when we're apart is think about you, and all I do when we're together is panic. Because every second feels so important. And because I'm so out of control, I can't help myself. I'm not even mine anymore, I'm yours, and what if you decide that you don't want me? How *could* you want me like I want you?"

He was quiet. He wanted everything she'd just said to be the last thing he heard. He wanted to fall asleep with *I want you* in his ears.

"God," she said. "I told you I shouldn't talk. I didn't even answer your question."

eleanor

She hadn't even said anything nice about him. She hadn't told him that he was prettier than any girl, and that his skin was like sunshine with a suntan.

And that's exactly why she hadn't said it. Because all her feelings for him—hot and beautiful in her heart—turned to gobbledygook in her mouth.

She flipped the tape and pressed Play, and waited for Robert Smith to start singing before she climbed up onto her dad's brown leather couch.

"Why can't I see you?" Park asked. His voice sounded raw and pure. Like something just hatched.

"Because my stepfather is crazy."

"Does he have to know?"

"My mom will tell him."

"Does she have to know?"

Eleanor ran her fingers along the edge of the glass coffee table. "What do you mean?"

"I don't know what I mean. I just know that I need to see you. Like this."

"I'm not even allowed to talk to boys."

"Until when?"

"I don't know, never. This is one of those things that doesn't make sense. My mom doesn't want to do anything that could possibly irritate my stepfather. And my stepfather gets off on being mean. Especially to me. He hates me."

"Why?"

"Because I hate him."

"Why?"

She wanted, badly, to change the subject, but she didn't.

"Because he's a bad person. Just . . . trust me. He's the kind of bad that tries to kill anything good. If he knew about you, he'd do whatever he could to take you away from me."

"He can't take me away from you," Park said.

Sure he can, she thought. "He can take *me* away from *you,*" she said. "The last time he got really mad at me, he kicked me out and didn't let me come home for a year."

"Jesus."

"Yeah."

"I'm sorry."

"Don't be sorry," she said. "Just don't tempt him."

"We could meet at the playground."

"My siblings would turn me in."

"We could meet somewhere else."

"Where?"

"Here," he said. "You could come here."

"What would your parents say?"

"It's nice to meet you, Eleanor, would you like to stay for dinner?"

She laughed. She wanted to say it wouldn't work, but maybe it would. Maybe.

"Are you sure you want them to meet me?" she asked.

"Yes," he said. "I want everyone to meet you. You're my favorite person of all time."

He kept making her feel like it was safe to smile. "I don't want to embarrass you . . ." she said.

"You couldn't."

Headlights shot across the living room.

"Damn," she said. "I think my dad's home." She got up and looked out the window.

Her dad and Donna were getting out of the Karmann Ghia. Donna's hair was a mess.

"Damn, damn, damn," she said. "I never said why I like you, and now I have to go."

"That's okay," he said.

"It's because you're kind," she said. "And because you get all my jokes . . ."

"Okay." He laughed.

"And you're smarter than I am."

"I am not."

"And you look like a protagonist." She was talking as fast as she could think. "You look like the person who wins in the end. You're so pretty, and so good. You have magic eyes," she whispered. "And you make me feel like a cannibal."

"You're crazy."

"I have to go." She leaned over so the receiver was close to the base.

"Eleanor—wait," Park said. She could hear her dad in the kitchen and her heartbeat everywhere.

"Eleanor—wait—*I love you.*"

"Eleanor?" Her dad was standing in the doorway. He was being quiet, in case she was asleep. She hung up the phone and pretended that she was.

20

eleanor

The next day was a blur.

Her dad complained that she'd eaten all the yogurt.

"I didn't eat it, I gave it to Matt."

Her dad only had seven dollars in his wallet, so that's what he gave her. When he was ready to take her home, she said she had to go the bathroom. She went up to the hall closet, found three brand-new toothbrushes, and shoved them into the front of her pants, along with a bar of Dove soap. Donna might have seen her (she was right there in the bedroom), but she didn't say anything.

Eleanor felt sorry for Donna. Her dad never laughed at anyone's jokes but his own.

When her dad dropped Eleanor off at her house, all the little kids ran out to see him. He gave them rides around the neighborhood in his new car.

Eleanor wished she had a phone to call the cops. *There's a guy driving around the Flats with a bunch of kids hanging out of a convertible. I'm pretty sure none of them have seat belts on and that he's been drinking Scotch all morning. Oh, and while you're here, there's another guy in the backyard smoking hash. In a school zone.*

When their dad finally left, Mouse couldn't stop talking about him. After a few hours, Richie told everybody to put their coats on. "We're going to a movie. All of us," he said, looking right at Eleanor.

Eleanor and the little kids climbed into the back of the truck and huddled against the cab, making faces at the baby, who got to sit inside. Richie drove down Park's street on the way out of the neighborhood, but Park wasn't outside, thank God. Of course, Tina and her Neanderthal boyfriend were out. Eleanor didn't even try to duck. What was the point. Steve whistled at her.

It was snowing on the way home from the movie. *(Short Circuit.)* Richie drove slow, which meant that even more snow fell on them, but at least nobody flew out of the truck.

Huh, Eleanor thought. *I'm not fantasizing about being thrown from a moving vehicle. Weird.*

When they drove by Park's house again in the dark, she wondered which window was his.

park

He regretted saying it. Not because it wasn't true. He loved her. Of course he did. There was nothing else to explain . . . everything Park felt.

But he hadn't meant to tell her like that. So soon. And over the phone. Especially knowing how she felt about *Romeo and Juliet*.

Park was waiting for his little brother to change clothes. Every Sunday, they got dressed up, in nice pants and sweaters, and had dinner with their grandparents. But Josh was playing Super Mario and wouldn't turn it off. (He was about to get to the infinity turtle for the first time.)

"I'm going over!" Park yelled to his parents. "I'll see you there."

He ran across the yard because he didn't feel like putting on a coat.

His grandparents' house smelled like chicken-fried chicken. His grandma had only four Sunday dinners in her repertoire—chicken-fried chicken, chicken-fried steak, pot roast, and corned beef—but they were all good.

His grandpa was watching TV in the living room. Park stopped to give him half a hug, then went into the kitchen and hugged his grandma. She was so small, even Park towered over her. All the women in his family were tiny, and all the men were huge. Only Park's DNA had missed the memo. Maybe the Korean genes scrambled everything.

That didn't explain Josh's hugeness, though. Josh looked like the Korean genes had skipped him altogether. His eyes were brown and just barely almondy—almond-flavored. And his hair was dark, but not even close to black. Josh looked like a big German or Polish kid whose eyes kind of crinkled when he smiled.

Their grandmother looked nothing but Irish. Or maybe Park only thought that because everyone in his dad's family made such a big deal about being Irish. Park got a KISS ME, I'M IRISH T-shirt every year for Christmas.

He set his grandparents' table without being asked, because it had always been his job. When his mom got there, he hung out in the kitchen with her and his grandma, and listened to them gossip about the neighbors.

"I heard from Jamie that Park's going steady with one of those kids who live over with Richie Trout," his grandma said.

It shouldn't surprise Park that his dad had already told his grandma. His dad could never keep a secret.

"Everybody talking about Park's girlfriend," his mom said, "except for Park."

"I heard she's a redhead," his grandma said.

Park pretended to read the newspaper. "You shouldn't listen to gossip, Grandma."

"Well, I wouldn't have to," his grandma said, "if you'd just introduce us to her."

He rolled his eyes. Which made him think of Eleanor. Which almost made him feel like telling them about her, just so he'd have a reason to say her name.

"Well, my heart goes out to any child living in that house," his grandma said. "That Trout boy has never been any good. He smashed out our mailbox while your dad was in the service. I know it was him because he was the only one in the neighborhood with an El Camino. He grew up in that little house, you know, until his parents moved someplace even more redneck than here. Wyoming, I think it was. They probably moved to get away from him."

"Tishhhh," his mom said. Grandma was a little sharp for his mom's taste sometimes.

"We thought he'd moved out West, too," she said, "but now he's back with an older wife who looks like a movie star and a whole house full of redheaded stepchildren. Gil told your grandpa that they've got a big old dog living there, too. I never . . ."

Park felt like he should defend Eleanor. But he wasn't sure how.

"It doesn't surprise me that you have a thing for redheads," his grandma said. "Your grandfather was in love with a redhead. Lucky for me, she wouldn't have anything to do with him."

What would Park's grandmother say if he did introduce her to Eleanor? What would she say to the neighbors?

And what would his mother say?

He watched his mom mash potatoes with a masher as big as her arm. She was wearing stone-washed jeans and a pink V-neck sweater with fringed leather boots. There was a gold angel charm hanging around her neck and gold crosses hanging from her ears. She'd be the most popular girl on the bus. He couldn't imagine her living anywhere but here.

eleanor

She'd never lied to her mother. Not about anything important, anyway. But on Sunday night, while Richie was at the bar, Eleanor told her mom that she might go over to a friend's house after school the next day.

"Who's that?" her mom asked.

"Tina," Eleanor said. It was the first name she thought of. "She lives in the neighborhood."

Her mom was distracted. Richie was late, and his steak was drying out in the oven. If she took it out, he'd be pissed that it was cold. But if she left it in, he'd be pissed that it was tough.

"Okay," she said. "I'm glad you're finally making friends."

21

eleanor

Would he look different?

Now that she knew that he loved her? (Or that he *had* loved her, at least for a minute or two on Friday night. At least enough to say so.)

Would he look different?

Would he look away?

He did look different. More beautiful than ever. When she got on the bus, Park was sitting tall in the seat, so she could see him. (Or maybe so that he could see her.) And when he let her into the seat, he sat back down again against her. They both slouched down low.

"That was the longest weekend of my life," he said.

She laughed and leaned into him.

"Are you over me?" he asked. She wished she could say things like that. That she could ask him questions like that, even in a joking way.

"Yeah," she said. "Over and over and over."

"Yeah?"

"Yeah, no."

She reached into his jacket and slipped the Beatles tape into his T-shirt pocket. He caught her hand and held it to his heart.

"What's this?" He pulled the tape out with his other hand.

"The greatest songs ever written. You're welcome."

He rubbed her hand against his chest. Just barely. Just enough to make her blush. "Thank you," he said.

She waited until they were at her locker to tell him the other thing. She didn't want anyone to hear. He was standing next to her and purposely bumping his backpack into her shoulder.

"I told my mom that I might go over to a friend's house after school."

"You did?"

"Yeah, it doesn't have to be today, though. I don't think she'll change her mind."

"No, today. Come over today."

"Don't you have to ask your mom?"

He shook his head. "She doesn't care. I can even have girls in my room, if I keep the door open."

"Girl-zzz? You've had enough girls in your room to require a ruling?"

"Oh, yeah," he said. "You know me."

I don't, she thought to herself, *not really.*

park

For the first time in weeks, Park didn't have that anxious feeling in his stomach on the way home from school, like he had to soak up enough of Eleanor to keep him until the next day.

He had a different anxious feeling. Now that he was actually introducing Eleanor to his mom, he couldn't help but see Eleanor the way his mom was going to.

His mom was a beautician who sold Avon. She never left the house without touching up her mascara. When Patti Smith was on *Saturday Night Live*, his mom had gotten upset—"Why she want to look like man? It's so sad."

Eleanor, today, was wearing her sharkskin suit jacket and an old plaid cowboy shirt. She had more in common with his grandpa than with his mom.

And it wasn't just the clothes. It was her.

Eleanor wasn't . . . nice.

She was good. She was honorable. She was honest. She would definitely help an old lady across the street. But nobody—not even the old lady—would ever say, *Have you met that Eleanor Douglas? What a nice girl.*

Park's mom liked nice. She loved nice. She liked smiling and small talk and eye contact . . . All things Eleanor sucked at.

Also, his mom didn't get sarcasm. And he was pretty sure it wasn't a language thing. She just didn't get it. She called David Letterman "the ugly, mean one on after Johnny."

Park realized that his hands were sweating and let go of Eleanor's. He put his hand on her knee instead, and that felt so good, so new, he stopped thinking about his mom for a few minutes.

When they got to his stop, he stood in the aisle and waited for her. But she shook her head. "I'll meet you there," she said.

He felt relieved. And then guilty. As soon as the bus pulled away, he ran to his house. His brother wouldn't be home yet, that was good. "Mom!"

"In here!" she called from the kitchen. She was painting her nails a pearly pink.

"Mom," he said. "Hey. Um, Eleanor's coming over in few minutes. My, um, my Eleanor. Now. Is that okay?"

"Right now?" She shook the bottle. *Click, click, click.*

"Yeah, don't make a big deal, okay? Just . . . be cool."

"Okay," she said. "I'm cool."

He nodded, then looked around the kitchen and the living room to make sure there was nothing weird sitting out. He checked his room, too. His mom had made his bed.

He opened the door before Eleanor knocked.

"Hi," she said. She looked nervous. Well, she looked angry, but he was pretty sure that was because she was nervous.

"Hey," he said. This morning, all he'd been able to think about was how to get more servings of Eleanor into his day, but now that she was here . . . he wished he would've thought this through. "Come on in," he said. "And smile," he whispered at the second-to-last second, "okay?"

"What?"

"*Smile.*"

"Why?"

"Never mind."

His mom was standing in the doorway to the kitchen.

"Mom, this is Eleanor," he said.

His mom smiled broadly.

Eleanor smiled, too, but it was all messed up. She looked like she was squinting into a bright light or getting ready to tell someone bad news.

He thought he saw his mom's pupils widen, but he was probably imagining it.

Eleanor went to shake his mom's hand, but she waved them in the air, like *sorry, my nails are wet,* a gesture that Eleanor didn't seem to recognize.

"It's nice to meet you, Eleanor." *Ell-a-no.*

"It's nice to meet you," Eleanor said, still squinty and weird.

"You live close enough to walk?" his mom asked.

Eleanor nodded.

"That's nice," his mom said.

Eleanor nodded.

"You kids want some pop? Some snacks?"

"No," Park said, cutting her off. "I mean . . ."

Eleanor shook her head.

"We're just going to watch some TV," he said, "okay?"

"Sure," his mom said. "You know where to find me."

She went back in the kitchen, and Park walked over to the couch. He wished he lived in a split-level or a house with a finished basement.

Whenever he went over to Cal's house in west Omaha, Cal's mom sent them downstairs and left them alone.

Park sat on the couch. Eleanor sat at the other end. She was staring at the floor and chewing on the skin around her fingernails.

He turned on MTV and took a deep breath.

After a few minutes, he scooted toward the middle of the couch. "Hey," he said. Eleanor stared at the coffee table. There was big bunch of red glass grapes on the table. His mom loved grapes. *"Hey,"* he said again.

He scooted closer.

"Why did you tell me to smile?" she whispered.

"I don't know," he said, "because I was nervous."

"Why are you nervous? This is your house."

"I know, but I've never brought anyone like you home before."

She looked at the television. There was a Wang Chung video on. Eleanor stood up suddenly. "I'll see you tomorrow."

"No," he said. He stood up, too. "What? Why?"

"Just. I'll see you tomorrow," she said.

"No," he said. He took her arms by the elbow. "You just got here. What is it?"

She looked up at him painfully, "Anyone like me?"

"That's not what I meant," he said. "I meant anyone I care about."

She took a breath and shook her head. There were tears on her cheeks. "It doesn't matter. I shouldn't be here, I'm going to embarrass you. I'm going home."

"No." He pulled her closer. "Calm down, okay?"

"What if your mom sees me crying?"

"That . . . wouldn't be great, but I don't want you to leave." He was afraid that if she left now, she'd never come back. "Come on, sit next to me."

Park sat down and pulled Eleanor down next to him, so he was sitting between her and the kitchen.

"I hate meeting new people," she whispered.

"Why?"

"Because they never like me."

"I liked you."

"No, you didn't. I had to wear you down."

"I like you now." He put his arm around her.

"Don't. What if your mom comes in?"

"She won't care."

"I care," Eleanor said, pushing him away. "It's too much. You're making me nervous."

"Okay," he said, giving her space. "Just don't leave."

She nodded and looked at the TV.

After a while, maybe twenty minutes, she stood up again.

"Stay a little longer," he said. "Don't you want to meet my dad?"

"I super don't want to meet your dad."

"Will you come back tomorrow?"

"I don't know."

"I wish I could walk you home."

"You can walk me to the door." He did.

"Will you tell your mom I said good-bye? I don't want her to think I'm rude."

"Yeah."

Eleanor stepped out onto his porch.

"Hey," he said. It came out hard and frustrated. "I told you to smile because you're pretty when you smile."

She walked to the bottom of the steps, then looked back at him. "It'd be better if you thought I was pretty when I don't."

"That's not what I meant," he said, but she was walking away.

When Park went inside, his mother came out to smile at him. "Your Eleanor seems nice," she said.

He nodded and went to his room. *No,* he thought, falling into his bed. *No, she doesn't.*

eleanor

He was probably going to break up with her tomorrow. Whatever. At least she wouldn't have to meet his dad. God, what must his dad be like? He looked just like Tom Selleck; Eleanor had seen a family portrait sitting on their TV cabinet. Park in grade school, by the way? Extremely cute. Like, *Webster* cute. The whole family was cute. Even his white brother.

His mom looked exactly like a doll. In *The Wizard of Oz*—the book, not the movie—Dorothy goes to this place called the Dainty China Country, and all the people are tiny and perfect. When Eleanor was little and her mom read her the story, Eleanor had thought the Dainty China people were Chinese. But they were actually ceramic, or they'd *turn* ceramic if you tried to sneak one back to Kansas.

Eleanor imagined Park's dad, Tom Selleck, tucking his Dainty China person into his flak jacket and sneaking her out of Korea.

Park's mom made Eleanor feel like a giant. Eleanor couldn't be that much taller than her, maybe three or four inches. But Eleanor was *so much* bigger. If you were an alien who came to Earth to study its life-forms, you wouldn't even think the two of them were the same species.

When Eleanor was around girls like that—like Park's mom, like Tina, like most of the girls in the neighborhood—she wondered where they put their organs. Like, how could you have a stomach and intestines and kidneys, and still wear such tiny jeans? Eleanor knew that she was fat, but she didn't feel *that* fat. She could feel her bones and muscles just underneath all the chub, and they were big, too. Park's mom could wear Eleanor's rib cage like a roomy vest.

Park was probably going to break up with her tomorrow, and not even because she was huge. He was going to break up with her because she was a huge mess. Because she couldn't even be around regular people without freaking out.

It was just too much. Meeting his pretty, perfect mom. Seeing his normal, perfect house. Eleanor hadn't known there were houses like that in this crappy neighborhood—houses with wall-to-wall carpeting and little baskets of potpourri everywhere. She didn't know there were *families* like that. The only upside to living in this effed-up neighborhood was that everybody else was effed up, too. The other kids might hate Eleanor for being big and weird, but they weren't going to hate on her for having a broken family and a broke-down house. That was kind of the rule around here.

Park's family didn't fit. They were the Cleavers. *And* he'd told her that his grandparents lived in the house next door, which had flower boxes, for Christ's sake. His family was practically the Waltons.

Eleanor's family had been messed up even before Richie came around and sent everything straight to hell.

She would never belong in Park's living room. She never felt like she belonged anywhere, except for when she was lying on her bed, pretending to be somewhere else.

22

eleanor

When Eleanor got to their seat the next morning, Park didn't stand up
to let her in. He just scooted over. It didn't seem like he wanted to look
at her; he handed her some comic books, then turned away.

Steve was being really loud. Maybe he was always this loud. When
Park was holding her hand, Eleanor couldn't even hear herself *think*.

Everyone in the back of the bus was singing the Nebraska fight song.
There was some big game coming up this weekend, against Oklahoma
or Oregon or something. Mr. Stessman was giving them extra credit all
week for wearing red. You wouldn't think Mr. Stessman would be
prone to all this Husker crap, but it seemed like nobody was immune.

Except Park.

Park was wearing a U2 shirt today with a picture of a little boy on
the chest. Eleanor had been up all night thinking about how he was

probably done with her, and now she just wanted to put herself out of her misery.

She pulled at the edge of his sleeve.

"Yeah?" Park said softly.

"Are you over me?" she asked. It didn't come out like a joke. Because it wasn't.

He shook his head, but looked out the window.

"Are you mad at me?" she asked.

His fingers were locked loosely together in his lap, like he was thinking about praying. "Sort of."

"I'm sorry," she said.

"You don't even know why I'm mad," he said.

"I'm still sorry."

He looked at her then and smiled a little. "Do you want to know?" he asked.

"No."

"Why not?"

"Because it's probably for something I can't help."

"Like what?" he asked.

"Like for being weird," she said. "Or . . . for hyperventilating in your living room."

"I feel like that was partly my fault."

"I'm sorry," she said.

"Eleanor, stop, *listen,* I'm mad because I feel like you decided to leave my house as soon as you walked in, maybe even before that."

"I felt like I shouldn't be there," she said. She didn't say it loud enough to be heard over the creeps in the back. (Seriously. Their singing was even worse than their shouting.) "I didn't feel like you wanted me there," she said, a little louder.

The way Park looked at her then, biting his bottom lip, she knew she was at least a little bit right.

She'd wanted to be all wrong.

She'd wanted him to tell her that he *did* want her at his house, that he wanted her to come back and try again.

Park said something, but she couldn't hear him, because now the kids in the back were chanting. Steve was standing at the back of the aisle, waving his gorilla arms like a conductor.

"*Go. Big. Red.*"

"*Go. Big. Red.*"

"*Go. Big. Red.*"

She looked around. Everyone was saying it.

"*Go. Big. Red.*"

"*Go. Big. Red.*"

Eleanor's fingertips went cold. She looked around again, and realized that they were all looking at her.

"*Go. Big. Red.*"

Realized that they meant it for her.

"*Go. Big. Red.*"

She looked at Park. He knew it, too. He was staring straight ahead. His fists were clenched tight at his sides. He looked like someone she'd never met.

"It's okay," she said.

He closed his eyes and shook his head.

The bus was parking in front of their school, and Eleanor couldn't wait to get off. She forced herself to stay in her seat until it stopped, and to calmly walk forward. The chanting broke up into laughter. Park was right behind her, but he stopped as soon as he was off the bus. He threw his backpack on the ground and took off his coat.

Eleanor stopped, too. "Hey," she said, "wait, *no*. What are you doing?"

"I'm ending this."

"No. Come on. It's not worth it."

"You are," he said fiercely, looking at her. "*You're* worth it."

"This isn't for me," she said. She wanted to pull at him, but she didn't feel like he was hers to hold back. "I don't want this."

"I'm tired of them embarrassing you."

Steve was getting off the bus, and Park clenched his fists again.

"Embarrassing me?" she said. "Or embarrassing you?"

He looked back at her, stricken. And she knew again that she was right. *Damn it*. Why did he keep letting her be right about all the crappy stuff?

"If this is for me," she said, as fiercely as she could, "then listen to me. I don't *want* this."

He looked in her eyes. His eyes were so green, they looked yellow. He was breathing heavy, and his face was dark red under the gold.

"Is it for me?" she asked.

He nodded. He dug into her with his eyes. He looked like he was begging for something.

"It's okay," she said. "*Please*. Let's go to class."

He closed his eyes and, eventually, nodded. She bent over to get his coat, and heard Steve say, "That's right, Red. Show it off."

And then Park was gone.

When she turned to look, he was already shoving Steve back toward the bus. They looked like David and Goliath, if David had gotten close enough to let Goliath kick his ass.

Kids were yelling "Fight!" and running from every direction. Eleanor ran, too.

She heard Park say, "I'm so sick of your mouth."

And she heard Steve say, "Are you serious with this?"

He pushed Park hard, but Park didn't fall. Park took a few steps back, then cranked his shoulder forward, spinning into the air and kicking Steve right in the mouth. The whole crowd gasped.

Tina screamed.

Steve sprang forward almost as soon as Park landed, swinging his giant fists and clubbing Park in the head.

Eleanor thought that she might be watching him die.

She ran to get between them, but Tina was already there. Then one of the bus drivers was there. And an assistant principal. All pushing them apart.

Park was panting and hanging his head.

Steve was holding his own mouth. There was a waterfall of blood on his chin. "Jesus Christ, Park, what the fuck? I think you knocked out my tooth."

Park lifted his head. His whole face was covered with blood. He staggered forward and the assistant principal caught him. "*Leave . . . my girlfriend . . . alone.*"

"I didn't know she was really your girlfriend!" Steve shouted. A bunch more blood spilled out of his mouth.

"Jesus, Steve. It shouldn't matter."

"It matters," Steve spat. "You're my friend. I didn't know she was your girlfriend."

Park put his hands on his knees and shook his head, splattering the sidewalk. "Well, she is."

"All right," Steve said. "Jesus."

There were enough adults now to herd the boys to the building. Eleanor carried Park's coat and his backpack to her locker. She didn't know what to do with them.

She didn't know what to do with herself either. She didn't know how to feel.

Was she supposed to be happy that Park had called her his girl-friend? It's not like he'd given her any choice in the matter—and it's not like he'd said it happily. He said it with his head down, with his face dripping blood.

Should she be worried about him? Could he still have brain dam-age, even though he'd been talking? Could he still stroke out, or fall into a coma? Whenever anyone in her family was fighting, her mother would start yelling, *Not in the head, not in the head!*

Also, was it wrong to be so worried about Park's face?

Steve had the kind of face that could take or leave teeth. A few gaps in Steve's smile would just add to the big, creepy goon look he was rocking.

But Park's face was like art. And not weird, ugly art either. Park had the sort of face you painted because you didn't want history to forget it.

Was Eleanor supposed to be mad at him still? Was she supposed to be indignant? Was she supposed to shout at him when she saw him in English class, *Was that for me? Or for you?*

She hung his trench coat in her locker and leaned in to take a deep breath. It smelled like Irish Spring and a little bit like potpourri and like something she couldn't describe any way other than *boy.*

Park wasn't in English or history, and he wasn't on the bus after school. Neither was Steve. Tina walked by Eleanor's seat with her head in the air; Eleanor looked away. Everybody else on the bus was talking about the fight. "Fucking *Kung Fu,* fucking David Carradine." And "Fuck David Carradine—fucking Chuck Norris."

Eleanor got off at Park's stop.

park

He was suspended for two days.

Steve was suspended for two weeks because this was his third fight of the year. Park felt kind of bad about that—because Park was the one who'd started the fight—but then he thought about all the other ridiculous crap Steve did every day and never got busted for.

Park's mom was so mad, she wouldn't come get him. She called his dad at work. When his dad showed up, the principal thought he was Steve's dad.

"Actually," his dad said, pointing at Park, "that one's mine."

The school nurse said Park didn't have to go the hospital, but he looked pretty bad. He had a black eye and probably a broken nose.

Steve did have to go the hospital. His tooth was loose, and the nurse was pretty sure he'd broken his finger.

Park waited in the office with ice on his face while his dad talked to the principal. The secretary brought him a Sprite from the teacher's lounge.

His dad didn't say anything until they were driving.

"Taekwondo is the art of self-defense," he said sternly.

Park didn't answer. His whole face was throbbing; the nurse wasn't allowed to give out Tylenol.

"Did you really kick him in the face?" his dad asked.

Park nodded.

"That had to be a jump kick."

"Jump reverse hook," Park groaned.

"No way."

Park tried to give his dad a dirty look, but any look at all felt like getting hit in the face with rocks.

"He's lucky you wear those little tennis shoes," his dad said, "even in the middle of winter. . . . Seriously, a jump reverse hook?"

Park nodded.

"Huh. Well, your mom is going to hit the goddamn roof when she sees you. She was at your grandma's house, crying, when she called me."

His dad was right. When Park walked in, his mom was practically incoherent.

She took him by the shoulders and looked up at his face, shaking her head. "Fighting!" she said, stabbing her index finger into his chest. "Fighting like white-trash dumb monkey . . ."

He'd seen her this mad at Josh before—he'd seen her throw a basket of silk flowers at Josh's head—but never at him.

"Waste," she said, "waste! Fighting! Can't trust you with own face."

His dad tried to put his hand on her shoulder, but she shook him off.

"Get the boy a steak, Harold," his grandma said, sitting Park at the kitchen table and inspecting his face.

"I'm not wasting a steak on that," his grandpa said.

His dad went to the cupboard to get Park some Tylenol and a glass of water.

"Can you breathe?" his grandma asked.

"Through my mouth," Park said.

"Your dad broke his nose so many times, he can only breathe through one nostril. That's why he snores like a freight train."

"No more taekwondo," his mom said. "No more fighting."

"Mindy . . . ," his dad said. "It was one fight. He was sticking up for some girl the kids pick on."

"She's not some girl," Park growled. His voice made every bone in his head vibrate with pain. "She's my girlfriend."

He hoped so, anyway.

"Is it the redhead?" his grandma asked.

"Eleanor," he said. "Her *name*—is *Eleanor*."

"No girlfriend, no," his mom said, folding her arms. "Grounded."

eleanor

When Eleanor rang the doorbell, Magnum, P.I., answered.

"Hi," she said, trying to smile. "I go to school with Park. I have his books and stuff."

Park's dad looked her up and down, but not like he was checking her out, thank God. More like he was sizing her up. (Which was also uncomfortable.) "Are you Helen?" he asked.

"Eleanor," she said.

"Eleanor, right . . . Just a second."

Before she could tell him that she just wanted to drop off Park's stuff, he walked away. He left the door open, and Eleanor could hear him talking to someone, probably in the kitchen, probably Park's mom. "Come on, Mindy. . . ." And, "Just for a few minutes . . ." And then, right before he came back to the door, "With a nickname like Big Red, I expected her to be a lot bigger."

"I was just dropping this off," Eleanor said when he pushed the screen open.

"Thanks," he said, "come on in."

Eleanor held up Park's backpack.

"Seriously, kid," he said. "Come on in and give it to him yourself. I'm sure he wants to see you."

Don't be, she thought.

But she followed him through the living room, down the short hall to Park's room.

His dad knocked softly and peeked in the door. "Hey. Sugar Ray. Someone's here to see you. You want to powder your nose first?"

He opened the door for Eleanor, then walked away.

Park's room was small, but it was packed with stuff. Stacks of books and tapes and comic books. Model airplanes. Model cars. Board games. A rotating solar system hung over his bed like one of those things you put over a crib.

Park was on his bed, trying to prop himself up on his elbows, when she walked in.

She gasped when she saw his face. It looked so much worse than it had earlier.

One of his eyes was swollen shut, and his nose was thick and purple. It made her want to cry. And to kiss him. (Because apparently everything made her want to kiss him. Park could tell her that he had lice and leprosy and parasitic worms living in his mouth, and she would still put on fresh ChapStick. *God.*)

"Are you okay?" she asked. Park nodded and sat up against his headboard. She set down his bag and his coat, and walked over to the bed. He made room for her, so she sat down.

"Whoa," she said, falling backwards, tipping Park on his side.

He groaned and grabbed her arm.

"Sorry," she said. "Oh my God, sorry, are you okay? I wasn't expecting a *waterbed.*" Just saying that word made her giggle.

Park laughed a little, too. It sounded like snorting. "My mom bought it," he said. "She thinks they're good for your back."

He was keeping both his eyes mostly shut, even the good one, and he didn't open his mouth when he talked.

"Does it hurt to talk?" she asked.

He nodded. He hadn't let go of her arm, even though she'd recovered her balance. If anything, he was holding it tighter.

She reached up with her other hand and lightly touched his hair. Brushed it out of his face. It felt smooth and sharp at the same time, like she could feel each strand under her fingertips.

"I'm sorry," he said.

She didn't ask why.

There were tears pooling in the slit of his left eye and slipping down his right cheek. She started to wipe them away, but she didn't want to touch him.

"It's okay . . ." she said. She let her hand settle in her lap.

She wondered if he was still trying to break up with her. If he was, she wouldn't hold it against him.

"Did I ruin everything?" he asked.

"Every-what?" she whispered, as if listening might hurt him, too.

"Every-us."

She shook her head, even though he probably couldn't see her. "Not. Possible," she said.

He ran his hand down her arm and squeezed her hand. She could see the muscles flex in his forearm and just under the sleeve of his T-shirt.

"I think you might have ruined your face," she said.

He groaned.

"Which is okay," she said, "because you were way too cute for me, anyway."

"You think I'm cute?" he said thickly, pulling on her hand.

She was glad he couldn't see her face. "I think you're . . ."

Beautiful. Breathtaking. Like the person in a Greek myth who makes one of the gods stop caring about being a god.

Somehow the bruises and swelling made Park even more beautiful. His face looked ready to break out of its chrysalis.

"They're still going to make fun of me," she blurted. "This fight doesn't change that. You can't start kicking people every time someone thinks I'm weird or ugly. . . . Promise me you won't try. Promise me that you'll try not to care."

He pulled on her hand again, and shook his head, gingerly.

"Because it doesn't matter to me, Park. If you like me," she said, "I swear to God, nothing else matters."

He leaned back into his headboard and pulled her hand to his chest.

"Eleanor, how many times do I have to tell you," he said, through his teeth, "that I don't like you. . . ."

Park was grounded, and he wouldn't be back at school until Friday.

But nobody bothered Eleanor the next day on the bus. Nothing bothered her all day long.

After gym class, she found more pervy stuff written on her

chemistry book—*pop that cherry*, written in globby purple ink. Instead of scribbling it out, Eleanor tore off the cover and threw it away. She might be broke and pathetic, but she could still scrounge up another brown paper bag.

When Eleanor got home after school, her mom followed her into the kids' room. There were two new pairs of Goodwill jeans folded on the top bunk.

"I found some money when I was doing laundry," her mom said. Which meant that Richie had accidentally left money in his pants. If he came home drunk, he'd never ask about it—he'd just assume he spent it at the bar.

Whenever her mom found money, she tried to spend it on things Richie would never notice. Clothes for Eleanor. New underwear for Ben. Cans of tuna fish and bags of flour. Things that could be hidden in drawers and cupboards.

Her mom had become some sort of genius double agent since she hooked up with Richie. It was like she was keeping them all alive behind his back.

Eleanor tried the jeans on before anybody else got home. They were a little big, but much nicer than anything else she had. All her other pants had something wrong with them—a broken zipper or a tear in the crotch—some flaw she had to hide by constantly pulling down her shirt. It would be nice to have jeans that didn't do anything worse than sag.

Maisie's present was a bag of half-dressed Barbies. When Maisie got home, she laid all the dolls out on the bottom bunk, trying to put together one or two complete outfits for them.

Eleanor climbed onto the bed with her and helped comb and braid their frayed hair.

"I wish there'd been a Ken in there," Maisie said.

On Friday morning, when Eleanor got to her bus stop, Park was already waiting there for her.

23

park

His eye went from purple to blue to green to yellow.

"How long am I grounded?" he asked his mother.

"Long enough to make you sorry you fight," she said.

"I *am* sorry," he said.

But he wasn't really. The fight had changed something on the bus. Park felt less anxious now—more relaxed. Maybe it was because he'd stood up to Steve. Maybe it was because he had nothing left to hide. . . .

Plus nobody on the bus had ever seen anybody kick like that in real life.

"It *was* pretty fantastic," Eleanor said on the way to school, a few days after he came back. "Where did you learn to do that?"

"My dad's been making me go to taekwondo since kindergarten. . . .

It was actually kind of a stupid, show-offy kick. If Steve had been thinking, he could have grabbed my leg or pushed me."

"If Steve had been *thinking* . . ." she said.

"I thought you'd think it was lame," he said.

"I did."

"Lame and fantastic?"

"Those are both your middle names. . . ."

"I want to try again."

"Try what again? Your *Karate Kid* thing? I think that would be less fantastic. You've got to know when to walk away. . . ."

"No, I want you to come over again. Would you?"

"It doesn't matter," she said. "You're grounded."

"Yeah . . ."

eleanor

Everybody at school knew that Eleanor was the reason Park Sheridan kicked Steve Murphy in the mouth.

There was a new kind of whispering when she walked down the halls.

Somebody in geography asked her if it was true that they were fighting *over* her. "No!" Eleanor said. "For Christ's sake."

Later she wished that she would have said *Yes!*—because if that had gotten back to Tina, oh my God, it would have made her furious.

On the day of the fight, DeNice and Beebi wanted Eleanor to tell them every gory detail. Especially the gory details. DeNice even bought Eleanor an ice cream cone to celebrate.

"Anyone who whups Steve Murphy's sorry ass deserves a medal," DeNice said.

"I didn't go near Steve's ass," Eleanor said.

"But you were the cause of the ass-whupping," DeNice said. "I heard your boy kicked him so hard, Steve cried blood."

"That's not true," Eleanor said.

"Girl, you need to learn a lesson about standing in your own light," DeNice said. "If my Jonesy kicked Steve's ass, I'd be walking around this place singing that song from *Rocky*. Nuh-nuh, nuhhh, nuh-nuh, nuhhh . . ."

That made Beebi giggle. Everything DeNice said made Beebi giggle. They'd been best friends since grade school, and the better that she got to know them, the more Eleanor felt like it was an honor that they'd let her into their club.

Granted, it was a weird club.

DeNice was wearing her overalls today with a pink T-shirt, pink and yellow hair ribbons, and a pink bandanna tied around her leg. When they were standing in line for ice cream, some boy walked by and told DeNice that she looked like a black Punky Brewster.

DeNice didn't even flinch. "I don't need to worry about that riff-raff," she said to Eleanor. "I got a man."

Jonesy and DeNice were engaged. He'd already graduated and was working as an assistant manager at ShopKo. They were getting married as soon as DeNice was legal.

"And your man's fine," Beebi said, giggling.

When Beebi giggled, Eleanor giggled, too. Beebi's laugh was that contagious. And she always had a manic, surprised look in her eyes—that look people get when they can't keep a straight face.

"Eleanor wouldn't think he's fine," DeNice teased. "She's only interested in stone-cold killers."

park

"How long am I grounded?" Park asked his father.

"That's not up to me, that's up to your mother." His dad was sitting on the couch, reading *Soldier of Fortune*.

"She says forever," Park said.

"I guess it's forever, then."

It was almost Christmas break. If Park was grounded during Christmas break, he'd have to go three weeks without seeing Eleanor.

"Dad . . ."

"I've got an idea," his dad said, setting down the magazine. "You can be ungrounded as soon as you learn to drive a stick. Then you can drive your girlfriend around. . . ."

"What girlfriend?" his mother said. She came in the front door, carrying groceries. Park got up to help her. His dad got up to give her a welcome-home tongue kiss.

"I told Park I'd unground him if he learned how to drive."

"I know how to drive!" Park shouted from the kitchen.

"Learning how to drive an automatic is like learning how to do a girl push-up," his dad said.

"No girl," his mother said. "Grounded."

"But for how long?" Park asked, walking back into the living room. His parents were sitting on the couch. "You can't ground me forever."

"Sure we can," his dad said.

"Why?" Park asked.

His mother looked agitated. "You're grounded until you stop thinking about that trouble girl."

Park and his dad both broke character to look at her.

"What trouble girl?" Park asked.

"Big Red?" his dad asked.

"I don't like her," his mother said adamantly. "She comes to my house and cries, very weird girl, and then next thing I know, you're kicking friends and school is calling, face broken. . . . And everybody, everybody, tell me that family is trouble. Just trouble. I don't want it."

Park took a breath and held it. Everything inside him felt too hot to let out.

"Mindy . . ." his dad said, holding a *wait a minute* hand up to Park.

"No," she said, "*no*. No weird white girl in my house."

"I don't know if you've noticed, but weird white girls are my only option," Park said as loudly as he could. Even this angry, he couldn't yell at his mother.

"There are other girls," his mother said. "Good girls."

"She *is* a good girl," Park said. "You don't even know her."

His dad was standing, pushing Park toward the door. "Go," he said sternly. "Go play basketball or something."

"Good girls don't dress like boys," his mother said.

"Go," his dad said.

Park didn't feel like playing basketball, and it was too cold outside without his coat. He stood in front of his house for a few minutes, then stomped over to his grandparents' house. He knocked, then opened the door; they never locked it.

They were both in the kitchen, watching *Family Feud*. His grandmother was making Polish sausage.

"Park!" she said. "I must have known you were coming. I made way too many Tater Tots."

"I thought you were grounded," his grandpa said.

"Hush, Harold, you can't be grounded from your own grandparents. . . . Are you feeling okay, honey? You look flushed."

"I'm just cold," Park said.

"Are you staying for dinner?"

"Yeah," he said.

After dinner, they watched *Matlock*. His grandmother crocheted. She was working on a blanket for somebody's baby shower. Park stared at the TV, but didn't take anything in.

His grandmother had filled the wall behind the TV with framed eight-by-ten photographs. There were pictures of his dad and his dad's older brother who died in Vietnam, and pictures of Park and Josh from every school year. There was a smaller photo of his parents, on their wedding day. His dad was in his dress uniform, and his mom was wearing a pink miniskirt. Somebody had written *Seoul, 1970* in the corner. His dad was twenty-three. His mom was eighteen, only two years older than Park.

Everybody had thought she must be pregnant, his dad had told him. But she wasn't. "Practically pregnant," his dad said, "but that's a different thing. . . . We were just in love."

Park hadn't expected his mom to like Eleanor, not right away—but he hadn't expected her to reject her, either. His mom was so nice to everybody. *Your mother's an angel,* his grandma always said. It's what everybody always said.

His grandparents sent him home after *Hill Street Blues*.

His mom had gone to bed, but his dad was sitting on the couch, waiting for him. Park tried to walk past.

"Sit down," his dad said.

Park sat down.

"You're not grounded anymore," his dad said.

"Why not?"

"It doesn't matter why not. You're not grounded, and your mother is sorry, you know, for everything she said."

"You're just saying that," Park said.

His dad sighed. "Well, maybe I am. But that doesn't matter either. Your mother wants what's best for you, right? Hasn't she always wanted what's best for you?"

"I guess. . . ."

"So she's just worried about you. She thinks she can help you pick out a girlfriend the same way she helps you pick out your classes and your clothes—"

"She doesn't pick out my clothes."

"Jesus, Park, could you just shut up and listen?"

Park sat quietly in the blue easy chair.

"This is new to us, you know? Your mother's sorry. She's sorry that she hurt your feelings, and she wants you to invite your girlfriend over to dinner."

"So that she can make her feel bad and weird?"

"Well, she is kind of weird, isn't she?"

Park didn't have the energy to be angry. He sighed and let his head fall back on the chair.

His dad kept talking. "Isn't that why you like her?"

Park knew he should still be mad.

He knew there were big chunks of this situation that were completely uncool and out of order.

But he wasn't grounded anymore, he was going to get to spend more time with Eleanor. . . . Maybe they'd even find a way to be alone. Park couldn't wait to tell her. He couldn't wait for morning.

24

eleanor

It was a terrible thing to admit. But sometimes, Eleanor slept right through the yelling.

Especially after she'd been back a couple months. If she were to wake up every time Richie got angry . . . If she got scared every time she heard him yelling in the back room . . .

Sometimes Maisie would wake her up, crawling into the top bunk. Maisie wouldn't let Eleanor see her cry during the day, but she shook like a little baby and sucked her thumb at night. All five of them had learned to cry without making any noise. "It's okay," Eleanor would say, hugging her. "It's okay."

Tonight, when Eleanor woke up, she knew something was different.

She heard the back door slam open. And she realized that, before she'd been quite awake, she'd heard men's voices outside. Men cursing.

There was more slamming in the kitchen—and then gunshots. Eleanor knew they were gunshots, even though she'd never heard them before.

Gang members, she thought. Drug dealers. Rapists. Gang members who were also drug-dealing rapists. She could imagine a thousand heinous people who might have some bone to pick out of Richie's skull— even his friends were scary.

She must have started to get out of bed as soon as she heard the gunshots. She was already on the bottom bunk, crawling over Maisie. "Don't move," she whispered, not sure whether Maisie was awake.

Eleanor opened the window just enough to fit through. There wasn't any screen. She climbed out and ran as lightly as she could off the porch. She stopped at the house next door—an old guy named Gil lived there. He wore suspenders with T-shirts and gave them dirty looks when he was sweeping his sidewalk.

Gil took forever to answer the door, and when he did, Eleanor realized she'd used up all her adrenaline knocking.

"Hi," she said weakly.

He looked mean and mad as spit. Gil could dirty-look Tina right under the table, and then he'd probably kick her.

"Can I use your phone?" she asked. "I need to call the police."

"What?" Gil barked. His hair was oiled down, and he even wore suspenders with his pajamas.

"I need to call 911," she said. She sounded like she was trying to borrow a cup of sugar. "Or maybe you could call 911 for me? There are men in my house with . . . guns. Please."

Gil didn't seem impressed, but he let her in. His house was really nice inside. She wondered if he used to have a wife—or if he just really liked ruffles. The phone was in the kitchen. "I think there are men in my house," Eleanor told the 911 operator. "I heard gunshots."

Gil didn't tell her to leave, so she waited for the police in his kitchen. He had a whole pan of brownies on the counter, but he didn't offer any. His refrigerator was covered with magnets shaped like states, and he had an egg timer that looked like a chicken. He sat at the kitchen table and lit a cigarette. He didn't offer her one of those either.

When the police pulled up, Eleanor walked out of the house, feeling silly suddenly about her bare feet. Gil shut the door behind her.

The cops didn't get out of their car. "You called 911?" one of them asked.

"I think there's somebody in my house," she said shakily. "I heard people yelling and gunshots."

"All right," he said. "Hang on a minute, and we'll go in with you."

With me, Eleanor thought. She wasn't going back in there at all. What was she going to say to the Hells Angels in her living room?

The police officers—two big guys in tall black boots—parked and followed her up onto the porch.

"Go ahead," one said, "open the door."

"I can't. It's locked."

"How'd you get out?"

"The window."

"Then go back through the window."

The next time she called 911, she was going to request cops who wouldn't send her alone into an occupied building. Did firemen do this, too? *Hey, kid, you go in first and unlock the door.*

She climbed in the window, climbed over Maisie (still sleeping), ran into the living room, opened the front door, then ran back into her room and sat on the bottom bunk.

"This is the police," she heard.

Then she heard Richie cussing, "What the fuck?"

Her mom: "What's going on?"

"This is the police."

Her brothers and sisters were waking up and crawling to one another frantically. Someone stepped on the baby and he started to cry.

Eleanor heard the police tramping through the house. She heard Richie shouting. The bedroom door flew open, and their mom came in like Mr. Rochester's wife, in a long, torn, white nightgown.

"Did you call them?" she asked Eleanor.

Eleanor nodded. "I heard gunshots," she said.

"Shhhh," her mother said, rushing to the bed and pressing her hand too hard over Eleanor's mouth. "Don't say anything more," she hissed. "If they ask, say it was a mistake. This was all a mistake."

The door opened, and her mother moved her hand away. Two flash-lights shot around the room. Her siblings were all awake and crying. Their eyes flashed like cats.

"They're just scared," her mother said. "They don't know what's happening."

"There's nobody here," the cop said to Eleanor, shining his light in her direction. "We checked the yard and the basement."

It was more of an accusation than an assurance.

"I'm sorry," she said. "I thought I heard something. . . ."

The lights went out, and Eleanor heard all three men talking in the living room. She heard the police officers on the porch, with their heavy boots, and she heard them drive away. The window was still open.

Richie came into the room then—he never came into their room. Eleanor felt a new flood of adrenaline.

"What were you thinking?" he said softly.

She didn't say anything. Her mother held her hand, and Eleanor locked her jaw shut.

"Richie, she didn't know," her mom said. "She just heard the gun."

"What the fuck," he said, slamming his fist into the door. The veneer splintered.

"She thought she was protecting us—it was a mistake."

"Are you trying to get rid of me? Did you think you could get rid of me?"

Eleanor hid her face in her mother's shoulder. It wasn't a protection. It was like hiding behind the thing in the room he was most likely to hit.

"It was a mistake," her mother said gently. "She was trying to help."

"You never call them here," he said to Eleanor, his voice dying, his eyes wild. "Never again."

And then, shouting, "I can get rid of all of you!" He banged the door closed behind him.

"Back to bed," her mother said. "Everybody—"

"But, Mom . . . ," Eleanor whispered.

"In bed," her mom said, helping Eleanor up the ladder to her bunk. Then her mom leaned in close, her mouth touching Eleanor's ear. "It was Richie," she whispered. "There were kids playing basketball in the park, being loud. . . . He was just trying to scare them. But he doesn't have a license, and there are other things in the house—he could have been arrested. No more tonight. Not a breath."

She knelt down with the boys for a minute, petting and hushing, then floated out of the room.

Eleanor could swear she heard five hearts racing. Every one of them was stifling a sob. Crying inside out. She climbed out of her bed and into Maisie's.

"It's okay," she whispered to the room. "It's okay now."

25

park

Eleanor seemed off that morning. She didn't say anything while they waited for the bus. When they got on, she dropped onto their seat and leaned against the wall.

Park pulled on her sleeve, and she not-even-half smiled. "Okay?" he asked.

She glanced up at him. "Now," she said.

He didn't believe her. He pulled on her sleeve again.

She fell against him and hid her face in his shoulder.

Park laid his face in her hair and closed his eyes.

"Okay?" he asked.

"Almost," she said.

She pulled away when the bus stopped. She never let him hold her hand once they were off the bus. She wouldn't touch him in the hall-ways. *People will look at us,* she always said.

He couldn't believe that still mattered to her. Girls who don't want to be looked at don't tie curtain tassels in their hair. They don't wear men's golf shoes with the spikes still attached.

So today he stood by her locker and only thought about touching her. He wanted to tell her his news—but she seemed so far away, he wasn't sure she'd hear him.

eleanor

Where would she go this time?

Back to the Hickmans'?

Hey, remember that time when my mom asked if I could stay with you guys for a few days, and then she didn't come back for a year? I really appreciate the fact that you didn't turn me into Child Protective Services. That was very Christian of you. Do you still have that foldout couch?

Fuck.

Before Richie moved in, Eleanor only knew that word from books and bathroom walls. *Fucking woman. Fucking kids. Fuck you, you little bitch—who the fuck touched my stereo?*

Eleanor hadn't seen it coming the last time. When Richie kicked her out.

She couldn't have seen it coming, because she never thought it could happen. She never thought he'd try—and she never *ever* thought her mom would go along with it. (Richie must have recognized before Eleanor that her mother's allegiances had shifted.)

It was embarrassing to think about the day that it happened—embarrassing, on top of everything else—because it really was Elea-nor's fault. She really was asking for it.

She was in her room, typing song lyrics on an old manual type-writer that her mom had brought home from the Goodwill. It needed new ribbon (Eleanor had a box full of cartridges that didn't fit), but it still worked. She loved everything about that typewriter; the way the keys felt, the sticky, crunchy noise they made. She even liked the way it smelled, like metal and shoe polish.

She was bored that day, the day it happened.

It was too hot to do anything but lie around or read or watch TV. Richie was in the living room. He hadn't gotten out of bed until two or three, and everybody could tell he was in a bad mood. Her mom was walking around the house in nervous circles, offering Richie lemonade and sandwiches and aspirin. Eleanor hated it when her mom acted like that. Relentlessly submissive. It was humiliating to be in the same room.

So Eleanor was upstairs, typing song lyrics. "Scarborough Fair."

She heard Richie complaining. "What the fuck is that noise?" And, "Fuck, Sabrina, can't you shut her up?"

Her mom tiptoed up the stairs and ducked her head into Eleanor's room. "Richie isn't feeling well," she said. "Can you put that away?" She looked pale and anxious. Eleanor hated that look.

She waited for her mother to get back downstairs. Then, without really thinking about why, Eleanor deliberately pressed a key.

A

Crunch-lap.
Her fingertips trembled over the keyboard.

RE

Crch-crch-lap-tap.
Nothing happened. No one stirred. The house was hot and stiff and as quiet as a library in hell. Eleanor closed her eyes and jerked her chin into the air.

YOU GOING TO SCRABOROUGH FAIR PARSLEY
SAAGE ROSEMAYRY AND THYME

Richie came up the stairs so fast, in Eleanor's head he was flying. In Eleanor's head, he burst open the door by hurling a ball of fire at it.

He was on her before she could brace herself, tearing the typewriter from her hands and throwing it into the wall so hard, it broke through the plaster and hung for a moment in the lath.

Eleanor was too shocked to make out what he was shouting at her. FAT and FUCK and BITCH.

He'd never come this close to her before. Her fear of him crushed her back. She didn't want him to see it in her eyes, so she pressed her face into her hands in her pillow.

FAT and FUCK and BITCH. And I WARNED YOU SABRINA.

"I hate you," Eleanor whispered into the pillow. She could hear things slamming. She could hear her mother in the doorway, talking softly, like she was trying to put a baby back to sleep.

FAT and FUCK and BITCH and BEGGING FOR IT, JUST FUCKING BEGGING FOR IT.

"I hate you," Eleanor said louder. "I hate you, I hate you, I hate you."

FUCK THIS.

"I hate you."

FUCK ALL OF YOU.

"Fuck you."

STUPID BITCHES.

"Fuck you, fuck you, fuck you."

WHAT DID SHE JUST SAY?

In Eleanor's head, the house shook.

Her mother was pulling on her then, trying to pull her out of bed. Eleanor tried to go with her, but she was too scared to stand up. She wanted to flatten herself to the floor and crawl away. She wanted to pretend that the room was full of smoke.

Richie was roaring. Her mother pulled Eleanor to the top of the stairs, then pushed her down. He was right behind them.

Eleanor fell against the banister and practically ran to the front door on all fours. She got outside and kept running to the end of the sidewalk.

Ben was sitting on the porch, playing with his Hot Wheels. He stopped and watched Eleanor run by.

Eleanor wondered if she should keep running, but where would she go? Even when she was a little girl, she never fantasized about running away. She could never imagine herself past the edge of the yard. Where would she go? Who would take her?

When the front door opened again, Eleanor took a few steps into the street.

It was just her mom. She took Eleanor's arm and started walking quickly toward the neighbor's house.

If Eleanor would have known then what was about to happen, she would have run back to tell Ben good-bye. She would have looked for Maisie and Mouse and kissed them each hard on the cheek. Maybe she would have asked to go back inside to see the baby.

And if Richie had been inside waiting for her, maybe she would have dropped to her knees and begged him to let her stay. Maybe she would have said anything he wanted her to.

If he wanted that now—if he wanted her to beg for forgiveness, for mercy, if that was the price she had to pay to stay—she'd do it.

She hoped he couldn't see that.

She hoped none of them could see what was left of her.

park

She ignored Mr. Stessman in English class.

In history, she stared out the window.

On the way home, she wasn't irritable; she wasn't anything at all.

"Okay?" he asked.

She nodded her head against him.

When she got off the bus at her stop, Park still hadn't told her. So he jumped up and followed her, even though he knew she didn't want him to.

"Park . . ." she said, looking nervously down the street to her house.

"I know," he said, "but I wanted to tell you . . . I'm not grounded anymore."

"You're not?"

"Uh-uh." He shook his head.

"That's great," she said.

"Yeah . . ."

She looked back at her house.

"It means you can come over again," he said.

"Oh," she said.

"I mean, if you want to." This wasn't going like he thought it would. Even when Eleanor was looking at him, she wasn't looking at him.

"Oh," she said.

"Eleanor? Is everything okay?"

She nodded.

"Do you still . . ." He hung on to the backpack straps across his chest. "I mean, do you still want to? Do you still miss me?"

She nodded. She looked like she was going to cry. Park hoped she wouldn't cry at his house again. . . . If she ever came back. It felt like she was slipping away.

"I'm just really tired," she said.

26

eleanor

Did she miss him?

She wanted to lose herself in him. To tie his arms around her like a tourniquet.

If she showed him how much she needed him, he'd run away.

27

eleanor

Eleanor felt better the next morning. Mornings usually got the best of her.

This morning, she woke up with that stupid cat curled up against her like it couldn't tell that she'd never liked him or cats in general.

And then her mom gave her a fried-egg sandwich that Richie hadn't wanted, and pinned an old, chipped glass flower to Eleanor's jacket.

"I found it at the thrift shop," her mom said. "Maisie wanted it, but I saved it for you." She smudged vanilla behind Eleanor's ears.

"I might go to Tina's house after school," Eleanor said.

"Okay," her mom said. "Have fun."

Eleanor hoped that Park would be waiting for her at the bus stop, but she wouldn't blame him if he wasn't.

He was. He was standing there in the half light, wearing a gray trench coat and black high-tops, and watching for her.

She ran past the last few houses to get to him. "Good morning," she said, shoving him with both hands.

He laughed and stepped back. "Who are *you*?"

"I'm your girlfriend," she said. "Ask anybody."

"No . . . my girlfriend is sad and quiet and keeps me up all night worrying about her."

"Bummer. Sounds like you need a different girlfriend."

He smiled and shook his head.

It was cold and half dark, and Eleanor could see Park's breath. She resisted the urge to try to swallow it.

"I told my mom that I was going to a friend's house after school . . ." she said.

"Yeah?"

Park was the only person she knew who wore his backpack actually on his shoulders, not slung over one side—and he was always holding on to the straps, like he'd just jumped out of a plane or something. It was extremely cute. Especially when he was being shy and letting his head hang forward.

She pulled the front of his bangs. "Yeah."

"Cool," he said, smiling, all shiny cheeks and full lips.

Don't bite his face, Eleanor told herself. *It's disturbing and needy and never happens in situation comedies or movies that end with big kisses.*

"I'm sorry about yesterday," she said.

He hung on to his straps and shrugged. "Yesterday happens."

God, it was like he wanted her to eat his face clean off.

park

He almost told her all the things his mom had said about her.

It seemed like it was wrong to keep secrets from Eleanor.

But it seemed like it would be *more* wrong to share that kind of secret. It would just make Eleanor even more nervous. She might even refuse to come over. . . .

And she was so happy today. She was a different person. She kept squeezing his hand. She even bit his shoulder when they were getting off the bus.

Plus, if he told her, at the very least she was going to want to go home and change. She was wearing an orange argyle sweater today, way too big, with her silky green tie and baggy painter's jeans.

Park didn't know if Eleanor even had any girls' clothes—and he didn't care. He kind of liked that she didn't. Maybe that was another gay thing about him, but he didn't think so, because Eleanor wouldn't look like a guy even if you cut off her hair and gave her a mustache. All the men's clothes she wore just called attention to how much of a girl she was.

He wasn't going to tell her about his mom. And he wasn't going to tell her to smile. But if she bit him again, he was going to lose something.

"Who are you?" he asked when she was still smiling in English class.

"Ask anybody," she said.

eleanor

In Spanish class today, they were supposed to write a letter in Spanish to a friend. Señora Bouzon put on an episode of ¿Qué Pasa, USA? while they worked on it.

Eleanor tried to write a letter to Park. She didn't get very far.

Estimado Señor Sheridan,
Mi gusta comer su cara.
Besos,
Leonor

For the rest of the day, whenever Eleanor felt nervous or scared, she told herself to be happy instead. (It didn't really make her feel better, but it kept her from feeling worse. . . .)

She told herself that Park's family must be decent people because they'd raised a person like Park. Never mind that this principle didn't hold true in her own family. It wasn't like she had to face his family alone. Park would be there. That was the whole point. Was there any place so horrible that she wouldn't go there to be with Park?

She saw him after seventh hour in a place she'd never seen him before, carrying a microscope down the hall on the third floor. It was at least twice as nice as seeing him somewhere she expected him to be.

28

park

He called his mom during lunch to tell her that Eleanor was coming over. His counselor let him use her phone. (Mrs. Dunne loved the opportunity to be good in a crisis, so all Park had to do was imply that it was a emergency.)

"I just wanted to tell you that Eleanor is coming over after school," he told his mom. "Dad said it was all right."

"Fine," his mother said, not even pretending that she was okay with it. "Is she staying for dinner?"

"I don't know," Park said. "Probably not."

His mother sighed.

"You have to be nice to her, you know."

"I'm nice to everybody," his mom said. "You know that."

He could tell Eleanor was nervous on the bus. She was quiet, and she kept running her bottom lip through her teeth, making it go white, so that you could see that her lips had freckles, too.

Park tried to get her to talk about *Watchmen;* they'd just read the fourth chapter. "What do you think of the pirate story?" he asked.

"What pirate story?"

"You know, there's that character who's always reading a comic book about pirates, the story within the story, the *pirate* story."

"I always skip that part," she said.

"You skip it?"

"It's boring. Blah, blah, blah—pirates!—blah, blah, blah."

"Nothing Alan Moore writes can be blah-blah-blahed," Park said solemnly.

Eleanor shrugged and bit her lip.

"I'm beginning to think you shouldn't have started reading comics with a book that completely deconstructs the last fifty years of the genre," he said.

"All I'm hearing is blah, blah, blah, genre."

The bus stopped near Eleanor's house. She looked at him.

"We may as well get off at my stop," Park said, "right?"

Eleanor shrugged again.

They got off at his stop, along with Steve and Tina and most of the people who sat at the back of the bus. All the back-of-the-bus kids hung out in Steve's garage when he wasn't working, even in winter.

Park and Eleanor trailed behind them.

"I'm sorry I look so stupid today," she said.

"You look like you always do," he said. Her bag was hanging at the end of her arm. He tried to take it, but she pulled away.

"I always look stupid?"

"That's not what I meant. . . ."

"It's what you said," she muttered.

He wanted to ask her not to be mad right now. Like, anytime but now. She could be mad at him for no reason all day tomorrow, if she wanted to.

"You really know how to make a girl feel special," Eleanor said.

"I've never pretended to know anything about girls," he answered.

"That's not what I heard," she said. "I heard you were allowed to have girl-*zzz* in your room. . . ."

"They were there," he said, "but I didn't learn anything."

They both stopped on his porch. He took her bag from her and tried not to look nervous. Eleanor was looking down the walk, like she might bolt.

"I meant that you don't look any different than you usually look," he said softly, just in case his mom was standing on the other side of the door. "And you always look nice."

"I never look nice," she said. Like he was an idiot.

"I like the way you look," he said. It came out more like an argument than like a compliment.

"That doesn't mean it's nice." She was whispering, too.

"Fine then, you look like a hobo."

"A hobo?" Her eyes lit.

"Yeah, a gypsy hobo," he said. "You look like you just joined the cast of *Godspell*."

"I don't even know what that is."

"It's terrible."

She stepped closer to him. "I look like a hobo?"

"Worse," he said. "Like a sad hobo clown."

"And you like it?"

"I love it."

As soon as he said it, she broke into a smile. And when Eleanor smiled, something broke inside him.

Something always did.

eleanor

It was probably a good thing that Park's mom opened the door when she did because Eleanor was thinking about kissing him, and no way was that a good idea—Eleanor didn't know the first thing about kissing.

Of course, she'd watched a million kisses on TV (thank you, Fonzie), but TV never showed you the mechanics of it. If Eleanor tried to kiss Park, it would be like a real-life version of some little girl making her Barbie kiss Ken. Just smashing their faces together.

Besides, if Park's mom had opened the door right in the middle of a big, awkward kiss, she'd hate Eleanor even more.

Park's mom *did* hate her; you could tell. Or maybe she just hated the *idea* of Eleanor, of a girl seducing her firstborn son right in her own living room.

Eleanor followed Park into the living room and sat down. She tried to look extra polite. When his mom offered them a snack, Eleanor said, "That would be great, thank you." His mom was looking at Eleanor like she was something somebody had spilled on the baby blue couch. She brought out cookies, then left them alone.

Park seemed so happy. Eleanor tried to concentrate on how nice it was to be with him—but it was taking too much of her concentration, just keeping herself together.

It was the little things about Park's house that really freaked her out. Like all the glass grapes hanging from everything. And the curtains that matched the sofa that matched the little doily-napkins under the lamps.

You'd think that nobody interesting could grow up in a house as nice and boring as this one—but Park was the smartest, funniest guy she'd ever met, and this was his home planet.

Eleanor wanted to feel superior to Park's mom and her Avon-lady house. But instead, she kept thinking about how nice it must be to live in a house like this one. With your own room. And your own parents. And six different kinds of cookies in the cupboard.

park

Eleanor was right: She never looked nice. She looked like art, and art wasn't supposed to look nice; it was supposed to make you feel something.

Eleanor sitting next to him on the couch made Park feel like someone had opened a window in the middle of the room. Like someone had replaced all the air in the room with brand-new, improved air (now with twice the freshness).

Eleanor made him feel like something was happening. Even when they were just sitting on the couch.

She wouldn't let him hold her hand, not in his house, and she wouldn't stay for dinner. But she said she'd come back tomorrow—if his parents said it was okay, which they did.

His mom was being perfectly nice so far. She wasn't turning on the charm, like she did for her clients and the neighbors, but she wasn't being rude either. And if she wanted to hide in the kitchen every time Eleanor came over, Park thought, that was her prerogative.

Eleanor came over again on Thursday afternoon and Friday. And on Saturday, while they were playing Nintendo with Josh, his dad asked her to stay for dinner.

Park couldn't believe it when she said yes. His dad put the leaf into the dining room table, and Eleanor sat right next to Park. She was nervous, he could tell. She barely touched her sloppy joe, and after a while her smile started to go all grimacey around the edges.

After dinner, they all watched *Back to the Future* on HBO, and his mom made popcorn. Eleanor sat with Park on the floor, leaning against the couch, and when he surreptitiously took her hand, she didn't pull away. He rubbed the inside of her palm because he knew she liked it. It made her eyelids dip like she was going to fall asleep.

When the movie was over, Park's dad insisted that Park walk Eleanor home.

"Thanks for having me, Mr. Sheridan," she said. "And thank you for dinner, Mrs. Sheridan. It was delicious, I had a great time." She didn't even sound like she was being sarcastic.

When they got to the door, she called back, "Good night!"

Park closed the door behind them. You could almost see all the nervous niceness draining out of Eleanor. He wanted to hug her, to help wring it out.

"You can't walk me home," she said with her usual edge. "You know that, right?"

"I know. But I can walk you partway."

"I don't know. . . ."

"Come on," he said, "it's dark. No one will see us."

"Okay," she said, but she put her hands in her pockets. They both walked slowly.

"Your family is really great," she said after a minute. "Really."

He took her arm. "Hey, I want to show you something." He pulled her into the next driveway, between a pine tree and an RV.

"Park, this is trespassing."

"It's not. My grandparents live here."

"What do you want to show me?"

"Nothing, really. I just want to be alone with you for a minute."

He pulled her to the back of the driveway, where they were almost completely hidden by a line of trees and the RV and the garage.

"Seriously?" she said. "That was so lame."

"I know," he said, turning to her. "Next time, I'll just say, 'Eleanor, follow me down this dark alley, I want to kiss you.'"

She didn't roll her eyes. She took a breath, then closed her mouth. He was learning how to catch her off guard.

She pushed her hands deeper in her pockets, so he put his hands on her elbows. "Next time," he said, "I'll just say, 'Eleanor, duck behind these bushes with me, I'm going to lose my mind if I don't kiss you.'"

She didn't move, so he thought it was probably okay to touch her face. Her skin was as soft as it looked, white and smooth as freckled porcelain.

"I'll just say, 'Eleanor, follow me down this rabbit hole. . . .'"

He laid his thumb on her lips to see if she'd pull away. She didn't.

He leaned closer. He wanted to close his eyes, but he didn't trust her not to leave him standing there.

When his lips were almost touching hers, she shook her head. Her nose rubbed against his.

"I've never done this before," she said.

"S'okay," he said.

"It's not, it's going to be terrible."

He shook his head. "It's not."

She shook her head a little more. Just a little. "You're going to regret this," she said.

That made him laugh, so he had to wait a second before he kissed her.

It wasn't terrible. Eleanor's lips were soft and warm, and he could feel her pulse in her cheek. It was good that she was so nervous—because it forced him not to be. It steadied him to feel her trembling.

He pulled away before he wanted to. He hadn't done this enough to know how to breathe.

When he pulled away, her eyes were mostly closed. His grandparents had a light on, on their front porch, and Eleanor's face caught every bit of it. She looked like she should be married to the man in the moon.

Her face dropped after a second, and he let his hand fall to her shoulder.

"Okay?" he whispered.

She nodded. He pulled her closer and kissed the top her head. He tried to find her ear under all that hair.

"Come here," he said. "I want to show you something."

She laughed. He lifted her chin.

The second time was even less terrible.

eleanor

They walked together from his grandparents' driveway to the alley; then Park waited there in the shadows and watched Eleanor walk home alone.

She told herself not to look back.

Richie was home, and everybody except her mom was watching TV. It wasn't *that* late; Eleanor tried to act like there was nothing strange about her coming home in the dark.

"Where have you been?" Richie said.

"At a friend's house."

"What friend?"

"I told you, honey," her mom said, stepping into the room, drying a pan. "Eleanor has a girlfriend in the neighborhood. Lisa."

"Tina," Eleanor said.

"Girlfriend, huh?" Richie said. "Giving up on men already?" He thought that was pretty funny.

Eleanor went into the bedroom and closed the door. She didn't turn on the light. She climbed into bed in her street clothes, opened the curtains, and wiped the condensation off the window. She couldn't see the alley or anything moving outside.

The window fogged over again. Eleanor closed her eyes and laid her forehead against the glass.

29

eleanor

When she saw Park standing at the bus stop on Monday morning, she started giggling. Seriously, giggling like a cartoon character . . . when their cheeks get all red, and little hearts start popping out of their ears . . .

It was ridiculous.

park

When he saw Eleanor walking toward him on Monday morning, Park wanted to run to her and sweep her up in his arms. Like some guy in the soap operas his mom watched. He hung on to his backpack to hold himself back. . . .

It was kind of wonderful.

eleanor

Park was just her height, but he seemed taller.

park

Eleanor's eyelashes were the same color as her freckles.

eleanor

They talked about the *White Album* on the way to school, but just as an excuse to stare at each other's mouths. You'd think they were lip-reading.

Maybe that's why Park kept laughing, even when they were talking about "Helter Skelter"—which wasn't the Beatles' funniest song, even before Charles Manson got a hold of it.

30

park

"Hey," Cal said, taking a bite out of his Rib-a-Que sandwich. "You should come to the basketball game with us Thursday. And don't even try to tell me you don't like basketball, Spud."

"I don't know. . . ."

"Kim's going to be there."

Park groaned. "Cal . . ."

"Sitting next to me," Cal said. "Because we're totally going out."

"Wait, seriously?" Park covered his mouth to keep a chunk of sandwich from flying out. "Are we talking about the same Kim?"

"Is that so hard to believe?" Cal opened his carton of milk completely and drank out of it like a cup. "She wasn't even into you, you know. She was just bored, and she thought you were mysterious and quiet—like, 'still waters run deep.' I told her that sometimes still waters just run still."

"Thanks."

"But she's totally into me now, so you can hang out with us if you want. The basketball games are a blast. They sell nachos and everything."

"I'll think about it," Park said.

He wasn't going to think about it. He wasn't going anywhere without Eleanor. And she didn't seem like the basketball-game type.

eleanor

"Hey, girl," DeNice said after gym class. They were in the locker room, changing back into their street clothes. "So I've been thinking, you've got to go to Sprite Nite with us this week. Jonesy's got his car fixed, and he's got this Thursday off. We are going to do it right, right, right, all through the night, night, night."

"You know I'm not allowed to go out," Eleanor said.

"I know that you're not allowed to go to your boyfriend's house either," DeNice said.

"I heard that," Beebi said.

Eleanor should never have told them about Park's house, but she'd been dying to tell *somebody*. (This was how people ended up in jail after committing the perfect crime.) "Keep it down," she said. "God."

"You should come," Beebi said. Her face was perfectly round, with dimples so deep that when she smiled, she looked tufted, like a cushion. "We have so much fun. I'll bet you've never even been dancing before."

"I don't know . . ." Eleanor said.

"Is this about your man?" DeNice asked. "Because he can come, too. He don't take up much space."

Beebi giggled, so Eleanor giggled, too. She couldn't imagine Park dancing. He'd probably be really good at it, if all the Top 40 music didn't make his ears bleed. He was good at everything.

Still . . . She couldn't imagine the two of them going out with DeNice or Beebi. Or anybody. Thinking about going out with Park, in public, was kind of like thinking about taking your helmet off in space.

park

His mom said that if they were going to hang out every night after school, which they definitely were, they had to start doing homework.

"She's probably right," Eleanor said on the bus. "I've been faking it in English all week."

"You were faking it today? Seriously? It didn't sound like it."

"We did Shakespeare last year at my old school. . . . But I can't fake it in math. I can't even . . . what's the opposite of faking it?"

"I can help you with your math, you know. I'm already through algebra."

"Gosh, Wally, that'd be dreamy."

"Or not," he said. "I could *not* help you with your math."

Even her mean, smirky smile made him crazy.

They tried to study in the living room, but Josh wanted to watch TV, so they took their stuff into the kitchen.

His mom said it was okay; then said she had stuff to do in the garage. Whatever.

Eleanor moved her lips when she read. . . .

Park kicked her gently under the table, and threw crumpled-up pieces of paper into her hair. They were almost never alone, and now that they almost-practically were, he felt kind of frantic for her attention.

He flipped her algebra book closed with his pen.

"Seriously?" She tried to open it again.

"No," he said, pulling it toward him.

"I thought we were studying."

"I know," he said, "I just . . . we're alone."

"Sort of . . ."

"So we should be doing alone things."

"You sound so creepy right now. . . ."

"I meant talking." He wasn't sure what he meant. He looked down at the table. Eleanor's algebra book was covered with her handwriting, the lyrics to one song wrapped and coiled around the title of another. He saw his name written in tiny cursive letters—your own name always stands out—and hidden in the chorus of a Smiths song.

He felt himself grin.

"What?" Eleanor asked.

"Nothing."

"What."

He looked back at the book. He was going to think about this later, after she went home. He was going to think about Eleanor sitting in class, thinking about him, carefully writing his name someplace she thought only she would see.

And then he noticed something else. Written just as small, just as carefully, in all lowercase letters. *i know your a slut you smell like cum*

"What," Eleanor said, trying to pull the book away.

Park held on to it. He felt the Bruce Banner blood rushing to his face. "Why didn't you tell me that this was still happening?"

"That what was still happening?"

He didn't want to say it, he didn't want to point to it. He didn't want their eyes on those words together.

"This," he said, waving his hand over the words.

She looked—and immediately started scrubbing the bad writing out with her pen. Her face was skim milk, and her neck went red and blotchy.

"Why didn't you tell me?" he said.

"I didn't know it was there."

"I thought this had stopped."

"Why would you think that?"

Why *had* he thought that? Because she was with him now?

"I just . . . Why didn't you tell me about this?"

"Why would I tell you?" she asked. "It's gross and embarrassing." She was still scribbling.

He put his hand over her wrist. "Maybe I could help."

"Help how?" She shoved the book toward him. "Do you want to kick it?"

He clenched his teeth. She took the book back and put it in her bag.

"Do you know who's doing it?" he asked.

"Are you going to kick *them*?"

"Maybe . . ."

"Well . . ." she said, "I've narrowed it down to people who don't like me. . . ."

"It couldn't be just anyone. It would have to be somebody who could get to your books without you knowing about it."

Ten seconds ago, Eleanor had looked mean as a cat. Now she looked resigned, slumped over the table with her fingertips at her temples. "I don't know. . . ." She shook her head. "It seems like it always happens on gym days."

"Do you leave your books in the locker room?"

She rubbed her eyes with both hands. "I feel like now you're intentionally asking me stupid questions. You're like the worst detective ever."

"Who doesn't like you in gym class?"

"Ha." She was still covering her face. "Who *doesn't* like me in gym class."

"You need to take this seriously," he said.

"No," she said firmly, squeezing her hands into fists, "this is exactly the sort of thing I *shouldn't* take seriously. That's exactly what Tina and her henchgirls want me to do. If they think they're getting to me? They'll never leave me alone."

"What does Tina have to do this?"

"Tina is the queen of the people in my gym class who don't like me."

"Tina would never do anything this bad."

Eleanor looked hard at him. "Are you kidding? Tina's a monster. She's what would happen if the devil married the wicked witch, and they rolled their baby in a bowl of chopped evil."

Park thought of the Tina who sold him out in the garage and made fun of people on the bus. . . . But then he thought of all the times that Steve had gone after Park, and Tina had pulled him back.

"I've known Tina since we were kids," he said. "She's not that bad. We used to be friends."

"You don't act like friends."

"Well, she's dating Steve now."

"Why does that matter?"

Park couldn't think of how to answer.

"Why does it matter?" Eleanor's eyes were dark slits in her face. If he lied to her about this, she'd never forgive him.

"None of it matters now," he said. "It's stupid. . . . Tina and I went together in the sixth grade. Not that we ever went anywhere or did anything."

"Tina? You went with *Tina*?"

"It was the sixth grade. It was nothing."

"But you were boyfriend and girlfriend? Did you hold hands?"

"I don't remember."

"Did you kiss her?"

"None of this matters."

But it did. Because it was making Eleanor look at him like he was a stranger. It was making him *feel* like a stranger. He knew that Tina had a mean streak, but he also knew that she wouldn't go this far.

What did he know about Eleanor? Not much. It was like she didn't want him to know her better. He felt everything for Eleanor, but what did he really *know*?

"You always write in lowercase letters. . . ." Saying this out loud seemed like a good idea only for as long as the words were on his tongue, but he kept talking. "Did you write those things yourself?"

Eleanor paled from pale to ashen. It was like all the blood in her body rushed to her heart, all at once. Her speckled lips hung open.

Then she snapped out of it. She started stacking her books.

"If I were going to write a note to myself, calling myself a dirty slut," she said it matter-of-factly, "you're right, I might not use capital letters. But I would definitely use an apostrophe . . . and probably a period. I'm a huge fan of punctuation."

"What are you doing?" he asked.

She shook her head and stood up. He couldn't for the life of him think of how to stop her.

"I don't know who's been writing on my books," she said coolly. "But I think we just solved the mystery of why Tina hates me so much."

"Eleanor . . ."

"No," she said, her voice catching. "I don't want to talk anymore."

She walked out of the kitchen just as Park's mom was coming in from the garage. His mom looked at Park with a face he was beginning to recognize. *What do you see in this weird white girl?*

park

That night, Park lay in bed thinking about Eleanor thinking about him, writing his name on her book.

She'd probably already scribbled that out, too.

He tried to think about why he'd defended Tina.

Why did it matter to him whether Tina was good or bad? Eleanor was right: He and Tina weren't friends. They weren't anything like friends. They hadn't even been friends in the sixth grade.

Tina had asked Park to go with her, and Park had said yes—because everybody knew that Tina was the most popular girl in class. Going with Tina was such powerful social currency, Park was still spending it.

Being Tina's first boyfriend kept Park out of the lowest neighborhood caste. Even though they all thought Park was weird and yellow, even though he had never fit in . . . They couldn't call him a freak or a chink or a fag, because—well, *first,* because his dad was a giant and a veteran and from the neighborhood. But second, because what would that say about Tina?

And Tina had never turned on Park or pretended he didn't happen. In fact . . . Well. There were times when he thought she wanted something to happen between them again.

Like, a few times, she'd come over to Park's house on the wrong day for her hair appointment—and ended up in Park's room, trying to find something for them to talk about.

On homecoming night, when she came over to have her hair put up, she'd stopped in Park's room to ask what he thought of her strapless blue dress. She'd had him untangle her necklace from the hair at the back of her neck.

Park always let these opportunities pass like he didn't see them.

Steve would kill him if he hooked up with Tina.

Plus, Park didn't want to hook up with Tina. They didn't have anything in common—like, *nothing*—and it wasn't the kind of nothing that can be exotic and exciting. It was just boring.

He didn't even think Tina really liked him, deep down. It was more like she didn't want him to get over her. And not-so-deep down, Park didn't want Tina to get over him.

It was nice to have the most popular girl in the neighborhood offering herself to him every now and then.

Park rolled onto his stomach and pressed his face into his pillow. He'd thought he was over caring what people thought about him. He'd thought that loving Eleanor proved that.

But he kept finding new pockets of shallow inside himself. He kept finding new ways to betray her.

31

eleanor

There was just one more day of school left before Christmas vacation. Eleanor didn't go. She told her mother she was sick.

park

When he got to the bus stop Friday morning, Park was ready to apologize. But Eleanor didn't show up. Which made him feel a lot less like apologizing . . .

"What now?" he said in the direction of her house. Were they supposed to break up over this? Was she going to go three weeks without talking to him?

He knew it wasn't Eleanor's fault that she didn't have a phone, and

that her house was the Fortress of Solitude, but . . . Jesus. It made it
so easy for her to cut herself off whenever she felt like it.

"I'm sorry," he said at her house, too loudly. A dog started barking
in the yard behind him. "Sorry," Park muttered to the dog.

The bus turned the corner and heaved to a stop. Park could see Tina
in the back window, watching him.

I'm sorry, he thought, not looking back again.

eleanor

With Richie at work all day, she didn't have to stay in her room, but
she did anyway. Like a dog who won't leave its kennel.

She ran out of batteries. She ran out of things to read. . . .

She lay in bed so much, she actually felt dizzy when she got up Sunday afternoon to eat dinner. (Her mom said Eleanor had to come out of
her crypt if she was hungry.) Eleanor sat on the living room floor next
to Mouse.

"Why are you crying?" he asked. He was holding a bean burrito,
and it was dripping onto his T-shirt and the floor.

"I'm not," she said.

Mouse held the burrito over his head and tried to catch the leak
with his mouth. "Yeh oo are."

Maisie looked up at Eleanor, then back at the TV.

"Is it because you hate Dad?" Mouse asked.

"Yes," Eleanor said.

"Eleanor," her mother said, walking out of the kitchen.

"No," Eleanor said to Mouse, shaking her head. "I told you, I'm not
crying." She went back to her room and climbed into bed, rubbing her
face in the pillow.

Nobody followed her to see what was wrong.

Maybe her mom realized that she'd pretty much forfeited the right
to ask questions for all eternity when she dumped Eleanor at somebody's house for a year.

Or maybe she just didn't care.

Eleanor rolled onto her back and picked up her dead Walkman. She took out the tape and held it up to the light, turning the reels with her fingertip and looking at Park's handwriting on the label.

Never mind the Sex Pistols . . . Songs Eleanor might like.

Park thought she'd written those awful things on her books herself.

And he'd taken Tina's side against hers. *Tina's.*

She closed her eyes again and remembered the first time that he kissed her. . . . How she'd let her neck bend back, how she'd opened her mouth. How she'd believed him when he said she was special.

park

A week into break, his dad asked Park if he and Eleanor had broken up.

"Sort of," Park said.

"That's too bad," his dad said.

"It is?"

"Well, it must be. You're acting like a four-year-old lost at Kmart. . . ."

Park sighed.

"Can't you get her back?" his dad asked.

"I can't even get her to talk to me."

"It's too bad you can't talk to your mother about this. The only way I know how to land a girl is to look sharp in a uniform."

eleanor

A week into break, Eleanor's mom woke her up before sunrise. "Do you want to walk to the store with me?"

"No," Eleanor said.

"Come on, I could use the extra hands."

Her mom walked fast, and she had long legs. Eleanor had to take extra steps just to keep up. "It's cold," she said.

"I told you to wear a hat." Her mom had told her to wear socks, too, but they looked ridiculous with Eleanor's Vans.

It was a forty-minute walk.

When they got to the grocery store, her mom bought them each a day-old cream horn and a cup of twenty-five-cent coffee. Eleanor dumped Coffee-Mate and Sweet'N Low in hers, and followed her mom to the bargain bin. Her mom had this thing about being the first person to go through all the smashed cereal boxes and dented cans. . . .

Afterwards, they walked to the Goodwill, and Eleanor found a stack of old *Analog* magazines and settled in on the least-disgusting couch in the furniture section.

When it was time to go, her mom came up from behind her with an incredibly ugly stocking cap and pulled it over her head.

"Great," Eleanor said, "now I have lice."

She felt better on the way home. (Which was probably the point of this whole field trip.) It was still cold, but the sun was shining, and her mom was humming that Joni Mitchell song about clouds and circuses.

Eleanor almost told her everything.

About Park and Tina and the bus and the fight, about the place between his grandparents' house and the RV.

She felt it all right at the back of her throat, like a bomb—or a tiger—sitting on the base of her tongue. Keeping it in made her eyes water.

The plastic shopping bags were cutting into her palms. Eleanor shook her head and swallowed.

park

Park rode his bike by her house over and over one day until her step-dad's truck was gone and one of the other kids came outside to play in the snow.

It was the older boy; Park couldn't remember his name. The kid scuttled up the steps nervously when Park stopped in front of the house.

"Hey, wait," Park said, "please, *hey* . . . is your sister home?"

"Maisie?"

"No, Eleanor . . ."

"I'm not telling you," the boy said, running in the house.

Park jerked his bike forward and pedaled away.

32

eleanor

The box of pineapple arrived on Christmas Eve. You'd have thought Santa Claus had shown up in person with a bag of toys for each of them.

Maisie and Ben were already fighting over the box. Maisie wanted it for her Barbies. Ben didn't have anything to put in it, but Eleanor still hoped he'd win.

Ben had just turned twelve, and Richie said he was too old to share a room with girls and babies. Richie brought home a mattress and put it in the basement, and now Ben had to sleep down there with the dog and Richie's free weights.

In their old house, Ben wouldn't even go down to the basement to put clothes in the wash—and that basement had at least been dry and mostly finished. Ben was scared of mice and bats and spiders and anything that started moving when the lights went out. Richie had already yelled at him, twice, for trying to sleep at the top of the stairs.

The pineapple came with a letter from their uncle and his wife. Eleanor's mom read it first, and it made her get all teary. "Oh, Eleanor," she said excitedly, "Geoff wants you to come up for the summer. He says there's a program at his university, a camp for gifted high school students—"

Before Eleanor could even think about what that meant—St. Paul, a camp where nobody knew her, where nobody was Park—Richie was shooting it down.

"You can't send her up to Minnesota by herself."

"My brother's there."

"What does he know about teenage girls?"

"You know I lived with him in high school."

"Yeah, and he let you get pregnant. . . ."

Ben was lying solidly on top of the pineapple box, and Maisie was kicking him in the back. They were both shouting.

"It's just a fucking box!" Richie yelled. "If I knew that you wanted boxes for Christmas, I would have saved myself some money."

That silenced everyone. Nobody had expected Richie to buy Christmas presents. "I should make you wait until Christmas morning," he said, "but I'm sick of watching this."

He put his cigarette in his mouth and put his boots on. They heard the truck door open, and then Richie was back with a big ShopKo bag. He started throwing boxes onto the floor.

"Mouse," he said. A remote control monster truck.

"Ben." A big racetrack.

"Maisie . . . 'cause you like to sing." Richie pulled out a keyboard, an actual electronic keyboard. It was probably some off-brand, but still. He didn't drop it on the floor. He handed it to Maisie.

"And Little Richie . . . where's Little Richie?"

"He's taking a nap," their mom said.

Richie shrugged and threw a teddy bear onto the floor. The bag was empty, and Eleanor felt cold with relief.

Then Richie took out his wallet and pulled out a bill. "Here, Eleanor, come get it. Buy yourself some normal clothes."

She looked at her mother, who stood blank-faced in the kitchen doorway, then walked over to take the money. It was a fifty.

"Thank you." Eleanor said it as flatly as possible. Then she went to sit on the couch. The little kids were all opening their presents.

"Thanks, Dad," Mouse kept saying. "Oh man, thanks, Dad!"

"Yeah," Richie said, "you're welcome. You're welcome. That's a real Christmas."

Richie stayed home all day to watch the little kids play with their toys. Maybe the Broken Rail wasn't open on Christmas Eve. Eleanor went to her bedroom to get away from him. (And to get away from Maisie's new keyboard.)

She was tired of missing Park. She just wanted to see him. Even if he *did* think she was a perverted psychopath who wrote herself badly punctuated threats. Even if he *had* spent his formative years tongue-kissing Tina. None of it was vile enough to make Eleanor stop wanting him. (*How vile would that have to be?* she wondered.)

Maybe she should just go over to his house right now and pretend that nothing had happened. Maybe she would, if it weren't Christmas Eve. Why didn't Jesus ever work *with* her.

Later, her mom came in to say they were going to the store to buy groceries for Christmas dinner.

"I'll come out and watch the kids," Eleanor said.

"Richie wants us all to go," her mom said, smiling, "as a family."

"But, Mom . . ."

"None of this, Eleanor," she said softly, "we're having a good day."

"Mom, come on—he's been drinking all day."

Her mom shook her head. "Richie's fine, he never has a problem with driving."

"I don't think the fact that he drinks and drives all the time is a very good argument."

"You just can't stand this, can you?" her mom said quietly, angrily, stepping into the room and shutting the door behind her. "Look," she said, "I know that you're going through—" She looked at Eleanor, then shook her head again. "—*something*. But everyone else in this house is having a great day. Everyone else in this house deserves a great day.

"We're a family, Eleanor. All of us. Richie, too. And I'm sorry that that makes you so unhappy. I'm sorry that things aren't perfect here all the time for you. . . . But this is our life now. You can't keep throwing tantrums about it, you can't keep trying to undermine this family—I won't *let* you."

Eleanor clenched her jaw.

"I have to think of everyone," her mom said. "Do you understand? I have to think of myself. In a few years, you'll be on your own, but Richie is my husband."

She almost sounded sane, Eleanor thought. If you didn't know that she was acting rational on the far side of crazy.

"Get up," her mother said, "and put on your coat."

Eleanor put on her coat and her new hat and followed her brothers and sisters into the back of the Isuzu.

When they got to Food 4 Less, Richie waited in the truck while everybody else went in. As soon as they were inside, Eleanor put the wadded-up fifty in her mother's hand.

Her mother didn't thank her.

park

They were shopping for Christmas dinner, and it was taking forever because it always made Park's mom nervous to cook for his grand-mother.

"What kind of stuffing Grandma like?" his mom asked.

"Pepperidge Farm," Park said, standing on the back of the cart and popping a wheelie.

"Pepperidge Farm original? Or Pepperidge Farm corn bread?"

"I don't know, original."

"If you don't know, don't tell me. . . . Look," she said, looking over his shoulder. "There's your Eleanor."

El-la-no.

Park whipped around and saw Eleanor standing by the meat case with all four of her redheaded brothers and sisters. (Except none of them had red hair standing next to Eleanor. Nobody did.)

A woman walked up to the cart and set down a turkey.

That must be Eleanor's mom, Park thought, she looked just like her. But sharper and with more shadows. Like Eleanor, but taller. Like Eleanor, but tired. Like Eleanor, after the fall.

Park's mom was staring at them, too.

"Mom, come on," Park whispered.

"Aren't you going to say hi?" she asked.

Park shook his head, but didn't turn away. He didn't think Eleanor would want him to, and even if she did, he didn't want to get her in trouble. What if her stepdad was here, too?

Eleanor looked different, drabber than usual. There was nothing hanging from her hair or magpie-tied to her wrists. . . .

She still looked beautiful. His eyes missed her as much as the rest of him. He wanted to run to her and tell her—tell her how sorry he was and how much he needed her.

She didn't see him.

"Mom," he whispered again, "come on."

Park thought his mom might say something more about it in the car, but she was quiet. When they got home, she said she was tired. She asked Park to bring in the groceries; then she spent the rest of the afternoon in her room with the door closed.

His dad went in to check on her at dinner time, and an hour later, when they both came out, his dad said they were going to Pizza Hut for dinner. "On Christmas Eve?" Josh said. They always had waffles and watched movies on Christmas Eve. They'd already rented *Billy*

Jack. "Get in the car," his dad said. Park's mom's eyes were red, and she didn't bother reapplying her eye makeup before they left.

When they got home, Park went straight to his room. He just wanted to be alone to think about seeing Eleanor—but his mom came in a few minutes later. She sat on his bed without making a single wave.

She held out a Christmas present. "This . . . is for your Eleanor," she said. "From me."

Park looked at the gift. He took it, but shook his head. "I don't know if I'll have a chance to give it to her."

"Your Eleanor," she said, "she come from big family."

Park shook the present gently.

"I come from big family," his mom said. "Three little sisters. Three little brothers." She held out her hand, as if she were patting six heads.

She'd had a wine cooler with dinner, and you could tell. She almost never talked about Korea.

"What were their names?" Park asked.

His mom's hand settled softly in her lap.

"In big family," she said, "everything . . . everybody spread so thin. Thin like paper, you know?" She made a tearing gesture. "You know?"

Maybe two wine coolers.

"I'm not sure," Park said.

"Nobody gets enough," she said. "Nobody gets what they need. When you always hungry, you get hungry in your head." She tapped her forehead. "You know?"

Park wasn't sure what to say.

"You don't know," she said, shaking her head. "I don't want you to know. . . . I'm sorry."

"Don't be sorry," he said.

"I'm sorry for how I welcomed your Eleanor."

"Mom, it's okay. This isn't your fault."

"I don't think I say this right. . . ."

"It's okay, Mindy," Park's dad said softly from the doorway. "Come to bed, honey." He walked over to the bed and helped Park's mom up, then stood with his arm wrapped protectively around her. "Your mom just wants you to be happy," he said to Park. "Don't puss out on our account."

His mother frowned, like she wasn't sure whether that counted as a dirty word.

Park waited until the TV was off in his parents' room. Then he waited a half hour after that. Then he grabbed his coat and slipped out the back door, on the far side of the house.

He ran until he got to the end of the alley.

Eleanor was so close.

Her stepdad's truck was in the driveway. Maybe that was good; Park wouldn't want him coming home while Park was standing there on the front porch. All the lights were off, as far as Park could tell, and there was no sign of the dog. . . .

He climbed the steps as quietly as possible.

He knew which room was Eleanor's. She'd told him once that she slept by the window, and he knew she had the top bunk. He stood to the side of the window, so he wouldn't cast a shadow. He was going to tap softly, and if anyone but Eleanor looked out, he was going to run for his life.

Park tapped the top of the glass. Nothing happened. The curtain, or the sheet or whatever it was, didn't move.

She was probably sleeping. He tapped a little harder and got ready to run. The side of the sheet opened just a sliver, but he couldn't see in.

Should he run? Should he hide?

He stepped in front of the window. The sheet opened wider. He could see Eleanor's face: she looked terrified.

Go, she mouthed.

He shook his head.

Go, she mouthed again. Then she pointed away. *School.* At least that's what he thought she said. Park ran away.

eleanor

All Eleanor could think was that, if somebody were breaking in through *this* window, how was she supposed to escape and call 911?

Not that the police would even come after last time. But at least she could wake that bastard Gil up and eat his goddamn brownies.

Park was the last person she expected to see standing there.

Her heart leapt out to him before she could stop it. He was going to get them both killed. Shots had been fired for less.

As soon as he disappeared from the window, she slipped off the bed like that stupid cat and put her bra and shoes on in the dark. She was wearing a great big T-shirt and a pair of her dad's old flannel pajama pants. Her coat was in the living room, so she put on a sweater.

Maisie had fallen asleep watching TV, so it was relatively easy to climb over her bed and out the window.

He'll kick me out for real this time, Eleanor thought, tiptoeing across the porch. *That would be his best Christmas ever.*

Park was waiting on the school steps. Where they'd sat and read *Watchmen*. As soon as he saw her, he stood up and ran to her. Like, actually *ran*.

He ran to her—and took her face in both of his hands. And then he was kissing her before she could say no. And she was kissing him back before she could remind herself that she wasn't ever going to kiss anybody again, especially not him, because look how miserable it had made her.

She was crying, and so was Park. When she put her hands on his cheeks, they were wet.

And warm. He was so warm.

She bent her neck back and kissed him like she never had before. Like she wasn't scared of doing it wrong.

He pulled away to say he was sorry, and she shook her head no, because even though she really did want him to be sorry, she wanted to kiss him more.

"I'm sorry, Eleanor." He held her face against his. "I was wrong about everything. *Everything.*"

"I'm sorry, too," she said.

"For what?"

"For acting mad at you all the time."

"It's okay," he said, "sometimes I like it."

"But not always."

He shook his head.

"I don't even know why I do it," she said.

"It doesn't matter."

"I'm not sorry about getting mad about Tina."

He pressed his forehead against hers until it hurt. "Don't even say her name," he said. "She's nothing and you're . . . everything. You're everything, Eleanor."

He kissed her again, and she opened her mouth.

They stayed outside until Park couldn't rub any warmth back into her hands. Until her lips were numb from cold and kissing.

He wanted to walk her back home, but she told him that would be suicidal.

"Come see me tomorrow," he said.

"I can't, it's Christmas."

"The next day, then."

"The next day," she said.

"And the day after that."

She laughed. "I don't think your mom would like that. I don't think she likes me."

"You're wrong," he said. "Come."

Eleanor was climbing the front steps when she heard him whispering her name. She turned back, but she couldn't see him in the shadows.

"Merry Christmas," he said.

She smiled, but didn't answer.

33

eleanor

Eleanor slept until noon on Christmas Day. Until her mom finally came in and told her to wake up.

"Are you okay?" her mom asked.

"I'm asleep."

"You look like you're getting a cold."

"Does that mean I can go back to sleep?"

"I guess so. Look, Eleanor—" Her mother stepped away from the door, and her voice dropped. "—I'm going to talk to Richie about this summer. I think I can get him to change his mind about that camp."

Eleanor opened her eyes. "No. No, I don't want to go."

"But I thought you'd jump at the chance to get out of here."

"No," Eleanor said, "I don't want to have to leave everybody . . . again." Saying it made her feel like 100 percent jerk, but she'd say anything to spend the summer with Park. (And she wasn't even going to tell herself that he'd probably be sick of her by then.) "I want to stay home," she said.

Her mom nodded. "Okay," she said, "then I won't mention it. But if you change your mind . . ."

"I won't," Eleanor said.

Her mom left the room, and Eleanor pretended to go back to sleep.

park

He slept until noon on Christmas Day, until Josh came in and sprayed him with one their mom's salon water bottles.

"Dad says that if you don't get up, he's going to let me have all your presents."

Park beat Josh back with a pillow.

Everybody else was waiting for him, and the whole house smelled like turkey. His grandma wanted him to open her present first—a new KISS ME, I'M IRISH T-shirt. A size bigger than last year's, which meant it would be a size too big.

His parents gave him a fifty-dollar gift certificate to Drastic Plastic, the punk rock record store downtown. (Park was surprised that they'd think of that. And he was surprised that DP sold gift certificates. Not very punk.)

He also got two black sweaters he might actually wear, some Avon cologne in a bottle shaped like an electric guitar, and an empty key ring—which his dad made sure everybody noticed.

Park's sixteenth birthday had come and gone, and he didn't even care anymore about getting his license and driving himself to school. He wasn't going to give up his only guaranteed time with Eleanor.

She'd already told him that as awesome as last night was—and they both agreed it was awesome—she couldn't risk sneaking out again.

"Any one of my siblings could have woken up, they still could, and they would definitely tell on me. They have very confused alliances."

"But if you're quiet . . ."

That's when she'd told him that, most nights, she shared a room with all her brothers and sisters. *All* of them. A room about the size of his, she said, "minus the waterbed."

They were sitting against the back door of the elementary school, in a little alcove where no one would see them unless they were really looking, and where the snow didn't fall directly on their faces. They sat next to each other, facing each other, holding hands.

There was nothing between them now. Nothing stupid and selfish just taking up space.

"So you have two brothers and two sisters?"

"Three brothers, one sister."

"What are their names?"

"Why?"

"I'm just curious," he said. "Is it classified?"

She sighed. "Ben, Maisie . . ."

"Maisie?"

"Yeah. Then Mouse—Jeremiah. He's five. Then the baby. Little Richie."

Park laughed. "You call him 'Little Richie'?"

"Well, his dad is Big Richie, not that he's very big either. . . ."

"I know, but like Little Richard? 'Tutti Frutti'?"

"Oh my God, I never thought of that. Why haven't I ever thought of that?"

He pulled her hands to his chest. He still hadn't managed to touch Eleanor anywhere below the chin or above the elbow. He didn't think she'd necessarily stop him if he tried, but what if she did? That'd be awful. Anyway, her hands and her face were excellent.

"Do you guys get along?"

"Sometimes . . . They're all crazy."

"How can a five-year-old be crazy?"

"Oh my God, Mouse? He's the craziest of them all. He's always got a hammer or a jackrabbit or something stuck in his back pocket, and he refuses to wear a shirt."

Park laughed. "How is Maisie crazy?"

"Well, she's *mean*. For starters. And she fights like a street person. Like, take-off-your-earrings fights."

"How old is she?"

"Eight. No, nine."

"What about Ben?"

"Ben . . ." She looked away. "You've seen Ben. He's almost Josh's age. He needs a haircut."

"Does Richie hate them, too?"

Eleanor pushed his hands forward. "Why do you want to talk about this?"

He pushed back. "*Because*. It's your life. Because I'm interested. It's like you've got all these weird barriers set up, like you only want me to have access to this tiny part of you. . . ."

"Yes," she said, crossing her arms. "Barriers. Caution tape. I'm doing you a favor."

"Don't," he said. "I can handle it." He put his thumb between her eyebrows and tried to smooth out the frown. "This whole stupid fight was about keeping secrets."

"Keeping secrets about your demonic ex-girlfriend. I don't have any demonic ex-anythings."

"Does Richie hate your brothers and sister, too?"

"Stop saying his name." She was whispering.

"I'm sorry," Park whispered back.

"He hates everybody, I think."

"Not your mom."

"Especially her."

"Is he mean to her?"

Eleanor rolled her eyes and wiped her cheek with her pajama sleeve. "Uh. Yeah."

Park took her hands again. "Why doesn't she leave?"

She shook her head. "I don't think she can. . . . I don't think there's enough of her left."

"Is she scared of him?" he asked.

"Yeah . . ."

"Are you scared of him?"

"Me?"

"I know you're scared of getting kicked out, but are you scared of him?"

"No." She lifted up her chin. "No . . . I just have to lie low, you know? Like as long as I stay out of his way, I'm fine. I just have to be invisible."

Park smiled.

"What?" she asked.

"You. Invisible."

She smiled. He let go of her hands and held her face. Her cheeks were cold, and her eyes were fathomless in the dark.

She was all he could see.

Eventually it was too cold to stay out there. Even the insides of their mouths were freezing.

eleanor

Richie said Eleanor had to come out of her room for Christmas dinner. Fine. She really was getting a cold, so at least it didn't seem like she'd been faking it all day.

Dinner was awesome. Her mom could really cook when she had actual food to work with. (Something other than legumes.)

They had turkey with stuffing, and mashed potatoes swimming with dill and butter. For dessert, there was rice pudding and pepper cookies, which her mom only ever made on Christmas.

At least that had been the rule back when her mom used to make all kinds of cookies, all year long. The little kids didn't know what they were missing now. When Eleanor and Ben were little, their mom baked constantly. There were always fresh cookies in the kitchen when Eleanor got home from school. And real breakfast every morning . . . Eggs and bacon, or pancakes and sausage, or oatmeal with cream and brown sugar.

Eleanor used to think that that was why she was so fat. But look at her now—she was starving all the time, and she was still enormous.

They all tore into Christmas dinner like it was their last meal, which it practically was, at least for a while. Ben ate both the turkey legs, and Mouse ate an entire plate of mashed potatoes.

Richie had been drinking all day again, so he was all kinds of festive at dinner—laughing too much and too loud. But you couldn't enjoy the fact that he was in a good mood, because it was the kind of good mood that was just on the edge of a bad one. They were all waiting for him to cross over. . . .

Which he did, as soon as he realized there was no pumpkin pie.

"What the fuck is this?" he said, flicking his spoon in the risalamande.

"It's rice pudding," Ben said, stupid with turkey.

"I know it's pudding," Richie said. "Where's the pumpkin pie, Sabrina?" he shouted into the kitchen. "I told you to make a real Christmas dinner. I gave you money for a real Christmas dinner."

Her mother stood in the doorway to the kitchen. She still hadn't sat down to eat. "It's . . ."

It's a traditional Danish Christmas dessert, Eleanor thought. *My grandmother made it, and her grandmother made it, and it's better than pumpkin pie. It's special.*

"It's . . . just that I forgot to buy pumpkin," her mother said.

"How could you forget the fucking pumpkin on Christmas," Richie said, hurling the stainless steel bowl of rice pudding. It hit the wall near her mother and sprayed weepy chunks everywhere.

Everyone but Richie stayed still.

He stood up unsteadily from his chair. "I'm going to go buy some pumpkin pie . . . so this family can have a real fucking Christmas dinner."

He walked to the back door.

As soon as they heard his truck tear out, Eleanor's mom picked up the bowl with what was left of the rice pudding, then skimmed the top off the pile of pudding on the floor.

"Who wants cherry sauce?" she said.

They all did.

Eleanor cleaned up the rest of the pudding, and Ben turned on the TV. They watched *The Grinch* and *Frosty the Snowman*, and *A Christmas Carol*.

Their mom even sat down to watch with them.

Eleanor couldn't help but think that if the Ghost of Christmas Past showed up, he'd be disgusted with their whole situation. But Eleanor felt full and happy when she fell asleep.

34

eleanor

Park's mom didn't seem surprised to see Eleanor the next day. He must have warned them she was coming.

"Eleanor," his mom said extra nicely, "Merry Christmas, come in."

When Eleanor walked into the living room, Park had just gotten out of the shower, which was embarrassing for some reason. His hair was wet and his T-shirt was kind of sticking to him. He was really happy to see her. That was obvious. (And nice.)

She didn't know what to do with his present, so when he walked over to her, she shoved it at him.

He smiled, surprised. "This is for me?"

"No," she said, "it's . . ." She couldn't think of anything funny to say. "Yeah, it's for you."

"You didn't have to get me anything."

"I didn't. Really."

"Can I open it?"

She still couldn't think of anything funny, so she nodded. At least his family was in the kitchen, so nobody was watching them.

The present was wrapped in stationery. Eleanor's favorite stationery, watercolor paintings of fairies and flowers.

Park peeled off the paper carefully and looked at the book. It was *The Catcher in the Rye*. A really old edition. Eleanor had decided to leave the dust jacket on because it was neat-looking, even though it still had a thrift-shop price scrawled on the front with grease pencil.

"I know it's pretentious," she said. "I was going to give you *Watership Down,* but that's about rabbits, and not everybody wants to read about rabbits. . . ."

He looked at the book, smiling. For a terrible second, she thought he was going to open the front cover. And she really didn't want him to read what she'd written. (Not while she was standing right here.)

"Is this your book?" he asked.

"Yeah, but I've already read it."

"Thank you," he said, grinning at her. When he was really happy, his eyes disappeared into his cheeks. "Thank you."

"You're welcome," she said, looking down. "Just don't kill John Lennon or anything."

"Come here," he said, pulling on the front of her jacket.

She followed him to his room but stopped at the door like there was an invisible fence. Park set the book on his bed, then grabbed two small boxes off a shelf. They were both wrapped in Christmas paper with big red bows.

He came and stood in the doorway with her; she leaned back against the jamb.

"This one is from my mom," he said, holding up a box. "It's perfume. Please don't wear it." His eyes flicked down for a second, then back up at her. "This one is from me."

"You didn't have to get me a present," she said.

"Don't be stupid."

When she didn't take the present, he took her hand and pressed the box into it.

"I tried to think of something that nobody would notice but you," he said, pushing his bangs off his face. "That you wouldn't have to explain to your mom . . . Like, I was going to buy you a really nice pen, but then . . ."

He was watching her open it, which made her nervous. She accidentally tore the wrapping paper. He took the paper from her, and she opened a small gray box.

There was a necklace inside. A thin silver chain with a small pendant, a silver pansy.

"I'll understand if you can't take it," Park said.

She shouldn't take it, but she wanted it.

park

Dumb. He should have gotten the pen. Jewelry was so public . . . and personal, which was why he'd bought it. He couldn't buy Eleanor a pen. Or a bookmark. He didn't have bookmarklike feelings for her.

Park had used most of his car stereo money to buy the necklace. He'd found it at the jewelry store in the mall where people try on engagement rings.

"I kept the receipt," he said.

"No," Eleanor said, looking up at him. She looked anxious, but he wasn't sure what kind. "No. It's beautiful," she said, "thank you."

"Will you wear it?" he asked.

She nodded.

He ran his hand through his hair and held on to the back of his neck, trying to rein himself in. "Now?"

Eleanor looked at him for a second, then nodded again. He took the necklace out of the box and carefully fastened it around her neck. Just like he'd imagined himself doing when he bought it. That might even be *why* he bought it—so he'd have this moment, with his hands warm on the back of her neck, under her hair. He ran his fingertips along the chain and settled the pendant on her throat.

She shivered.

Park wanted to pull on the chain, to pull it into his chest and anchor her there.

He pulled his hands away self-consciously and leaned back against the doorjamb.

eleanor

They were sitting in the kitchen, playing cards. Speed. She'd taught Park how to play, and she could always beat him for the first few rounds. But after that, she'd get sloppy. (Maisie always started winning after a few rounds, too.)

Playing cards in Park's kitchen, even if his mom was in there, was better than just sitting in the living room, thinking about all the things they'd be doing if they were alone.

His mom asked how her Christmas was, and Eleanor said it was nice. "What do you have for holiday dinner?" his mom asked. "Turkey or ham?"

"Turkey," Eleanor said, "with dill potatoes . . . My mom's Danish."

Park stopped playing to look at her. She popped her eyes at him. *What, I'm Danish, shut up,* she would have said if his mom hadn't been there.

"That's where you get beautiful red hair," his mom said knowingly.

Park smiled at Eleanor. She rolled her eyes.

When his mom left to run something over to his grandparents, Park kicked her under the table. He wasn't wearing shoes. "I didn't know you were Danish," he said.

"Is this the kind of scintillating conversation we're going to have now that we don't have any secrets?"

"Yes. Is your mom Danish?"

"Yes," she said.

"What's your dad?"

"An ass."

He frowned.

"What? You wanted honest and intimate. That's way more honest than 'Scottish.'"

"Scottish," Park said, and smiled.

Eleanor had been thinking about this new arrangement he wanted. This being totally open and honest with each other. She didn't think she could start telling Park the whole, ugly truth overnight.

What if he was wrong? What if he couldn't handle it?

What if Park realized that all the things he thought were so mysterious and intriguing about her were actually just . . . bleak?

When he asked about her Christmas, Eleanor told him about her mom's cookies and the movies, and how Mouse thought *The Grinch* was about "all the Hoots down in Hootville."

She half expected him to say, *Yeah, but* now *tell me all the terrible parts.* . . . Instead he laughed.

"Do you think your mom would be okay with me," he asked, "you know, if it wasn't for your stepdad?"

"I don't know . . . ," Eleanor said. She realized that she was holding on to the silver pansy.

Eleanor spent the rest of Christmas vacation at Park's house. His mom didn't seem to mind, and his dad was always inviting her to stay for dinner.

Eleanor's mom thought she was spending all that time with Tina. Once she'd said, "I hope you're not overstaying your welcome over there, Eleanor." And once she'd said, "Tina could come over here sometimes, too, you know," which they both knew was a joke.

Nobody brought friends into their house. Not the little kids. Not even Richie. And her mom didn't have friends anymore.

She used to.

When Eleanor's parents were still together, there were always people around. There were always parties. Men with long hair. Women in long dresses. Glasses of red wine everywhere.

And even after her dad left, there were still women. Single moms who brought over their kids, plus all the ingredients for banana daiquiris. They'd sit up late talking in hushed voices about their ex-husbands and speculating about new boyfriends, while the kids played Trouble and Sorry! in the next room.

Richie had started as one of those stories. It went like this:

Her mom used to walk to the grocery store early in the morning while the kids were still asleep. They didn't have a car back then either. (Her mom hadn't had a car of her own since high school.) Well, Richie would see her mom out walking every morning on his drive to work. One day he stopped and asked for her number. He said she was the prettiest woman he'd ever seen.

When Eleanor first heard about Richie, she was leaning against their old couch, reading a *Life* magazine, and drinking a virgin banana daiquiri. She wasn't exactly eavesdropping—all her mom's friends liked having Eleanor around. They liked that she watched their kids without complaining; they said she was wise beyond her years. If Eleanor was quiet, they sort of forgot she was in the room. And if they drank too much, they didn't care.

"Never trust a man, Eleanor!" they'd all shouted at her, at one point or another.

"Especially if he hates to dance!"

But when her mom told them that Richie said she was as pretty as a spring day, they'd all sighed and asked her to tell them more.

Of course he said she's the prettiest woman he's ever seen, Eleanor thought. *She undoubtedly is.*

Eleanor was twelve, and she couldn't imagine a guy fucking her mom over worse than her dad had.

She didn't know there were things worse than selfish.

Anyway. She always tried to leave Park's house before dinner—just in case her mom was right about wearing out her welcome—and because, if Eleanor left early, there was a better chance that she'd beat Richie home.

Hanging out with Park every day had really messed up her bath-taking routine. (A fact she was never ever going to tell him, no matter how sharey-carey they got.)

The only safe time to take a bath in her house was right after school. If Eleanor went over to Park's house right after school, she had to hope that Richie would still be at the Broken Rail when she got home that night. And then she had to take a really fast bath because the back door was right across from the bathroom, and it could open at any time.

She could tell that all this sneaky bath-taking was making her mom nervous, but it wasn't exactly Eleanor's fault. She'd considered taking a shower in the locker room at school, but that might be even more dangerous, Tina et al.

The other day at lunch, Tina had made a big point of walking by Eleanor's table and mouthing the C-word. The *c-u-n-t* word. (Richie didn't even use that word, which implied an unimaginable degree of filth.)

"What is her *problem*?" DeNice asked. Rhetorically.

"She thinks she's all that," Beebi said.

"She ain't all that," DeNice said. "Walking around here looking like a little boy in a miniskirt."

Beebi giggled.

"That hair is just wrong," DeNice said, still looking at Tina. "She needs to wake up a little earlier and try to decide whether she wants to look like Farrah Fawcett or Rick James."

Beebi and Eleanor both cracked up.

"I mean, pick one, girl," DeNice said, milking it. "Pick. One."

"Oh, girl!" Beebi said, slapping Eleanor's leg. "There's your man." They all looked out the cafeteria's glass wall. Park was walking by with a few other guys. He was wearing jeans and a T-shirt that said MINOR THREAT. He looked into the cafeteria and smiled when he saw Eleanor. Beebi giggled.

"He is *cute*," DeNice said. Like it was something certifiable.

"I know," Eleanor said. "I want to eat his face."

They all three giggled until DeNice called them back to order.

park

"So," Cal said.

Park was still smiling. Even though they were long past the cafeteria.

"You and Eleanor, huh?"

"Uh . . . yeah," Park said.

"Yeah," Cal said, nodding. "Everybody knows. I mean, I've known forever. I could tell by the way you stare at her in English. . . . I was just waiting for *you* to tell me."

"Oh," Park said, looking up at Cal. "Sorry. I'm going with Eleanor."

"Why didn't you tell me?"

"I figured you knew."

"I did know," Cal said. "But, you know, we're friends. We're supposed to talk about these things."

"I didn't think you'd get it. . . ."

"I don't get it. No offense. Eleanor still scares the crap out of me. But if you're getting it—you know, *getting* it—I want to know about it. I want the whole freaking report."

"This, actually," Park said. "This is why I didn't tell you."

35

eleanor

Park's mom asked him to set the table. That was Eleanor's cue to leave. The sun had almost set. She rushed down the steps before Park could stop her . . . and almost ran into his dad standing in the driveway.

"Hey, Eleanor," he said, startling her. He was messing around with something in the back of his truck.

"Hey," she said, rushing past him. He really did look an awful lot like Magnum, P.I. It wasn't something you got used to.

"Hey, wait, come here," he said.

She felt something go slightly wrong in her stomach. She stopped and stepped toward him, but only a little.

"Look," he said, "I'm getting tired of asking you to stay for dinner."

"Okay . . ." she said.

"What I mean is, I want you to feel like you have a standing invitation. You're just . . . welcome, okay?" He seemed uncomfortable, and it was making her uncomfortable. Way more uncomfortable than she usually felt around him.

"Okay . . ." she said.

"Look, Eleanor . . . I know your stepdad."

This could go a million different ways, she thought. All of them awful.

Park's dad kept talking, one hand on his truck, the other on the back of his neck, like he was in pain. "We grew up together. I'm older than Richie, but this is a small neighborhood, and I've put in my time at the Rail. . . ."

The sun was too far gone to see his face. Eleanor still wasn't sure what he was getting at.

"I know that your stepdad isn't an easy man to be around," Park's dad said finally, stepping toward her. "And I'm just saying, you know, that if it's easier to be over here, then you should just be here. That would make Mindy and me feel a lot better, okay?"

"Okay," she said.

"So this is the last time I'm going to ask you to stay for dinner."

Eleanor smiled, and he smiled back, and for a second he looked a lot more like Park than like Tom Selleck.

park

Eleanor on the couch, holding his hand. Across from him at the kitchen table with her homework . . .

Helping him carry in groceries for his grandmother. Politely eating everything his mom made for dinner, even if it was something completely disgusting like liver and onions . . .

They were always together, and it still wasn't enough.

He still hadn't found a way to put his arms all the way around her. And he still didn't have enough opportunities to kiss her. She wouldn't go to his room with him. . . .

"We can listen to music," he'd say.

"Your mom . . ."

"Doesn't care. We'll leave the door open."

"Where will we sit?"

"On my bed."

"God. No."

"On the floor."

"I don't want her to think I'm slutty."

He wasn't sure his mother even thought of Eleanor as a girl.

She liked Eleanor, though. More than she used to. Just the other day, his mom had said that Eleanor had excellent manners.

"She's very quiet," his mom said, like that was a good thing.

"She's just nervous," Park said.

"Why nervous?"

"I don't know," Park said. "She just is."

He could tell that his mom still hated Eleanor's clothes. She was always looking her up and down and shaking her head when she thought Eleanor wasn't looking.

Eleanor was unfailingly polite with his mom. She even tried to make small talk. One Saturday night after dinner, Park's mom was sorting her Avon shipment on the dining room table while Park and Eleanor played cards. "How long have you been a beautician?" Eleanor asked, looking over at all the bottles.

His mom loved that word.

"Since Josh start school. I get my GED, I go to beauty school, get license, get permit. . . ."

"Wow," Eleanor said.

"I always do hair," his mom said, "even before." She opened a pink bottle of lotion and smelled it. "Little girl . . . cut dolls' hair, paint on makeup."

"That sounds like my sister," Eleanor said. "I could never do any of that."

"Not so hard . . ." his mom said, looking up at her. His mom's eyes lit up. "Hey, I have good idea," she said. "I do your hair. We have make-over night."

Eleanor's mouth dropped open. She was probably picturing herself with feathered hair and fake eyelashes.

"Oh, no . . ." she said. "I couldn't. . . ."

"Yes," his mom said, "so much fun!"

"Mom, no," Park said, "Eleanor doesn't want a makeover. . . . She doesn't need a makeover," he added, as soon as he thought of it.

"Not big makeover," his mom said. She was already reaching for Eleanor's hair. "No cutting. Nothing we can't wash off."

Park looked at Eleanor, pleading. Hopefully, she'd know that he was pleading because it would make his mom happy, not because he thought there was anything wrong with her.

"No cutting?" Eleanor said.

His mom was fingering a curl. "Better light in the garage," she said, "come on."

eleanor

Park's mom put Eleanor in the shampoo chair and snapped her fingers at Park. To Eleanor's horror—to her ongoing horror—Park came over and started filling the sink with water. He took a pink towel down from a big stack and expertly Velcroed it around Eleanor's neck, carefully lifting out her hair.

"I'm sorry," he whispered. "Do you want me to leave?"

No, she mouthed, grabbing his shirt. *Yes,* she thought. She was already starting to dissolve with embarrassment. She couldn't feel the tips of her fingers.

But if Park left, there'd be no one to stop his mom if she decided to give Eleanor giant, claw-shaped bangs or a spiral perm. Or both.

Eleanor wouldn't try to stop her, no matter what; she was a guest in this garage. She'd eaten this woman's food and manhandled her son—she was in no position to argue.

Park's mom pushed him aside and laid Eleanor's head firmly back into the sink. "What kind of shampoo you use?"

"I don't know," Eleanor said.

"How you not know?" his mom asked, feeling her hair. "Feels too dry. Curly hair is dry, you know?"

Eleanor shook her head.

"Hmmm . . ." Park's mom said. She tipped Eleanor's head back into the water and told Park to go stick a hot-oil pack in the microwave.

It was really, really strange having Park's mom wash her hair. She was practically standing in Eleanor's lap; her angel necklace hung right over Eleanor's mouth. Plus, the whole process tickled like crazy. Eleanor didn't know whether Park was watching. She hoped not.

A few minutes later, her hair was hot-oiled and wrapped in a towel so tight, it hurt her forehead. Park was sitting across from her, trying to smile, but looking almost as uncomfortable as she felt.

His mom was going through box after box of Avon samples. "I know it's here somewhere," she said. "Cinnamon, cinnamon, cinnamon . . . A-ha!"

She wheeled her chair over to Eleanor. "Okay. Close eyes."

Eleanor stared at her. She was holding up a little brown pencil.

"Close eyes," she said again.

"Why?" Eleanor said.

"Don't worry. This wash off."

"But I don't wear makeup."

"Why not?"

Maybe Eleanor should say that she wasn't allowed to. That would sound nicer than, *Because makeup is a lie.*

"I don't know," Eleanor said. "It's just not me."

"Yes, you," his mom said, looking at the pencil. "Very good color for you. Cinnamon."

"Is that lipstick?"

"No, eyeliner."

Eleanor especially didn't wear eyeliner.

"What does it do?"

"It's makeup," his mom said, exasperated. "It makes you pretty."

Eleanor felt like she had something in her eye. Like fire.

"Mom . . ." Park said.

"Here," his mom said. "I'll show you." She turned to Park, and before either of them realized what she was planning, she had her thumb at the corner of his eye.

"Cinnamon too light," she muttered. She picked up a different pencil. "Onyx."

"Mom . . ." Park said painfully, but he didn't move.

His mom sat so that Eleanor could see, then deftly drew a line along Park's eyelashes. "Open." He did. "Nice . . . close." She did the other eye, too. Then she added another line under his eye and licked her thumb to wipe away a smudge. "There, nice."

"See?" she said, sitting back so that Eleanor could see. "Easy. Pretty."

Park didn't look pretty. He looked dangerous. Like Ming the Merciless. Or a member of Duran Duran.

"You look like Robert Smith," Eleanor said. But . . . yeah, she thought, *prettier*.

He looked down. Eleanor couldn't look away.

His mom swooped in between them. "Okay, now close eyes," she said to Eleanor. "Open. Nice . . . Close again . . ." It felt exactly like having someone draw on your eye with a pencil. Then it was over, and Park's mom was rubbing something cold on Eleanor's cheeks.

"This very easy routine," his mom said. "Foundation, powder, eyeliner, eye shadow, mascara, lip liner, lipstick, blush. Eight steps, take you fifteen minutes tops."

Park's mom was very businesslike, like someone with a cooking show on PBS. Pretty soon she was unwrapping Eleanor's hair and standing behind her.

Eleanor wanted to look at Park again, now that she could, but she didn't want him looking back. Her face felt so heavy and sticky, she probably looked like one of the Designing Women.

Park scooted his chair closer to hers and started bouncing his fist on her knee. It took Eleanor a second to realize he was challenging her to a game of Rock, Paper, Scissors.

She played along. God. Any excuse to touch him. Any excuse not to look at him directly. He'd rubbed his eyes, so he didn't look painted anymore—but he still looked like something Eleanor didn't have words for.

"That's how Park keep little kids busy during haircuts," his mom said. "You must look scared, Eleanor. Don't worry. I promise no cutting."

Eleanor and Park both made scissors.

His mom rubbed half a can of mousse into her hair, then blew it dry with a diffuser (which Eleanor had never heard of before but was apparently very, very important).

According to Park's mom, everything Eleanor was doing with her hair—washing it with whatever, brushing it, tying in beads and silk flowers—was dead wrong.

She should be diffusing and scrunching and, if possible, sleeping on a satin pillowcase.

"I think you look really good with bangs," his mom said. "Maybe next time, we try bangs."

There will never be a next time, Eleanor promised herself and God.

"Okay, all done." Park's mom was all smiles. "Look so pretty . . . Ready to see?" She turned Eleanor around to the mirror. "Ta-daa!"

Eleanor looked at her own lap.

"Have to look, Eleanor. Look, mirror, so pretty."

Eleanor couldn't. She could feel them both watching her. She wanted to disappear, to drop through a trapdoor. This whole thing was a bad idea. A terrible idea. She was going to cry; she was going to make a scene. Park's mom was going to go back to hating her.

"Hey, Mindy." Park's dad opened the door and leaned into the garage. "Phone call. Oh, hey, look at you, Eleanor, you look like a *Solid Gold* dancer."

"See?" his mom said. "I told you—pretty. Don't look in mirror until I come back. Looking in mirror best part."

She hurried into the house, and Eleanor hid her face in her hands, trying not to mess anything up. She felt Park's hands on her wrists.

"I'm sorry," he said. "I guess I knew you'd hate this, but I didn't think you'd hate it this much."

"It's just so embarrassing."

"Why?"

"Because . . . you're all looking at me."

"I'm always looking at you," he said.

"I know, I wish you'd stop."

"She's just trying to get to know you. This is her thing."

"Do I look like a *Solid Gold* dancer?"

"No . . ."

"Oh my God," she said, "I do."

"No, you look . . . just look."

"I don't want to."

"Look now," he said, "before my mom gets back."

"Only if you close your eyes."

"Okay, they're closed."

Eleanor uncovered her face and looked in the mirror. It wasn't as embarrassing as she thought—because it was like looking at a different person. Someone with cheekbones and giant eyes and really wet lips. Her hair was still curly, curlier than ever, but calmer somehow. Less deranged.

Eleanor hated it, she hated all of it.

"Can I open my eyes?" Park asked.

"No."

"Are you crying?"

"No." Of course she was. She was going to ruin her fake face, and Park's mom was going to go back to hating her.

Park opened his eyes and sat in front of Eleanor on the vanity. "Is it so bad?" he asked.

"It's not me."

"Of course it's you."

"I just, I look like I'm in costume. Like I'm trying to be something that I'm not."

Like she was trying to be pretty and popular. It was the *trying* part that was so disgusting.

"I think your hair looks really nice," Park said.

"It's not *my* hair."

"It is . . ."

"I don't want your mom to see me like this. I don't want to hurt her feelings."

"Kiss me."

"What?"

He kissed her. Eleanor felt her shoulders fall and her stomach untwist. Then it started twisting in the other direction.

She pulled away. "Are you kissing me because I look like someone else?"

"You don't look like someone else. Plus, that's crazy."

"Do you like me better like this?" she asked. "Because I'm never going to look like this again."

"I like you the same. . . . I kind of miss your freckles." He rubbed her cheeks with his sleeve. "There," he said.

"You look like a different person," she said, "and you're just wearing eyeliner."

"Do you like me better?"

She rolled her eyes, but she felt the heat in her neck. "You look different. You look unsettling."

"You look like *you*," he said. "You with the volume turned up."

She looked in the mirror again.

"The thing is," Park said. "I'm pretty sure my mom was holding back. I think she thinks this is the natural look."

Eleanor laughed. The door to the house opened.

"Awww, I told you guys to wait," his mom said. "Were you surprised?"

Eleanor nodded.

"Did you cry? Oh, I missed it!"

"Sorry if I messed it up," Eleanor said.

"No mess," his mom said, "waterproof mascara and stay-put foundation."

"Thank you," Eleanor said carefully. "I could hardly believe the difference."

"I'll make you a kit," his mom said. "These all colors I never use anyway. Here, sit down, Park. I trim your hair while we here. Looking shaggy . . ."

Eleanor sat in front of him and played Rock, Paper, Scissors on his knee.

park

She looked like a different person, and Park didn't *know* if he liked it better. Or at all.

He couldn't figure out why it upset her so much. Sometimes, it seemed like she was trying to hide everything that was pretty about her. Like she wanted to look ugly.

That was something his mother would say. Which is why he hadn't said it to Eleanor. (Did that count as holding back?)

He got why Eleanor tried so hard to look different. Sort of. It was because she *was* different—because she wasn't afraid to be. (Or maybe she was just *more* afraid of being like everyone else.)

There was something really exciting about that. He liked being near that, that kind of brave and crazy.

Unsettling, how? he'd wanted to ask her.

The next morning, Park took the Onyx eyeliner into the bathroom and put it on. He was messier than his mom, but he thought that might look better. More masculine.

He looked in the mirror. *This really make your eyes pop,* his mom always told her customers, and it was true. The eyeliner did makes his eyes pop. It also made him look even less white.

Then Park did his hair like he usually did—flared up in the middle, all messy and tall, like it was reaching for something. Usually, as soon as he did that, Park combed his hair out and down again.

Today he left it wild.

His dad flipped at breakfast. *Flipped.* Park tried to sneak out without seeing him, but his mom was nonnegotiable about breakfast. Park hung his head over the cereal bowl.

"What's wrong with your hair?" his dad asked.

"Nothing."

"Wait a minute, look at me. . . . I said *look at me.*"

Park lifted his head, but looked away.

"What the fuck, Park?"

"Jamie!" his mother said.

"Look at him, Mindy, he's wearing makeup! Are you fucking kidding me, Park?"

"No excuse to cuss," his mom said. She looked nervously at Park, like maybe this was her fault. Maybe it was. Maybe she shouldn't have tried out lipstick samples on him when he was in kindergarten. Not that he wanted to wear lipstick . . .

Probably.

"Like hell it isn't," his dad roared. "Go wash your face, Park."

Park stayed where he was.

"Go wash your face. Park."

Park took a bite of cereal.

"Jamie . . ." his mom said.

"No, Mindy. *No.* I let these boys do pretty much anything they damn well please. But, no. Park is not leaving this house looking like a girl."

"Plenty of guys wear makeup," Park said.

"What? What are you even talking about?"

"David Bowie," Park said. "Marc Bolan."

"I'm not listening to this. Wash your face."

"Why?" Park pressed his fists into the table.

"Because I said so. Because you look like a girl."

"So what else is new." Park shoved his cereal bowl away from him.

"What did you say?"

"I said, *what else is new.* Isn't that what you think?" Park felt tears on his cheeks, but he didn't want to touch his eyes.

"Go to school, Park," his mom said softly. "You miss your bus."

"Mindy . . ." his dad said, just barely restraining himself, "they'll tear him apart."

"You tell me Park all grown up now, almost man, make own decisions. So let him make own decisions. Let him go."

His dad didn't say anything; he'd never raise his voice to Park's mom. Park saw his opportunity and left.

He went to his own bus stop, not Eleanor's. He wanted to deal with Steve before he saw her. If Steve was going to beat the shit out of him for this, Park would prefer that Eleanor not be in the audience.

But Steve hardly mentioned it.

"Hey, Park, what the fuck, man, are you wearing makeup?"

"Yeah," Park said, holding on to his backpack.

Everyone around Steve tittered, waiting to see what would happen next.

"You kind of look like Ozzy, man," Steve said. "You look ready to bite the head off a fucking bat."

Everybody laughed. Steve bared his teeth at Tina and growled, and then it was over.

When Eleanor got on the bus, she was in a good mood. "You're here! I thought maybe you were sick when you weren't at my corner." He looked up at her. She looked surprised, then sat down quietly and looked at her hands.

"Do I look like one of the *Solid Gold* dancers?" he asked finally, when he couldn't take any more quiet.

"No," she said, sidelong glancing, "you look . . ."

"Unsettling?" he asked.

She laughed and nodded.

"Unsettling, *how*?" he asked her.

She kissed him with tongue. *On the bus.*

36

park

Park told Eleanor not to come over after school. He figured he was grounded. He washed his face as soon as he got home and sent himself to his room.

His mom came in to check on him.

"Am I grounded?" he asked.

"I don't know," she said. "Did you have a good day at school?"

Meaning, did anyone try to flush his face down the toilet?

"It was fine," he said.

A couple of kids had called Park names in the halls, but it didn't hurt like he thought it might. Lots of other people said he looked cool.

His mom sat on his bed. She looked like she'd had a long day. You could see her lipliner.

She stared at a jumble of *Star Wars* action figures piled up on the shelf over his bed. He hadn't touched them for years.

"Park," she said, "do you . . . *want* to look like girl? Is that what this about? Eleanor dress like boy. You look like girl?"

"No . . ." Park said. "I just like it. I like the way it feels."

"Like girl?"

"No," he said. "Like myself."

"Your dad . . ."

"I don't want to talk about him."

His mother sat for another minute, then left.

Park stayed in his room until Josh came to get him for dinner. His dad didn't look up when Park sat down.

"Where's Eleanor?" his dad asked.

"I thought I was grounded."

"You're not grounded," his dad said, concentrating on his meat loaf.

Park looked around the table. Only Josh would look back at him. "Are you going to talk to me about this morning?" Park asked.

His dad took another bite, chewed it carefully, then swallowed. "No, Park, at the moment, I can't think of a single thing I'd like to say to you."

37

eleanor

Park was right. They were never alone.

She thought about sneaking out again, but the risk was incomprehensible, and it was so effing cold out, she'd probably lose an ear to frostbite. Which her mom would definitely notice.

She'd already noticed the mascara. (Even though it was light brown and said SUBTLE, NATURAL LOOK right on the package.)

"Tina gave it to me," Eleanor said. "Her mom's an Avon lady."

If she just changed Park's name to "Tina" every time she lied, it only felt like one big lie instead of a million small ones.

It was kind of funny to think about hanging out at Tina's house every day, doing each other's nails, trying on lip gloss. . . .

It would be awful if her mom actually met Tina somewhere, but that didn't seem likely—her mom never talked to anybody in the neighborhood. If you weren't born in the Flats (if your family didn't go back ten generations, if your parents didn't have the same great-great-grandparents), you were an outsider.

Park always said that was why people left him alone, even though he was weird and Asian. Because his family had owned their land back when the neighborhood was still cornfields.

Park. Eleanor blushed whenever she thought about him. She'd probably always done that, but now it was worse. Because he was cute and cool before, but lately he seemed so much more of both.

Even DeNice and Beebi thought so.

"He looks like a rock star," DeNice said.

"He looks like El DeBarge," Beebi agreed.

He looked like himself, Eleanor thought, but bolder. Like Park with the volume turned way up.

park

They were never alone.

They tried to make the walk from the bus to Park's house last forever, and sometimes, they'd hang out on his front steps awhile . . . until his mom opened the door and told them to come in from the cold.

Maybe it would be better this summer. They could go outside. Maybe they could take walks. Maybe he'd get his driver's license after all. . . .

No. His dad hadn't even spoken to him since the day they fought.

"What's up with your dad?" Eleanor asked him. She was standing one step below him on his front stoop.

"He's mad at me."

"For what?"

"For not being like him."

Eleanor looked dubious. "Has he been mad at you for the last sixteen years?"

"Basically."

"But it always seemed like you got along . . ." she said.

"No," Park said, "never. I mean, we were kind of getting along for a while, because I finally got in a fight, and because he thought my mom was being too hard on you."

"I knew she didn't like me!" Eleanor poked Park's arm.

"Well, now she likes you," he said, "so now my dad is back to not liking me."

"Your dad loves you," she said. It seemed to really matter to her.

Park shook his head. "Only because he has to. He's disappointed in me."

Eleanor laid her hand on his chest, and his mom opened the door.

"Come in, come in," she said. "Too cold."

eleanor

"Your hair looks nice, Eleanor," Park's mom said.

"Thank you."

Eleanor wasn't diffusing, but she was using the conditioner Park's mom had given her. And she'd actually found a satin pillowcase in the stack of towels and stuff in her bedroom closet, which was practically a sign from God that He wanted Eleanor to take better care of her hair.

Park's mom really did seem to like her better now. Eleanor hadn't consented to another full-on makeover, but Park's mom was always trying new eyeshadows on her or messing with her hair while she sat at the kitchen table with Park.

"I should have had girl," his mom said.

I should have had a family like this, Eleanor thought. And it only sometimes made her feel like a traitor to think so.

38

eleanor

Wednesday nights were the worst.

Park had taekwondo, so Eleanor went straight home after school, took a bath, then tried to hide in her room all night, reading.

It was way too cold to play outside, so the little kids were crawling up the walls. When Richie came home, there was no place for anybody to hide.

Ben was so afraid that Richie would send him to the basement early that he was sitting in the bedroom closet, playing with his cars.

When Richie turned on *Mike Hammer,* their mom shooed Maisie into the bedroom, too, even though Richie said she could stay.

Maisie paced the room, bored and irritable. She walked over to the bunk bed.

"Can I come up?"

"No."

"Please . . ."

Their beds were junior-sized, smaller than a twin, just barely big enough for Eleanor. And Maisie wasn't one of those stringy, weightless nine-year-olds. . . . "Fine," Eleanor groaned.

She scooted over carefully, like she was on thin ice, and pushed her grapefruit box behind her into the corner.

Maisie climbed up and sat on Eleanor's pillow. "What're you reading?"

"Watership Down."

Maisie wasn't paying attention. She folded her arms and leaned toward Eleanor. "We know you have a boyfriend," she whispered.

Eleanor's heart stopped. "I don't have a boyfriend," she said blankly—and immediately.

"We already know," Maisie said.

Eleanor looked over at Ben, sitting in the closet. He stared at her without giving up a thing. Thanks to Richie, they were all experts in the blank-face department. They should find some family poker tournament. . . .

"Bobbie told us," Maisie said. "Her big sister goes with Josh Sheridan, and Josh says you're his brother's girlfriend. Ben said you weren't, and Bobbie laughed at him."

Ben didn't flinch.

"Are you going to tell Mom?" Eleanor asked. May as well cut to the chase.

"We haven't told her yet," Maisie said.

"Are you going to?" Eleanor resisted the urge to shove Maisie off the bed. Maisie would go nuclear.

"He'll make me leave, you know," Eleanor said fiercely. "If I'm lucky, that's the worst that'll happen."

"We're not going to tell," Ben whispered.

"But it's not fair," Maisie said, slumping against the wall.

"What?" Eleanor said.

"It's not fair that you get to leave all the time," Maisie said.

"What do you want me to do?" Eleanor asked. They both stared at her, desperate and almost . . . almost hopeful.

Everything anybody ever said in this house was desperate.

Desperate was white noise, as far as Eleanor was concerned—it was the *hope* that pulled at her heart with dirty little fingers.

She was pretty sure she was wired wrong somewhere, that her plugs were switched, because instead of softening toward them—instead of tenderness—she felt herself go cold and mean. "I can't take you with me," she said, "if that's what you're thinking."

"Why not?" Ben said. "We'll just hang out with the other kids."

"There *are* no other kids," Eleanor said. "It's not like that."

"You don't care about us," Maisie said.

"I do care," Eleanor hissed. "I just can't . . . *help* you."

The door opened, and Mouse wandered in. "Ben, Ben, Ben, where's my car, Ben? Where's my car? Ben?" He jumped on Ben for no reason. Sometimes you didn't know until after Mouse jumped on you whether he was hugging you or trying to kill you.

Ben tried to push Mouse off as quietly as he could. Eleanor threw a book at him. (A paperback. God.)

Mouse ran out of the room, and Eleanor leaned out of her bed to close the door. She could practically open her dresser without getting out of bed.

"I can't help you," she said. It felt like letting go of them in deep water. "I can't even help myself."

Maisie's face was hard.

"Please don't tell," Eleanor said.

Maisie and Ben exchanged looks again; then Maisie, still hard and gray, turned to Eleanor. "Will you let us use your stuff?"

"What stuff?" Eleanor asked.

"Your comics," Ben said.

"They're not mine."

"Your makeup," Maisie said.

They'd probably cataloged her whole freaking bed. Her grapefruit box was packed with contraband these days, all of it from Park. . . . They were already into everything, she was sure.

"You have to put it away when you're done," Eleanor said. "And the comics aren't mine, Ben, they're borrowed. You have to keep them nice. . . .

"And if you get caught"—she turned to Maisie—"Mom will take it all away. Especially the makeup. None of us will have it then."

They both nodded.

"I would have let you use some, anyway," she said to Maisie. "You just had to ask."

"Liar," Maisie said.

And she was right.

park

Wednesdays were the worst.

No Eleanor. And his dad ignored him all through dinner and taekwondo.

Park wondered if it was just the eyeliner that had done it—or if the eyeliner had been the pencil that broke the camel's back. Like Park had spent sixteen years acting weak and weird and girlie, and his dad had borne it on his massive shoulders. And then one day, Park put on makeup, and that was it, his dad just shrugged him off.

Your dad loves you, Eleanor said. And she was right. But it didn't matter. That was table stakes. His dad loved him in a completely obligatory way, like Park loved Josh.

His dad couldn't stand the sight of him.

Park kept wearing eyeliner to school. And he kept washing it off when he got home. And his dad kept acting like he wasn't there.

eleanor

It was just a matter of time now. If Maisie and Ben knew, their mom would find out. Either the kids would tell her, or she'd find some clue Eleanor had overlooked, or something. . . . It would be *something*.

Eleanor didn't have anywhere to hide her secrets. In a box, on her bed. At Park's house, a block away.

She was running out of time with him.

39

eleanor

Thursday night after dinner, Park's grandma came over to have her hair set, and his mom disappeared into the garage. His dad was messing with the plumbing under the sink, replacing the garbage disposal. Park was trying to tell Eleanor about a tape he'd bought. Elvis Costello. He couldn't shut up about it.

"There are a couple songs you might like, ballady stuff. But the rest is really fast."

"Like punk?" She wrinkled her nose. She could stand a few Dead Milkmen songs, but other than that, she hated Park's punk music. "I feel like they're yelling at me," she'd say when he tried to put punk on her mixed tapes. "Stop yelling at me, Glenn Danzig!"

"That's Henry Rollins."

"They all sound the same when they're yelling at me."

Lately, Park was really into New Wave music. Or post-punk or some-thing. He went through bands like Eleanor went through books.

"No," he said, "Elvis Costello is more musical. Gentler. I'll dub you a copy."

"Or you could just play it for me. Now."

Park tilted his head. "That would involve going into my room."

"Okay," she said, not quite casually.

"Okay?" he asked. "Months of no, and now, okay?"

"Okay," Eleanor said. "You're always saying that your mom doesn't care. . . ."

"My mom doesn't care."

"So?"

Park stood up jerkily, grinning, and pulled her up. He stopped at the kitchen. "We're going to listen to music in my room."

"Fine," his dad said from under the sink. "Just don't get anybody pregnant."

That should have been embarrassing, but Park's dad had a way of cutting past embarrassing. Eleanor wished he wasn't ignoring them all the time.

Park's mom probably let him have girls in his room because you could practically see into his room from the living room, and you had to walk by it to get to the bathroom.

But, to Eleanor, it still felt incredibly private.

She couldn't get over the fact that Park spent most of his time in this room horizontal. (It was only a ninety-degree difference, but imagining him that way blew all her fuses.) Also, he changed his clothes in here.

There was no place to sit but on his bed, which Eleanor wouldn't consider. So they sat between his bed and his stereo, where there was just enough room to sit with their legs bent.

As soon as they sat down, Park started fast-forwarding through the Elvis Costello tape. He had stacks and stacks of tapes, and Eleanor pulled a few out to look at them.

"Ah . . ." Park said, pained.

"What?"

"Those're alphabetized."

"It's okay. I know the alphabet."

"Right." He looked embarrassed. "Sorry. Whenever Cal comes over, he always messes them up. Okay, this is the song I wanted you to hear. Listen."

"Cal comes over?"

"Yeah, sometimes." Park turned up the volume. "It's been a while."

"Because now I just come over. . . ."

"Which is okay with me because I like you a lot more."

"But don't you miss your other friends?" she asked.

"You're not listening," he said.

"Neither are you."

He paused the tape, like he didn't want to waste this song as background music. "Sorry," he said. "We're talking about whether I miss Cal? I eat lunch with him almost every day."

"And he doesn't mind that you spend the rest of your time with me now? None of your friends mind?"

Park ran his hand through his hair. "I still see them all at school. . . . I don't know, I don't really miss them, I've never really missed anybody but you."

"But you don't miss me now," she said. "We're together all the time."

"Are you kidding? I miss you constantly."

Even though Park washed his face as soon as he got home, the black around his eyes didn't come off completely. It made everything he did lately seem more dramatic.

"*That's* crazy," she said.

Park started laughing. "I know. . . ."

She wanted to tell him about Maisie and Ben and their days being numbered, et cetera, but he wouldn't understand, and what did she expect him to do?

Park pushed Play.

"What's this song called?" she asked.

" 'Alison.' "

park

Park played Elvis Costello for her—and Joe Jackson, and Jonathan Richman and the Modern Lovers.

She teased him because it was all so pretty and melodic, and "in the same phylum as Hall and Oates," and he threatened to evict her from his room.

When his mom came to check on them, they were sitting with a hundred cassette tapes between them, and as soon as she walked away, Park leaned over and kissed Eleanor. It seemed like the best time not to get caught.

She was a little too far away, so he put his hand on her back and pulled her toward him. He tried to do it like it was something he did all the time, as if touching her someplace new wasn't like discovering the Northwest Passage.

Eleanor came closer. She put her hands on the floor between them and leaned into him, which was so encouraging that he put his other hand on her waist. And then it was too much to be almost-but-not-really holding her. Park rocked forward onto his knees and pulled her tighter.

Half a dozen cassette tapes cracked under their weight. Eleanor fell back, and Park fell forward.

"I'm sorry," she said. "Oh, God . . . look, what we did to *Meat Is Murder*."

Park sat back and looked at the tapes. He wanted to sweep them out of the way. "It's mostly just the cases, I think," he said. "Don't worry about it." He started picking up the broken plastic.

"The Smiths and the Smithereens . . ." she said. "We even broke them in alphabetical order."

He tried to smile at her, but she wouldn't look at him. "I should go," she said. "I think it's almost eight, anyway."

"Oh. Okay, I'll walk you."

She stood up and Park followed her. They walked outside and down the walk, and when they got to his grandparents' driveway, Eleanor didn't stop.

eleanor

Maisie smelled like an Avon lady, and she was made up like the whore of Babylon. They were definitely going to get caught. Talk about a house of effing cards. Jee. Zus.

And Eleanor couldn't even think strategy, because all she could think about was Park's hands on her waist and her back and her stomach—which all must feel like nothing he'd ever encountered. Everyone in Park's family was skinny enough to be in a Special K commercial. Even his grandma.

Eleanor could only be in that scene where the actress pinches an inch, then looks at the camera like the world is going to end.

Actually, she'd have to lose weight to be in that scene. You could pinch an inch—or two, or three—all over Eleanor's body. You could probably pinch an inch on her forehead.

Holding hands was fine. Her hands weren't a complete embarrassment. And kissing seemed safe because fat lips are okay—and because Park usually closed his eyes.

But there was no safe place on Eleanor's torso. There was no place from her neck to her knees where she had any discernible infrastructure.

As soon as Park touched her waist, she'd sucked in her stomach and pitched forward. Which led to all the collateral damage . . . which made her feel like Godzilla. (But even Godzilla wasn't fat. He was just ginormous.)

The maddening part was, Eleanor wanted Park to touch her again. She wanted him to touch her constantly. Even if it led to Park deciding that she was way too much like a walrus to remain his girlfriend . . . *That's* how good it felt. She was like one of those dogs who've tasted human blood and can't stop biting. A walrus who's tasted human blood.

40

eleanor

Park wanted Eleanor to start checking her books now, especially after gym class.

"Because if it is Tina," he said—you could tell that he still didn't believe that it was, "you need to tell somebody."

"Tell who?" They were sitting in his room, leaning against his bed, trying to pretend that Park didn't have his arm around her for the first time since she crushed his cassette tapes. Just barely, not quite around her.

"You could tell Mrs. Dunne," he said. "She likes you."

"Okay, so I tell Mrs. Dunne, and I show her whatever awful thing Tina has misspelled on my books—and then Mrs. Dunne asks, 'How do you know that Tina wrote that?' She'll be just as skeptical as you were, but without the complicated romantic history. . . ."

"There's no complicated romantic history," Park said.

"Did you kiss her?" Eleanor hadn't meant to ask that. Out loud. It was almost like she'd asked it so many times in her head that it leaked out.

"Mrs. Dunne? No. But we've hugged a lot."

"You know what I mean. . . . Did you kiss her?"

She was sure that he'd kissed her. She was sure that they'd done other stuff, too. Tina was so little, Park could probably wrap his arms all the way around her and shake his own hands at her waist.

"I don't want to talk about this," he said.

"Because you did," Eleanor said.

"It doesn't matter."

"It *does* matter. Was it your first kiss?"

"Yeah," he said, "and that's one of the reasons it doesn't count. It was like a practice pitch."

"What are the other reasons?"

"It was Tina, I was twelve, I didn't even like girls yet. . . ."

"But you'll always remember it," she said. "It was your first kiss."

"I'll remember that it didn't matter," Park said.

Eleanor wanted to let this go—the most trustworthy voices in her head were shouting, *Let it go!*

"But . . ." she said, "how could you kiss *her*?"

"I was twelve."

"But she's awful."

"She was twelve, too."

"But . . . how could you kiss her and then kiss me?"

"I didn't even know you existed." Park's arm suddenly made contact, full contact, with Eleanor's waist. He pressed into her side, and she sat up, instinctively, trying to spread herself thinner.

"There aren't even roads between Tina and me . . . ," she said. "How could you like us both? Did you have a life-changing head injury in junior high?"

Park put his other arm around her. "Please. Listen to me. It was nothing. It doesn't matter."

"It matters," Eleanor whispered. Now that his arms were around her, there was almost no space between them. "Because you were the first person I ever kissed. And that matters."

He set his forehead against hers. She didn't know what to do with her eyes or her hands.

"Nothing before you counts," he said. "And I can't even imagine an after."

She shook her head. "Don't."

"What?"

"Don't talk about after."

"I just meant that . . . I want to be the *last* person who ever kisses you, too. . . . That sounds bad, like a death threat or something. What I'm trying to say is, you're it. *This* is it for me."

"Don't." She didn't want him to talk like this. She'd meant to push him, but not this far.

"Eleanor . . ."

"I don't want to think about an after."

"That's what I'm saying, maybe there won't be one."

"Of course there will." She put her hands on his chest, so that she could push him away if she had to. "I mean . . . God, of course there will. It's not like we're going to get married, Park."

"Not now."

"Stop." She tried to roll her eyes, but it hurt.

"I'm not proposing," he said. "I'm just saying . . . I love you. And I can't imagine stopping. . . ."

She shook her head. "But you're twelve."

"I'm sixteen . . ." he said. "Bono was fifteen when he met his wife, and Robert Smith was fourteen—"

"Romeo, sweet Romeo . . ."

"It's not like that, Eleanor, and you know it." Park's arms were tight around her. All the playfulness in his voice was gone. "There's no reason to think we're going to stop loving each other," he said. "And there's every reason to think that we won't."

I never said I loved you, Eleanor thought.

And even after he kissed her, she kept her hands on his chest.

So. Anyway. Park wanted her to start checking her book covers. Especially after gym class. So now Eleanor waited until almost everybody else had changed and left the locker room, and then she carefully examined her books for anything suspicious.

It was all very clinical.

DeNice and Beebi usually waited with her. It meant that they were late for lunch sometimes, but it also meant that they could all change in relative privacy, which they should have thought of months ago.

There didn't seem to be anything pervy written on Eleanor's books today. In fact, Tina had ignored her all through class. Even Tina's sidekicks (even thuggy Annette) seemed bored with Eleanor.

"I think they've run out of ways to make fun of my hair," Eleanor said to DeNice while she looked over her algebra book.

"They could call you 'Ronald McDonald,'" DeNice said. "Have they called you that?"

"Or 'Wendy,'" Beebi said, lowering her voice and calling, "Where's the beef?"

"Shut *up*," Eleanor said, looking around the locker room. "Little pitchers."

"They're all gone," DeNice said. "Everybody's gone. They're all in the cafeteria, eating my Macho Nachos. Hurry up, girl."

"You go ahead," Eleanor said. "Get us a place in line. I still have to change."

"All right," DeNice said, "but stop looking at those books. You said it yourself, there's nothing there. Come on, Beebi."

Eleanor started packing up her books. She heard Beebi shout, "Where's the beef?" from the locker room door. Dork. Eleanor opened up her locker.

It was empty.

Huh.

She tried the one above it. Nothing. And nothing below. *No . . .*

Eleanor started over, opening all the lockers on the wall, then moving on to the next wall, trying not to panic. Maybe they'd just moved her clothes. *Ha. Funny. Super-good joke, Tina.*

"What are you doing?" Mrs. Burt asked.

"Looking for my clothes," Eleanor said.

"You should use the same locker every time, so it's easy to remember."

"No, somebody . . . I mean, I think somebody took them."

"Those little bitches . . ." Mrs. Burt sighed. Like she couldn't imagine a bigger hassle.

Mrs. Burt started opening lockers at the other end of the room. Eleanor checked the trash and the showers. Then Mrs. Burt called out from the bathroom. "Found them!"

Eleanor walked into the bathroom. The floor was wet, and Mrs. Burt was standing in a stall. "I'll get a bag," Mrs. Burt said, pushing past Eleanor.

Eleanor looked down at the toilet. Even though she knew what she was going to see there, it still felt like a wet slap in the face. Her new jeans and her cowboy shirt were in a dark pile in the bowl, and her shoes were crammed under the lip. Somebody had flushed the toilet, and there was water still spilling over the edge. Eleanor watched it run.

"Here," Mrs. Burt said, handing Eleanor a yellow Food 4 Less bag. "Fish 'em out."

"I don't want them," Eleanor said, backing away. She couldn't wear them anymore anyway. Everybody would know those were her toilet clothes.

"Well, you can't leave them there," Mrs. Burt said. "Fish them out." Eleanor stared at her clothes. "Come on," Mrs. Burt said.

Eleanor reached into the toilet and felt tears slipping down her cheeks. Mrs. Burt held the bag open. "You've got to stop letting them get to you, you know," she said. "You just encourage them."

Yeah, thanks, Eleanor thought, wringing out her jeans over the toilet. She wanted to wipe her eyes, but her hands were wet.

Mrs. Burt handed her the bag. "Come on," she said. "I'll write you a pass."

"For where?" Eleanor asked.

"Your counselor's office."

Eleanor took a sharp breath. "I can't walk down the hall like this."

"What do you want from me, Eleanor?" That was obviously a rhetorical question; Mrs. Burt wasn't even looking at her. Eleanor followed her to the coaches' office and waited for the pass.

As soon as she got out to the hallway, the tears came on hard. She couldn't walk through the school like this—in her *gym suit*. In front of boys . . . And everybody. In front of *Tina*. God, Tina was probably selling tickets outside the cafeteria. Eleanor couldn't do it. Not like this.

It wasn't just that her gym suit was ugly. (Polyester. One-piece. Red and white stripes with an extra-long white zipper.)

It was also *extremely* tight.

The shorts just barely cleared her underwear, and the fabric was stretched so tight over her chest, the seams were starting to pop under her arms.

She was a tragedy in that gym suit. A ten-car pileup.

People were already showing up for the next gym class. A few freshman girls looked at Eleanor, then started whispering. Her bag was dripping.

Before she could think it through, Eleanor turned the wrong way down the hall and headed for the door to the football field. She acted like she was *supposed* to be walking out out of the building in the middle of the day, like she was on some kind of weeping/half-dressed/drippy-bag mission.

The door clicked locked behind her, and Eleanor crouched against it, letting herself fall apart. Just for a minute. God. *God.*

There was a trash can sitting right outside the door, and she got up and hurled the Food 4 Less bag into it. She wiped her eyes with her gym suit. *Okay,* she told herself, taking a deep breath, *get it together. Don't let them get to you.* Those were her new jeans in the trash. And her favorite shoes. Her Vans. She walked over to the trash and shook her head, reaching down for the bag. *Fuck you, Tina. Fuck you to the moon.*

She took another deep breath and started walking.

There were no classrooms on this end of the school, so at least no one was watching her. She stuck close to the building, and when she turned the corner, she walked under the row of windows. She thought about walking right home, but that might be worse. It'd definitely be longer.

If she could just get to the front door, the counselors' offices were right inside. Mrs. Dunne would help her. Mrs. Dunne wouldn't tell her not to cry.

The security guard at the front door acted like girls were wandering in and out in their gym clothes all day long. He glanced at Eleanor's pass and waved her on.

Almost there, Eleanor thought. *Don't run, just a few more doors. . . .*

She really should have expected Park to walk through one of them.

Ever since the first day they'd met, Eleanor was always seeing him in unexpected places. It was like their lives were overlapping lines, like they had their own gravity. Usually, that serendipity felt like the nicest thing the universe had ever done for her.

Park walked out of a door on the opposite side of the hallway and stopped as soon as he saw her. She tried to look away, but she didn't do it soon enough. Park's face turned red. He stared at her. She pulled down her shorts and stumbled forward, running the last few steps to the counselors' offices.

"You don't have to go back there," her mom said after Eleanor had told her the whole story. (Almost the whole story.)

Eleanor thought for a moment about what she'd do if she didn't go back to school. Stay here all day? And then what?

"It's okay," she said. Mrs. Dunne had driven Eleanor home herself, and she'd promised to bring a padlock for her gym locker.

Eleanor's mom dumped the yellow plastic bag into the bathtub and started rinsing out the clothes, wrinkling her nose, even though they didn't smell.

"Girls are so mean . . ." she said. "You're lucky to have one friend you can trust."

Eleanor must have looked confused.

"Tina," her mom said. "You're lucky to have Tina."

Eleanor nodded.

She stayed home that night. Even though it was Friday, and Park's family always watched movies and made popcorn in the air popper on Fridays.

She couldn't face him.

All she'd see was the look on his face in the hallway. She'd feel like she was still standing there in her gym suit.

41

park

Park went to bed early. His mom kept bothering him about Eleanor. "Where's Eleanor tonight?" "She running late?" "You get in fight?"

Every time she said Eleanor's name, Park felt his face go hot.

"I can tell that something wrong," his mom said at dinner. "Did you get in fight? Did you break up again?"

"No," Park said. "I think maybe she went home sick. She wasn't on the bus."

"I have a girlfriend now," Josh said, "can she start coming over?"

"No girlfriend," their mom said, "too young."

"I'm almost thirteen!"

"Sure," their dad said, "your girlfriend can come over. If you're willing to give up your Nintendo."

"What?" Josh was stricken. "Why?"

"Because I said so," his dad said. "Is it a deal?"

"No! No way," Josh said. "Does Park have to give up Nintendo?"

"Yep. Is that okay with you, Park?"

"Fine."

"I'm like Billy Jack," their dad said, "a warrior and a shaman."

It wasn't much of a conversation, but it was the most his dad had said to Park in weeks. Maybe his dad had been bracing for the entire neighborhood to swarm the house with torches and pitchforks as soon as they saw Park with eyeliner. . . .

But almost nobody cared. Not even his grandparents. (His grandma said he looked like Rudolph Valentino, and he heard his grandpa tell his dad, "You should have seen what kids looked like while you were in Korea.")

"I'm going to bed," Park said, standing up from the table. "I don't feel well either."

"So if Park doesn't get to play Nintendo anymore," Josh asked, "can I put it in my room?"

"Park can play Nintendo whenever he wants," their dad said.

"God," Josh said, "everything you guys do is unfair."

Park turned off his light and crawled onto his bed. He lay on his back because he didn't trust his front. Or his hands, actually. Or his brain.

After he saw Eleanor today, it hadn't occurred to him, not for at least an hour, to wonder why she was walking down the hall in her gym suit. And it took him another hour to realize he should have said something to her. He could have said, *Hey* or *What's going on?* or *Are you okay?* Instead, he'd stared at her like he'd never seen her before.

He *felt* like he'd never seen her before.

It's not like he hadn't thought about it (a lot)—Eleanor under her clothes. But he could never fill in any of the details. The only women he could actually picture naked were the women in the magazines his dad every-once-in-a-while remembered to hide under his bed.

Magazines like that made Eleanor freak. Just mention Hugh Hefner, and she'd be off for half an hour on prostitution and slavery and the Fall of Rome. Park hadn't told her about his dad's twenty-year-old *Playboys,* but he hadn't touched them since he met her.

He could fill in some of the details now. He could picture Eleanor. He couldn't *stop* picturing her. Why hadn't he ever noticed how tight those gym suits were? And how short . . .

And why hadn't he expected her to be so grown up? To have so much negative space?

He closed his eyes and saw her again. A stack of freckled heart shapes, a perfectly made Dairy Queen ice cream cone. Like Betty Boop drawn with a heavy hand.

Hey, he thought. *What's going on. Are you okay?*

She must not be. She hadn't been on the bus on the way home. She hadn't come over after school. And tomorrow was Saturday. What if he didn't see her all weekend?

How could he even look at her now? He wouldn't be able to. Not without stripping her down to her gym suit. Without thinking about that long white zipper.

Jesus.

42

park

His family was going to the boat show the next day, then out to lunch, and maybe to the mall. . . .

Park took forever to eat his breakfast and take a shower.

"Come on, Park," his dad said sharply, "get dressed and put your makeup on."

Like he'd wear makeup to the boat show.

"Come on," his mom said, checking her lipstick in the hall mirror, "you know your dad hate crowds."

"Do I have to go?"

"You don't want to go?" She scrunched and fluffed the back of her hair.

"No, I do," Park said. He didn't. "But what if Eleanor comes over? I don't want to miss the chance to talk to her."

"Is something wrong? You sure you didn't fight?"

"No, no fight. I'm just . . . worried about her. And you know I can't call her house."

His mom turned away from the mirror. "Okay . . ." she said, frowning. "You stay. But vacuum, okay? And put away big pile of black clothes on your floor."

"Thanks," Park said. He hugged her.

"Park! Mindy!" His dad was standing at the front door. "Let's go!"

"Park staying home," his mom said. "We go."

His dad flashed him a look, but didn't argue.

Park wasn't used to being home alone. He vacuumed. He put his clothes away. He made himself a sandwich and watched a *Young Ones* marathon on MTV, then fell asleep on the couch.

When he heard the doorbell, he jerked up to answer it before he was awake. His heart was pounding, the way it does sometimes when you sleep too hard in the middle of the day, like you can't remember how to wake up.

He was sure it was Eleanor. He opened the door without checking.

eleanor

Their car wasn't in the driveway, so Eleanor figured Park's family wasn't home. They were probably off doing awesome family stuff. Eating lunch at Bonanza and having their portraits taken in matching sweaters.

She'd already given up on the door when it opened. And before she could act embarrassed and uncomfortable about yesterday—or pretend that she wasn't—Park was opening the screen door and pulling her in by her shirtsleeve.

He didn't even close the door before he put his arms around her, his entire arms, all down the length of her back.

Park usually held Eleanor with his hands on her waist, like they were slow-dancing. This wasn't slow-dancing. This was . . . something else. His arms were around her, and his face was in her hair, and there was no place for the rest of her to go but against him.

He was warm. . . . Like *really* warm and fuzzy-soft. Like a sleeping baby, she thought. (Sort of. Not exactly.)

She tried to feel embarrassed again.

Park kicked the door closed and fell back on it, pulling her even tighter. His hair was clean and straight and flopping into his eyes, and his eyes were nearly closed. Fuzzy. Soft.

"Were you sleeping?" she whispered. Like he still might be.

He didn't answer, but his mouth fell on hers, open, and her head fell back into his hand. He was holding her so close, there was nowhere to hide. She couldn't sit up or suck in or keep any secrets.

Park made a noise, and it hummed in her throat. She could feel all ten of his fingers. On her neck, on her back . . . Her own hands hung stupidly at her side. Like they weren't even in the same scene as his. Like *she* wasn't even in the same scene.

Park must have noticed because he pulled his mouth back. He tried to wipe it on the shoulder of his T-shirt, and he looked at her like he was seeing her for the first time since she got there.

"Hey . . ." he said, taking a breath, focusing. "What's going on? Are you okay?"

Eleanor looked at Park's face, so full of something she couldn't quite place. His chin hung forward, like his mouth didn't want to pull away from her, and his eyes were so green, they could turn carbon dioxide into oxygen.

He was touching her all the places she was afraid to be touched. . . .

Eleanor tried one last time to be embarrassed.

park

For a second, he thought he'd gone too far.

He hadn't even meant to, he was practically sleepwalking. And he'd been thinking about Eleanor, dreaming about her, for so many hours; wanting her made him stupid.

She was so still in his arms. He thought for a second that he'd gone too far, that he'd tripped a wire.

And then Eleanor touched him. She touched his neck.

It's hard to say why this was different from all the other times she'd touched him. *She* was different. She was still and then she wasn't.

She touched his neck, then drew a line down his chest. Park wished that he was taller and broader; he hoped she wouldn't stop.

She was so gentle compared to him. Maybe she didn't want him like he wanted her. But even if she wanted him half as much . . .

eleanor

This is how she touched him in her head.

From jaw to neck to shoulder.

He was so much warmer than she expected, and harder. Like all his muscles and bones were right on the surface, like his heart was beating just under his T-shirt.

She touched Park softly, gingerly, just in case she touched him wrong.

park

He relaxed against the door.

He felt Eleanor's hand on his throat, on his chest, then took her other hand and pressed it to his face. He made a noise like he was hurt and decided to feel self-conscious about it later.

If he was shy now, he wouldn't get anything that he wanted.

eleanor

Park was alive, and she was awake, and this was allowed.

He was hers.

To have and hold. Not forever, maybe—not forever, for sure—and not figuratively. But literally. And now. Now, he was hers. And he wanted her to touch him. He was like a cat who pushes its head under your hands.

Eleanor brought her hands down Park's chest with her fingertips apart, then brought them up again under his shirt.

She did it because she wanted to. And because once she started touching him the way she did in her head, it was hard to stop. And because . . . what if she never had the chance to touch him like this again?

park

When he felt her fingers on his stomach, he made the noise again. He held her to him and pushed forward, pushing Eleanor backwards—stumbling around the coffee table to the couch.

In movies, this happens smoothly or comically. In Park's living room, it was just awkward. They wouldn't let go of each other, so Eleanor fell back, and Park fell against her in the corner of the couch.

He wanted to look in her eyes, but it was hard when they were this close. "Eleanor . . ." he whispered.

She nodded.

"I love you," he said.

She looked up at him, her eyes shiny and black, then looked away. "I know," she said.

He pulled one of his arms out from under her and traced her outline against the couch. He could spend all day like this, running his hand down her ribs, into her waist, out to her hip and back again. . . . If he had all day, he would. If she weren't made of so many other miracles.

"You know?" he repeated. She smiled, so he kissed her. "You're not the Han Solo in this relationship, you know."

"I'm totally the Han Solo," she whispered. It was good to hear her. It was good to remember it was Eleanor under all this new flesh.

"Well, I'm not the Princess Leia," he said.

"Don't get so hung up on gender roles," Eleanor said.

Park ran his hand out to her hip and back again, catching his thumb under her sweater. She swallowed and lifted her chin.

He pulled her sweater up farther, and then, without thinking about why, he pulled up his shirt, too, and laid his bare stomach against hers.

Eleanor's face crumpled, and it made him come unhinged.

"You can be Han Solo," he said, kissing her throat. "And I'll be Boba Fett. I'll cross the sky for you."

eleanor

Things she knew now, that she hadn't known two hours ago:

- Park was covered with skin. Everywhere. And it was all just as smooth and honey-beautiful as the skin on his hands. It felt thick and richer in some places, more like crushed velvet than silk. But it was all his. And all wonderful.
- She was also covered with skin. And her skin was apparently covered with super-powered nerve endings that hadn't done a damn thing her whole life, but came alive like ice and fire and bee stings as soon as Park touched her. Wherever Park touched her.
- As embarrassed as she was of her stomach and her freckles and the fact that her bra was held together with two safety pins, she wanted Park to touch her more than she could ever feel embarrassed. And when he touched her, he didn't seem to care about any of those things. Some of them he even liked. Like her freckles. He said she was candy-sprinkled.
- She wanted him to touch her everywhere.
He'd stopped at the edge of her bra and only dipped his fingers into the back of her jeans—but it wasn't Eleanor who stopped him. She never would. When Park touched her, it felt better than anything she'd ever felt in her whole life. Ever. And she wanted to feel that way as much as she could. She wanted to stock up on him.

- Nothing was dirty. With Park.

Nothing could be shameful.

Because Park was the sun, and that was the only way Eleanor could think to explain it.

park

Once it started to get dark, he felt like his parents could walk in at any minute, like they should have been home a long time ago—and he didn't want them to find him like this, with his knee between Eleanor's legs and his hand on her hip and his mouth as far as it could reach down the neck of her sweater.

He pulled away from her and tried to think clearly again.

"Where are you going?" she asked.

"I don't know. Nowhere . . . My parents should be home soon, we should get it together."

"Okay," she said, and sat up. But she looked so bewildered and beautiful that he climbed back on top of her and pushed her all the way down.

A half hour later, he tried again. He stood up this time.

"I'm going to the bathroom," he said.

"Go," she said. "Don't look back."

He took a step, then looked back.

"I'll go," she said a few minutes later.

While she was gone, Park turned up the volume on the TV. He got them both Cokes and looked at the couch to see if it looked illicit. It didn't seem to.

When Eleanor came back, her face was wet.

"Did you wash your face?"

"Yeah . . ." she said.

"Why?"

"Because I looked weird."

"And you thought you could wash it off?"

He gave her the same once-over he'd given the couch. Her lips were swollen, and her eyes seemed wilder than usual. But Eleanor's sweaters were always stretched out, and her hair always looked tangled.

"You look fine," he said. "What about me?"

She looked at him, and then smiled. "Good . . ." she said. "Just really, really good."

He held out his hand to her, and pulled her onto the couch. Smoothly, this time.

She sat next to him and looked down at her lap.

Park leaned against her. "It's not going to be weird now," he said, "is it?"

She shook her head and laughed. "No," she said, and then, "only for a minute, only a little." He'd never seen her face so open. Her brows weren't pulled together, her nose wasn't scrunched. He put his arm around her, and she laid her head on his chest without any prompting.

"Oh, look," she said. "*The Young Ones.*"

"Yeah . . . Hey. You still haven't told me—what was going on yesterday? When I saw you? What was wrong?"

She sighed. "I was on my way to Mrs. Dunne's office because somebody in gym took my clothes."

"Tina?"

"I don't know, probably."

"Jesus . . ." he said, "that's terrible."

"It's okay." She actually sounded like it was.

"Did you find them? Your clothes?"

"Yeah . . . I really, really don't want to talk about it."

"Okay," he said.

Eleanor pressed her cheek into his chest, and Park hugged her. He wished that they could go through life like this. That he could physically put himself between Eleanor and the world.

Maybe Tina really was a monster.

"Park?" Eleanor said. "Just one more thing. I mean, can I ask you something?"

"You know you can ask me anything. We've got a deal."

She set her hand over his heart. "Did . . . the way you acted today have something to do with seeing me yesterday?"

He almost didn't want to answer. Yesterday's confusing lust felt even more inappropriate now that he knew the depressing backstory. "Yeah," he said quietly.

Eleanor didn't say anything for a minute or so. And then . . .

"Tina would be so pissed."

eleanor

When Park's parents got home, they seemed genuinely glad to see Eleanor. His dad had bought a new hunting rifle at the boat show, and he tried to show her how it worked.

"You can buy guns at a boat show?" Eleanor asked.

"You can buy anything at a boat show," his dad said. "Anything worth having."

"Books?" she asked.

"Books about guns and boats."

She stayed late because it was Saturday, and on the way home, she and Park stopped at his grandparents' driveway, as usual.

But tonight, Park didn't lean over and kiss her. Instead, he held her tight.

"Do you think we'll ever be alone like that again?" she asked. She felt the tears in her eyes.

"Ever? Yes. Soon? I don't know. . . ."

She hugged him as hard as she could, and then she walked home alone.

Richie was home and awake and watching *Saturday Night Live*. Ben was asleep on the floor, and Maisie was sleeping next to Richie on the couch.

Eleanor would have gone straight to bed, but she had to go to the bathroom. Which meant walking between him and the TV. Twice.

When she got to the bathroom, she pulled her hair back tight and washed her face again. She hurried back past the TV without looking up.

"Where have you been?" Richie asked. "Where do you *go* all the time?"

"To my friend's house," Eleanor said. She kept walking.

"What friend?"

"Tina," Eleanor said. She put her hand on the bedroom door.

"Tina," Richie said. There was a cigarette in his mouth, and he was holding a can of Old Milwaukee. "Tina's house must be fucking Disneyland, huh? You can't get enough."

She waited.

"Eleanor?" she heard her mom calling from the bedroom. She sounded half asleep.

"So, what'd you spend your Christmas money on?" Richie asked. "I told you to buy yourself something nice."

The bedroom door opened, and her mother came out. She was wearing Richie's bathrobe—one of those Asian souvenir robes, red satin with a big gaudy tiger.

"Eleanor," her mom said, "go to bed."

"I was just asking Eleanor what she bought with her Christmas money," Richie said.

If Eleanor made something up now, he'd want to see whatever it was. If she said she hadn't spent the money, he might want it back.

"A necklace," she said.

"A necklace," he repeated. He looked at her blearily, like he was trying to come up with something awful to say, but he just took another drink and leaned back in his chair.

"Good night, Eleanor," her mom said.

43

park

Park's parents almost never fought, and when they did, it was always about him or Josh.

His parents had been arguing in their bedroom for more than an hour, and when it was time to leave for Sunday dinner, their mom came out and told the boys to go ahead without them. "Tell Grandma I have headache."

"What did you do?" Josh asked Park as they cut through the front lawn.

"Nothing," Park said. "What did *you* do?"

"Nothing. It's you. When I went to the bathroom, I heard mom say your name."

But Park hadn't done anything. Not since the eyeliner—which he knew wasn't dead, but it seemed in remission. Maybe his parents knew somehow about yesterday. . . .

Even if they did, Park hadn't done anything with Eleanor that he'd ever been explicitly told not to do. His mom never talked to him about that kind of thing. And his dad hadn't said anything more than "Don't get anybody pregnant" since he told Park about sex in the fifth grade. (He'd told Josh at the same time, which was insulting.)

Anyway, they hadn't gone *that* far. He hadn't touched her anywhere that you couldn't show on television. Even though he'd wanted to.

He wished now that he had. It might be months before they were alone again.

eleanor

She went to Mrs. Dunne's office Monday morning before class, and Mrs. Dunne gave her a brand-new combination lock. It was hot pink.

"We talked to some of the girls in your class," Mrs. Dunne said, "but they all played dumb. We're still going to get to the bottom of this, I promise."

There is no bottom, Eleanor thought. *There's just Tina.*

"It's okay," she told Mrs. Dunne. "It doesn't matter."

Tina had watched Eleanor get on the bus that morning with her tongue on her top lip, like she was waiting for Eleanor to spaz out—or like she was trying to see whether Eleanor was wearing any toilet clothes. But Park was right there, practically pulling Eleanor into his lap—so it was easy to ignore Tina and everybody else. He looked so cute this morning. Instead of his usual scary, black band T-shirt, he was wearing a green shirt that said KISS ME, I'M IRISH.

He walked with her to the counselors' offices, and told her that if

anybody stole her clothes today, she was supposed to find him, immediately.

Nobody did.

Beebi and DeNice had already heard about what happened from
somebody in another class—which meant that the whole school knew.
They said they were never going to let Eleanor walk alone to lunch
again, Macho Nachos be damned.

"Those skanks need to know you have friends," DeNice said.

"Mmm-hmm," Beebi agreed.

park

His mom was waiting in the Impala Monday afternoon when Park and
Eleanor got off the bus. She rolled down the window.

"Hi, Eleanor, sorry, but Park has errand to run. We see you tomorrow, okay?"

"Sure," Eleanor said. She looked at him, and he reached out to
squeeze her hand as she walked away.

He got into the car. "Come on, come on," his mom said, "why you do
everything so slow? Here," she handed him a brochure. *State of Nebraska
Driver's Manual*. "Practice test at end," she said, "now, buckle up."

"Where are we going?" he asked.

"To get your driving license, dummy."

"Does Dad know?"

His mom sat on a pillow when she drove and hung forward on the
steering wheel. "He knows, but you don't have to talk to him about it,
okay? This is our business right now, you and me. Now, look at test.
Not hard. I pass on first try."

Park flipped to the back of the book and looked at the practice
exam. He'd studied the whole manual when he turned fifteen and got
his learner's permit.

"Is Dad going to be mad at me?" he asked.

"Whose business is this right now?"

"Ours," he said.

"You and me," she said.

Park passed the test on his first try. He even parallel parked the Impala, which was like parallel parking a Star Destroyer. His mom wiped his eyelids with a Kleenex before he had his picture taken.

She let him drive home. "So, if we don't tell Dad," Park asked, "does that mean I can't ever drive?" He wanted to drive Eleanor somewhere. Anywhere.

"I work on it," his mom said. "Meantime, you have your license if you need it. For emergency."

That seemed like a pretty weak excuse to get his license. Park had gone sixteen years without a driving emergency.

The next morning on the bus, Eleanor asked him what his big, secret errand was, and he handed her his license.

"What?" she said. "Look at you, look at this!"

She didn't want to give it back.

"I don't have any pictures of you," she said.

"I'll get you another one," he said.

"You will? Really?"

"You can have one of my school pictures. My mom has tons."

"You have to write something on the back," she said.

"Like what?"

"Like, 'Hey, Eleanor, KIT, LYLAS, stay sweet, Park.' "

"But I don't *L-Y* like an *S*," he said. "And you're not sweet."

"I'm sweet," she said, affronted, and holding back his license.

"No . . . you're other good things," he said, snatching it from her, "but not sweet."

"Is this where you tell me that I'm a scoundrel, and I say that I think you like me *because* I'm a scoundrel? Because we've already covered this—I'm the Han Solo."

"I'm going to write, 'For Eleanor, I love you. Park.' "

"God, don't write that, my mom might find it."

eleanor

Park gave her a school picture. It was from October, but he already looked so different now. Older. In the end, Eleanor hadn't let him write anything on the back, because she didn't want him to ruin it.

They hung out in his bedroom after dinner (Tater Tot casserole) and managed to sneak kisses while they looked through all of Park's old school pictures. Seeing him as a little kid just made her want to kiss him more. (Gross, but whatever. As long as she didn't want to kiss actual little kids, she wasn't going to worry about it.)

When Park asked her for a picture, she was relieved that she didn't have any to give him.

"We'll take one," he said.

"Um . . . okay."

"Okay, cool, I'll get my mom's camera."

"Now?"

"Why not now?"

She didn't have an answer.

His mom was thrilled to take her picture. This called for Makeover, Part II—which Park cut short, thank God, saying, "Mom, I want a photo that actually looks like Eleanor."

His mom insisted on taking a photo of them together, too, which Park didn't mind at all. He put his arm around her.

"Shouldn't we wait?" Eleanor asked. "For a holiday or something more memorable?"

"I want to remember tonight," Park said.

He was such a dork sometimes.

Eleanor must have been acting too happy when she got home because her mom followed her to the back of the house like she could smell it on her. (Happiness smelled like Park's house. Like Skin So Soft and all four food groups.)

"Are you going to take a bath?" her mom asked.

"Uh-huh."

"I'll watch the door for you."

Eleanor turned on the hot water and climbed into the empty bathtub. It was so cold by the back door that the bath water started cooling off before the tub was even full. Eleanor took baths in such a hurry, she was usually done by then.

"I ran into Eileen Benson at the store today," her mom said. "Do you remember her from church?"

"I don't think so," Eleanor said. Her family hadn't gone to church in three years.

"She had a daughter your age—Tracy."

"Maybe . . ."

"Well, she's pregnant," her mom said. "And Eileen's a wreck. Tracy got involved with a boy in their neighborhood, a black boy. Eileen's husband is having a fit."

"I don't remember them," Eleanor said. The tub was almost full enough to rinse her hair.

"Well, it just made me think about how lucky I am," her mom said.

"That you didn't get involved with a black guy?"

"No," her mom said. "I'm talking about you. How lucky I am that you're so smart about boys."

"I'm not smart about boys," Eleanor said. She rinsed her hair quickly, then stood up, covering herself with a towel while she got dressed.

"You've stayed away from them. That's smart."

Eleanor pulled out the drain and carefully picked up her dirty clothes. Park's photo was in her back pocket, and she didn't want it to get wet. Her mom was standing by the stove, watching her.

"Smarter than I ever was," her mom said. "And braver. I haven't been on my own since the eighth grade."

Eleanor hugged her dirty jeans to her chest. "You act like there are two kinds of girls," she said. "The smart ones and the ones that boys like."

"That's not far from the truth," her mom said, trying to put her hand on Eleanor's shoulder. Eleanor took a step back. "You'll see," her mom said. "Wait until you're older."

They both heard Richie's truck pull into the driveway.

Eleanor pushed past her mother and rushed to her bedroom. Ben and Mouse slipped in just behind her.

Eleanor couldn't think of a place safe enough for Park's photo, so she zipped it into the pocket of her school bag. After she'd looked at it again and again and again.

44

eleanor

Wednesday night wasn't the worst.

Park had taekwondo, but Eleanor still had Park, the memory of him, everywhere. (Everywhere he'd touched her felt untouchable. Everywhere he'd touched her felt safe.)

Richie had to work late that night, so her mom made Totino's Party Pizzas for dinner. They must have been on sale at Food 4 Less, because the freezer was stuffed with them.

They watched *Highway to Heaven* while they ate. Then Eleanor sat with Maisie on the living room floor, and they tried to teach Mouse "Down Down Baby."

It was hopeless. He could either remember the words or the clapping, but never both at once. It drove Maisie crazy. "Start again," she kept saying.

"Come help us, Ben," Eleanor said, "it's easier with four."

Down, down, baby
Down by the roller coaster
Sweet, sweet baby
I'll never let you go
Shimmy, shimmy, cocoa puff,
Shimmy . . .

"Oh my God, Mouse. Right hand first—*right* first. Okay. Start again. . . ."

Down, down, baby . . .

"Mouse!"

45

park

"I don't feel like cooking dinner," his mom said.

It was just the three of them—Park, his mom, and Eleanor—sitting on the couch, watching *Wheel of Fortune*. His dad had gone turkey hunting and wouldn't be home until late, and Josh was staying over at a friend's.

"I could heat up a pizza," Park said.

"Or we could go get pizza," his mom said.

Park looked at Eleanor; he didn't know what the rules were, as far as going out. Her eyes got big, and she shrugged.

"Yeah," Park said, grinning, "let's go get pizza."

"I feel too lazy," his mom said. "You and Eleanor go get pizza."

"You want me to drive?"

"Sure," his mom said. "You too scared?"

Jeez, now his mom was calling him pussy.

"No, I can drive. Do you want Pizza Hut? Should we call it in first?"

"You go where you want," his mom said. "I'm not even very hungry. You go. Eat dinner. See movie or something."

He and Eleanor both stared at her.

"Are you sure?" he asked.

"Yeah, go," she said. "I never get house to myself."

She was home all day, every day by herself, but Park decided not to mention it. He and Eleanor stood up cautiously from the couch. Like they were expecting his mom to say *April fools!* two weeks late.

"Keys on hook," she said. "Hand me my purse." She gave him twenty dollars from her wallet, and then ten more.

"Thanks . . ." Park said, still hesitant. "I guess we'll go now?"

"Not yet . . ." His mom looked at Eleanor's clothes and frowned. "Eleanor can't go out like that." If they wore the same size, she'd be forcing Eleanor into a stonewashed miniskirt about now.

"But I've looked like this all day," Eleanor said. She was wearing army surplus pants and a short-sleeved men's shirt over some kind of long-sleeved purple T-shirt. Park thought she looked cool. (He actually thought she looked adorable, but that word would make Eleanor gag.)

"Just let me fix your hair," his mom said. She pulled Eleanor into the bathroom and started pulling bobby pins out of her hair. "Down, down, down," she said.

Park leaned against the doorway and watched.

"It's weird that you're watching this," Eleanor said.

"It's nothing I haven't seen before," he said.

"Park probably help me do your hair on wedding day," his mom said.

He and Eleanor both looked at the floor. "I'll wait for you in the living room," he said.

In a few minutes, she was ready. Her hair looked perfect, every curl shiny and on purpose, and her lips were a glossy pink. He could tell from here that she'd taste like strawberries.

"Okay," his mom said, "go. Have fun."

They walked out to the Impala, and Park opened the door for Eleanor. "I can open my own door," she said. And by the time he got to his side, she'd leaned over the seat and pushed his door open.

"Where should we go?" he asked.

"I don't know," she said, sinking down in her seat. "Can we just get out of the neighborhood? I feel like I'm sneaking across the Berlin Wall."

"Oh," he said, "yeah." He started the car and looked over at her. "Get down more. Your hair glows in the dark."

"Thanks."

"You know what I mean."

He started driving west. There was nothing east of the Flats but the river.

"Don't drive by the Rail," she said.

"The what?"

"Turn right here."

"Okay . . ." He looked down at her—she was crouching on the floor—and laughed.

"It's not funny."

"It's kind of funny," he said. "You're on the floor, and I'm only getting to drive because my dad's out of town."

"Your dad wants you to drive. All you have to do is learn how to drive a stick."

"I already know how to drive a stick."

"Then what's the problem?"

"The problem is me," he said, feeling irritated. "Hey, we're out of the neighborhood, can you sit up now?"

"I'll sit up when we get to Twenty-fourth Street."

She sat up at Twenty-fourth Street, but they didn't talk again until Forty-second.

"Where are we going?" she asked.

"I don't know," he said. He really didn't. He knew how to get to school and how to get downtown, and that was it. "Where do you want to go?"

"I don't know," she said.

eleanor

She wanted to go to Inspiration Point. Which, as far as she knew, only existed on *Happy Days*.

And she didn't want to say to Park, "Hey, where do you kids go when you want to fog up the windows?" Because, what would he think of her? And what if he had an answer?

Eleanor was trying really hard not to be overawed by Park's driving skills, but every time he changed lanes or checked the rearview mirror, she caught herself swooning. He might as well be lighting a cigarette or ordering a Scotch on the rocks, it made him seem so much older. . . .

Eleanor didn't have her learner's permit. Her mom wasn't even allowed to drive, so getting Eleanor's license wasn't a priority.

"Do we have to go somewhere?" she asked.

"Well, we have to go *some*where . . ." Park said.

"But do we have to do something?"

"What do you mean?"

"Can't we just go somewhere and be together? Where do people go to be together? I don't even care if we get out of the car. . . ."

He looked over at her, then looked back, nervously, at the road. "Okay," he said. "Yeah. Yeah, just let me . . ."

He pulled into a parking lot and turned around.

"We'll go downtown."

park

They did get out of the car. Once they were downtown, Park wanted to show Eleanor Drastic Plastic and the Antiquarium and all the other record stores. She'd never even been to the Old Market, which was practically the only place *to* go in Omaha.

There were a bunch of other kids hanging out downtown, a lot of them looking much weirder than Eleanor. Park took her to his favorite pizza place. And then his favorite ice cream place. And his third-favorite comic book shop.

He kept pretending that they were on a real date, and then he'd remember that they were.

eleanor

Park held her hand the whole night, like he was her boyfriend. *Because he is your boyfriend, dummy,* she kept telling herself.

Much to the dismay of the girl working at the record store. She had eight holes in each ear, and she clearly thought Park was a whole closet full of cat's pajamas. The girl looked at Eleanor like, *Are you kidding me*? And Eleanor looked back like, *I know, right*?

They walked down every street of the market area, and then across the street, into a park. Eleanor didn't even know all this existed. She hadn't realized Omaha could be such a nice place to live. (In her head, this was Park's doing, too. The world rebuilt itself into a better place around him.)

park

They ended up at Central Park. Omaha's version. Eleanor had never been here before either, and even though it was wet and muddy and still kind of cold, she kept saying how nice it was.

"Oh, look," she said. "Swans."

"I think those are geese," he said.

"Well, they're the best-looking geese I've ever seen."

They sat on one of the park benches and watched the geese settle in on the bank of the man-made lake. Park put his arm around Eleanor and felt her lean against him.

"Let's keep doing this," he said.

"What?"

"Going out."

"Okay," she said. She didn't say anything about him learning how to drive a manual transmission. Which he appreciated.

"We should go to prom," he said.

"What?" She lifted up her head.

"Prom. You know, prom."

"I know what it is, but why would we go there?"

Because he wanted to see Eleanor in a pretty dress. Because he wanted to help his mom do her hair.

"Because it's prom," he said.

"And it's lame," she said.

"How do you know?"

"Because the theme is 'I Want to Know What Love Is.'"

"That's not such a bad song," he said.

"Are you drunk? It's Foreigner."

Park shrugged and pulled one of her curls straight. "I know that prom is lame," he said. "But it's not something you can go back and do. You only get one chance."

"Actually, you get three chances. . . ."

"Okay, will you go to prom with me next year?"

She started laughing. "Yeah," she said, "sure. We can go next year. That will give my mouse and bird friends plenty of time to make me a dress. Totally. Yes. Let's go to prom."

"You think it's never going to happen," he said. "You'll see. I'm not going anywhere."

"Not until you learn how to drive a stick."

She was relentless.

eleanor

Prom. Right. That was going to happen.

The amount of chicanery it would take to slip prom past her mother . . . it boggled the mind.

Though now that Park had suggested it, Eleanor could almost see it working. She could tell her mom that she was going to prom with Tina.

(Good old Tina.) And she could get ready at Park's house; *his* mom would love that. The only thing Eleanor would have to figure out was the dress. . . .

Did they even make prom dresses in her size? She'd have to shop in the mother-of-the-bride section. And she'd have to rob a bank. Seriously. Even if a hundred-dollar-bill fell right out of the sky, Eleanor could never spend it on something as stupid as a prom dress.

She'd spend it on new Vans. Or a decent bra. Or a boom box . . .

Actually, she'd probably just give it to her mom.

Prom. As if.

park

After she'd agreed to go to next year's prom with him, Eleanor also agreed to accompany Park to his first cotillion, the Academy Awards after-party, and any and all "balls" to which he received invitations.

She giggled so much, the geese complained.

"Go on and honk," Eleanor said. "You think you can intimidate me with your swanlike good looks, but I'm not that kind of girl."

"Lucky for me," Park said.

"Why is that lucky for you?"

"Never mind." He wished he hadn't said it. He'd meant to be funny and self-deprecatory, but he didn't actually want to talk about how she managed to be attracted to him.

Eleanor was studying him coolly. "You're the reason that goose thinks I'm shallow," she said.

"I think it's a gander, right?" Park said. "The males are ganders?"

"Oh, right, gander. That suits him. Pretty boy . . . So, why is that lucky for you?"

"Because," he said, like both syllables hurt.

"Because, why?" she asked.

"Isn't that my line?"

"I thought I could you ask you anything . . ." she said. "Because, why?"

"Because of my All-American good looks." He ran his hand through his hair and looked down at the mud.

"Are you saying that you're not good looking?" she asked.

"I don't want to talk about this," Park said, hanging on to the back of his neck. "Can we go back to talking about prom?"

"Are you saying it just so that I'll tell you how cute you are?"

"*No,*" he said. "I'm saying it because it's kind of obvious."

"It's not obvious . . ." Eleanor said. She turned on the bench so she was facing him and pulled his hand down.

"Nobody thinks Asian guys are hot," Park said finally. He had to look away from her when he said it—way away, he turned his head completely. "Not here, anyway. I assume Asian guys do all right in Asia."

"That's not true," Eleanor argued. "Look at your mom and dad. . . ."

"Asian girls are different. White guys think they're exotic."

"But . . ."

"Are you trying to come up with a super-hot Asian guy, so you can prove me wrong? Because there aren't any. I've had my whole life to think about this."

Eleanor folded her arms. Park looked out at the lake.

"What about that old TV show," she said, "with the karate guy . . ."

"*Kung Fu?*"

"Yeah."

"That actor was white, and that character was a monk."

"What about . . ."

"There aren't any," Park said. "Look at *M*A*S*H*. The whole show takes place in Korea, and the doctors are always flirting with Korean girls, right? But the nurses don't use their R and R to go to Seoul to pick up hot Korean guys. Everything that makes Asian girls seem exotic makes Asian guys seem like girls."

The gander was still honking at them. Park picked up a chunk of melting snow and tossed it halfheartedly in the goose's direction. He still couldn't look at Eleanor.

"I don't know what any of that has to do with me," she said.

"It has everything to do with me," he answered.

"No." She put her hand on his chin and made him face her. "It doesn't. . . . I don't even know what it means that you're Korean."

"Beyond the obvious?"

"Yeah," she said, "*exactly*. Beyond the obvious."

Then she kissed him. He loved it when she kissed him first.

"When I look at you," she said, leaning into him, "I don't know if I'm thinking you're cute *because* you're Korean, but I don't think it's in spite of it. I just know that I think you're cute. Like, *so cute,* Park . . ."

He loved it when she said his name.

"Maybe I'm really attracted to Korean guys," she said, "and I don't even know it."

"Good thing I'm the only Korean guy in Omaha," he said.

"And good thing I'm never getting out of this dump."

It was getting cold, and probably late; Park wasn't wearing a watch. He stood up and pulled Eleanor to her feet. They held hands and cut through the park to get to the car.

"*I* don't even know what it means to be Korean . . ." he said.

"Well, I don't know what it means to be Danish and Scottish," she said. "Does it matter?"

"I think so. Because it's the number one thing people use to identify me. It's my main thing."

"I'm telling you," she said, "I think your main thing might be that you're cute. You're *practically* adorable."

Park didn't mind the word *adorable*.

eleanor

They'd parked on the far side of the Market, and the lot was mostly empty by the time they got back. Eleanor felt tense and reckless again. Maybe it was something about this car. . . .

The Impala might not look pervy on the outside, not like a fully carpeted custom van or something—but the inside was a different story. The front seat was almost as big as Eleanor's bed, and the backseat was an Erica Jong novel just waiting to happen.

Park opened the door for her, then ran around the car to get in. "It's not as late as I thought," he said, looking at the clock on the dash. Eight thirty.

"Yeah . . ." she said. She put her hand down on the seat between them. She tried to do it casually, but it came off pretty obvious.

Park laid his hand on top of hers.

It was just that kind of night. Every time she looked at him, he was looking back at her. Every time she thought about kissing him, he was already closing his eyes.

Read my mind now, she thought.

"Are you hungry?" he asked.

"No," she said.

"Okay." Park took his hand away and put the key in the ignition. Eleanor reached up and caught his sleeve before he could turn it.

He dropped the keys and, all in one motion, he turned and scooped her into his arms. Seriously, *scooped.* He was always stronger than she expected him to be.

If you were watching them now (and you totally could because the windows weren't fogged over yet), you'd think that Eleanor and Park did this kind of thing all the time. Not just the once before.

This time was already different.

They weren't moving forward in orderly steps, like a game of Mother May I. They weren't even kissing each other square on the mouth. (Lining things up neatly would take too long.) Eleanor climbed up his shirt, climbing on top of him. And Park kept pulling her to him, even when she couldn't come any closer.

She was wedged between Park and the steering wheel, and when he pushed his hand up her shirt, she leaned against the horn. They both jumped, and Park accidentally bit her tongue.

"Are you okay?" he asked.

"Yeah," she said, glad that he didn't pull his hand away. Her tongue didn't seem to be bleeding. "You?"

"Yeah . . ." He was breathing heavy, and it was wonderful. *I did this to him,* she told herself.

"Do you think . . ." he said.

"What?" He probably thought they should stop. *No,* she thought. *No, I don't think. Don't think, Park.*

"Do you think we should . . . Don't think I'm a creep, okay? Do you think we should get in the backseat?"

She pushed off him and slid over the backseat. God, it was huge, it was glorious.

Not even a second later, Park landed on top of her.

park

She felt so good underneath, even better than he'd expected. (And he'd expected her to feel like heaven, plus nirvana, plus that scene in *Willy Wonka* where Charlie starts to fly.) Park was breathing so hard, he couldn't get any air.

It seemed impossible that this could feel as good to Eleanor as it did to him—but she was making these faces. . . . She looked like a girl in a Prince video. If Eleanor was feeling anything like what he was feeling, how were they ever supposed to stop?

He pulled her shirt up over her head.

"Bruce Lee," she whispered.

"What?" That didn't seem right. Park's hands froze.

"Super-hot Asian guy. Bruce Lee."

"Oh . . ." He laughed, he couldn't help it. "Okay. I'll give you Bruce Lee. . . ."

She arched her back and he closed his eyes. He'd never get enough of her.

46

eleanor

Richie's truck was in the driveway, but the whole house was dark, thank God. Eleanor was sure that something would give her away. Her hair. Her shirt. Her mouth. She felt radioactive.

She and Park had been sitting in the alley for a while, in the front seat, just holding hands and feeling whiplashed. At least, that's how Eleanor felt. It wasn't that she and Park had gone too far, necessarily—but they'd gone a whole lot farther than she'd been prepared for. She'd never expected to have a love scene straight out of a Judy Blume book.

Park must be feeling strange, too. He sat through two Bon Jovi songs without even touching the radio. Eleanor had left a mark on his shoulder, but you couldn't see it anymore.

This was her mom's fault.

If Eleanor were allowed to have normal relationships with boys, she wouldn't have felt like she had to hit a home run the very first time she ended up in the backseat of a car—she wouldn't have felt like it might be her only time at bat. (And she wouldn't be making these stupid baseball metaphors.)

It hadn't been a home run, anyway. They'd stopped at second base. (At least, she thought it was second base. She'd heard conflicting definitions for the bases.) Still . . .

It was wonderful.

So wonderful that she wasn't sure how they'd survive never doing it again.

"I should go in," she said to Park after they'd been sitting in the car a half hour or more. "I'm usually home by now."

He nodded but didn't look up or let go of her hand.

"Okay," she said. "We're . . . okay, right?"

He looked up then. His hair had flattened out, and it fell in his eyes. He looked concerned. "Yeah," he said. "Oh. *Yeah*. I'm just . . ."

She waited.

He closed his eyes and shook his head, like he was embarrassed. "I . . . just really don't want to say good-bye to you, Eleanor. Ever."

He opened his eyes and looked straight into her. Maybe this was third base.

She swallowed. "You don't have to say good-bye to me *ever*," she said. "Just tonight."

Park smiled. Then he raised an eyebrow. Eleanor wished she could do that.

"Tonight . . ." he said, "but not ever?"

She rolled her eyes. She was talking like him now. Like an idiot. She hoped it was too dark in the alley for him to see her blush.

"Good-bye," she said, shaking her head. "I'll see you tomorrow." She opened the door to the Impala; it weighed as much as a horse. Then she stopped and looked back at him. "But we're okay, right?"

"We're perfect," he said, leaning forward quickly and kissing her cheek. "I'll wait for you to get in."

––––––––––

As soon as Eleanor slipped in the house, she could hear them fighting.

Richie was yelling about something, and her mom was crying. Eleanor moved toward her bedroom as quietly as she could.

All the little kids were on the floor, even Maisie. They were sleeping through the chaos. *I wonder how often I sleep through it,* Eleanor wondered. She managed to swing onto her bed without stepping on anybody, but she landed on the cat. He squawked, and she pulled him up and onto her lap. "Shhh," she breathed, scratching his neck.

Richie shouted again—"*My* house!"—and Eleanor and the cat both jumped. Something crunched beneath her.

She reached under her leg and pulled out a badly crumpled comic book. An *X-Men* annual. *Damn it, Ben.* She tried to smooth the comic out on her lap, but it was covered in some goop. The blanket felt wet, too; it was lotion or something. . . . No, liquid makeup. With little bits of broken glass. Eleanor carefully picked a shard out of the cat's tail and set it aside, then wiped her wet fingers on his fur. A length of oily-brown cassette tape was wrapped around his leg. Eleanor pulled it free. She looked down the bed and blinked until her eyes adjusted to the dark. . . .

Torn comic book pages.

Powder.

Little pools of green eyeshadow . . .

Miles of cassette tape.

Her headphones were snapped in half and hanging from the edge of the bunk. Her grapefruit box was at the end of the bed, and Eleanor knew before she reached for it that it would be light as air. Empty. The lid was ripped almost in half, and someone had written on it in bold black marker—with one of Eleanor's markers.

> *do you think you can make a fool of me? this is my house do you think you can hore around my neighborhood right under my nose and i'm not going to find out is that what you think? i know what you are and its over*

Eleanor stared at the lid and struggled to make the letters into words—but she couldn't get past the familiar spill of lowercase letters.

Somewhere in the house her mother was crying like she was never going to stop.

47

eleanor

Eleanor considered her options.

1.

48

eleanor

do i make you wet?

She pulled back the soiled blanket and set the cat on the clean sheet underneath. Then she climbed from the top bunk to the bottom. Her bookbag was sitting by the door. Eleanor unzipped it without getting off the bed and took Park's photo out of the side pocket. Then she was out the window and on the porch and running down the street faster than she'd ever run in gym class.

She didn't slow down until she was on the next block, and then only because she didn't know where to go. She was almost to Park's house—she couldn't go to Park's house.

pop that cherry

"Hey, Red."

Eleanor ignored the girl's voice. She looked back at the street. What if somebody had heard her leave the house? What if Richie came after her? She stepped off the sidewalk into someone's yard. Behind a tree.

"Hey. *Eleanor.*"

Eleanor looked around. She was standing in front of Steve's house. The garage door was mostly closed, propped open with a baseball bat. Eleanor could see someone moving inside, and Tina was walking down the driveway, holding a beer.

"*Hey,*" Tina hissed. She looked as disgusted with Eleanor as ever. Eleanor thought about running again, but her legs felt weak.

"Your stepfather's been looking for you," Tina said. "He's been driving around the neighborhood all goddamn night."

"What did you tell him?" Eleanor said. *Did Tina do this? Is that how he knew?*

"I asked him if his dick was bigger than his truck," Tina said. "I didn't tell him anything."

"Did you tell him about Park?"

Tina narrowed her eyes. Then shook her head. "But somebody's going to."

suck me off

Eleanor looked back at the street. She had to hide. She had to get away from him.

"What's wrong with you anyway?" Tina asked.

"Nothing." A pair of headlights stopped at the end of the block. Eleanor put her arms over her head.

"Come on," Tina said in a voice Eleanor had never heard before— concerned. "You just need to stay out of his way until he cools off."

Eleanor followed Tina up the driveway, crouching to get into the hazy, dark garage.

"Is that Big Red?" Steve was sitting on a couch. Mikey was there, too, on the floor, with one of the girls from the bus. There was hessian music, Black Sabbath, coming from a car up on blocks in the middle of the garage.

"Sit down," Tina said, pointing to the other end of the couch.

"You're in trouble, Big Red," Steve said. "Your daddy's looking for you." Steve was grinning from ear to ear. His mouth was bigger than a lion's.

"It's her stepdad," Tina said.

"*Stepdad!*" Steve shouted, throwing a beer can across the garage. "Your fucking *step*dad? Do you want me to kill him for you? I'm gonna kill Tina's, anyway. I could get them both in the same day. Buy one, get one . . ." He giggled. "Buy one, get one . . . free."

Tina opened a beer and shoved it into Eleanor's lap. Eleanor took it, just to have something to hold. "Drink up," Tina said.

Eleanor took a sip obediently. It tasted sharp and yellow.

"We should play quarters," Steve slurred. "Hey, Red, do you have any quarters?"

Eleanor shook her head.

Tina perched next to him on the arm of the couch and lit a cigarette. "We had quarters," she said. "We spent them on beer, remember?"

"Those weren't quarters," Steve said. "That was a ten."

Tina closed her eyes and blew smoke at the ceiling.

Eleanor closed her eyes, too. She tried to think about what she should do next, but nothing came to her. The music on the car radio switched from Sabbath to AC/DC to Zeppelin. Steve sang along; his voice was surprisingly light. "Hangman, hangman, turn your head awhile. . . ."

Eleanor listened to Steve sing song after song over the wet hammer of her heartbeat. The beer can went warm in her hand.

i know your a slut you smell like cum

She stood up. "I've got to get out of here."

"God," Tina said, "relax. He won't find you here. He's probably already at the Rail drinking it off."

"No," Eleanor said. "He's going to kill me."

It was true, she realized, even if it wasn't.

Tina's face was hard. "So, where you gonna go?"

"Away . . . I have to tell Park."

park

Park couldn't sleep.

That night, before they'd climbed back into the front seat of the Impala, he'd taken off all of Eleanor's layers and even unpinned her bra—then laid her down on the blue upholstery. She'd looked like a vision there, a mermaid. Cool white in the darkness, the freckles gathered on her shoulders and cheeks like cream rising to the top.

The sight of her. She still glowed on the inside of his eyelids.

It was going to be constant torture now that he knew what she was like under her clothes—and there wasn't a *next time* in their near future. Tonight was another fluke, a lucky break, a gift. . . .

"Park," someone said.

Park sat up in bed and looked around dumbly.

"Park." There was a knock at the window, and he scrambled over to it, pulling back the curtain.

It was Steve. Right behind the glass, grinning like a maniac. He must be hanging from the window ledge. Steve's face disappeared, and Park heard him fall heavily onto the ground. That asshole. Park's mom was going to hear him.

Park opened the window quickly and leaned out. He was going to tell Steve to go away, but then he saw Eleanor standing in the shadow of Steve's house with Tina.

Were they holding her hostage?

Was she holding a beer?

eleanor

As soon as Park saw her, he climbed out the window and hung four feet from the ground—he was going to break his ankles. Eleanor felt a sob catch in her throat.

He landed in a crouch like Spider-Man and ran toward her. She dropped the beer on the grass.

"Jesus," Tina said. "You're welcome. That was the last beer."

"Hey, Park, did I scare you?" Steve asked. "Did you think I was Freddy Krueger? *You think you was gonna get away from me?*"

Park got to Eleanor and took her arms. "What's wrong?" he asked. "What's going on?"

She started to cry. Like, majorly cry. She felt like herself again as soon as he touched her, and it was horrible.

"Are you bleeding?" Park asked, taking her hand.

"Car," Tina whispered, like it was a warning.

Eleanor pulled Park against the garage until the headlights had passed.

"What's going on?" he asked again.

"We should get back to the garage," Tina said.

park

He hadn't been in Steve's garage since grade school. They used to play foosball in here. Now there was the Camaro up on blocks and an old couch pushed against the wall.

Steve sat at one end of the couch and immediately lit a joint. He held it out to Park, but Park shook his head. The garage already smelled like a thousand joints had been smoked in here, then put out in a thousand beers. The Camaro was rocking a little bit, and Steve kicked the door. "Settle down, Mikey, you're gonna knock it over."

Park couldn't even imagine a turn of events that would have led Eleanor here—but she'd practically dragged him into the garage, and now she was huddled against him. Park still thought maybe they'd kidnapped her. Was he supposed to pay ransom?

"Talk to me," he said to the top of Eleanor's head. "What's going on?"

"Her stepdad is looking for her," Tina said. Tina was sitting on the arm of the couch with her legs in Steve's lap. She took the joint from him.

"Is that true?" Park asked Eleanor. She nodded into his chest. She wouldn't let him pull far enough away that he could look at her.

"Fucking stepdads," Steve said. "Motherfuckers, all of them." He burst into laughter. "Oh, fuck, Mikey, did you hear that?" He kicked the Camaro again. "Mikey?"

"I have to leave," Eleanor whispered.

Thank God. Park backed away from her and took her hand. "Hey, Steve, we're going back to my house."

"Be careful, man, he's been driving around in that shit-colored Micro Machine. . . ."

Park bent to clear the garage door. Eleanor stopped behind him. "Thank you," she said—he would swear that she was talking to Tina.

This night couldn't get any weirder.

He led Eleanor through his backyard, then around the back of his grandparents' house to the driveway, past the spot by the garage where they liked to kiss good-bye.

When they got to the RV, Park reached up and opened the screen door. "Go on," he said. "It's always unlocked."

He and Josh used to play in here. It was like a little house, with a bed at one end and a kitchen at the other. There was even a miniature stove and refrigerator. It had been a while since Park had been inside the RV—he couldn't stand up now without hitting his head on the ceiling.

There was a checkerboard-sized table against the wall with two seats. Park sat on one side and sat Eleanor down across from him. He reached for her hands—her right palm was streaked with blood, but she didn't seem to be in pain.

"Eleanor . . ." he said. "What's going on?" He was pleading.

"I have to leave," she said. She was looking across the table like she'd just seen a ghost. Like she was one.

"Why?" he said. "Is this about tonight?" In Park's head, it felt like everything must be about tonight. Like nothing that good and this bad could happen on the same night unless they were related. Whatever this was.

"No," Eleanor said, rubbing her eyes. "No. It's not about us. I mean . . ." She looked out the little window.

"Why is your stepdad looking for you?"

"Because he knows, because I ran away."

"Why?"

"Because he *knows*." Her voice caught. "Because it's him."

"What?"

"Oh God, I shouldn't have come here," she said. "I'm just making it worse. I'm sorry."

Park wanted to shake her, to shake through to her—she wasn't making any sense. Two hours ago, everything had been perfect between them, and now . . . Park had to get back to his house. His mom was still awake, and his dad was going to be home any minute.

He leaned over the table and took Eleanor by the shoulders. "Could we just start over?" he whispered. "Please? I don't know what you're talking about."

Eleanor closed her eyes and nodded wearily.

She started over.

She told him everything.

And Park's hands started shaking before she was halfway through.

"Maybe he won't hurt you," he said, hoping it was true, "maybe he's just trying to scare you. Here—" He pulled his hand inside his sleeve and tried to wipe Eleanor's face.

"No," she said. "You don't know, you don't see how . . . how he looks at me."

49

eleanor

How he looks at me.

    Like he's biding his time.

    Not like he wants me. Like he'll get around to me. When there's nothing and no one else left to destroy.

    How he waits up for me.

    Keeps track of me.

    How he's always there. When I'm eating. When I'm reading. When I'm brushing my hair.

    You don't see.

    Because I pretend not to.

50

park

Eleanor pushed her curls out of her face one by one, like she was gathering her wits by hand. "I have to go," she said.

She was making more sense now, and more eye contact, but Park still felt like someone had turned the world upside down and was shaking it.

"You could talk to your mom tomorrow," he said. "Everything might look different in the morning."

"You saw what he wrote on my books," she said evenly. "Would you want me to stay there?"

"I . . . I just don't want you to leave," he said. "Where would you go? To your dad's house?"

"No, he doesn't want me."

"But if you explained—"

"He doesn't *want* me."

"Then . . . where?"

"I don't know." She took a deep breath and squared her shoulders. "My uncle said I could spend the summer with him. Maybe he'll let me come up to St. Paul early."

"St. Paul, Minnesota."

She nodded.

"But . . ." Park looked in Eleanor's eyes, and her hands fell to the table.

"I know," she sobbed, slumping forward. "I know. . . ."

There was no room to sit at the table next to her, so he dropped to his knees and pulled her onto the dusty linoleum floor.

eleanor

"When are you leaving?" he asked. He pushed her hair out of her face and held it behind her head.

"Tonight," she said. "I can't go home."

"How are you going to get there? Have you called your uncle?"

"No. I don't know. I thought I'd take the bus."

She was going to hitchhike.

She figured she could walk as far as the interstate; then she'd stick out her thumb for station wagons and minivans. Family cars. If she hadn't been raped or murdered—or sold into white slavery—by Des Moines, she'd call her uncle collect. He'd come to get her, even if it was just to bring her home.

"You can't take the bus by yourself," Park said.

"I don't have a better plan."

"I'll drive you," he said.

"To the bus station?"

"To Minnesota."

"Park, no, your parents will never let you."

"So I won't ask."

"But your dad will kill you."

"No," he said. "He'll ground me."

"For life."

"Do you think I even care about that right now?" He held her face in his hands. "Do you think I care about anything but you?"

51

eleanor

Park said he'd come back after his dad got home and his parents were both asleep.

"It might be a while. Don't turn on the light or anything, okay?"

"Duh."

"And watch for the Impala."

"Okay."

He looked more serious than she'd seen him since the day he kicked Steve's ass. Or since her first day on the bus, when he'd ordered her to sit down. That was still the only time she'd heard him use the F-word.

He leaned into the RV and touched her chin.

"Please be careful," she said.

And then he was gone.

Eleanor sat back down at the table. She could see Park's driveway from there, through the lace curtains. She felt tired suddenly. She just wanted to lay her head down. It was already after midnight; it could be hours before Park came back. . . .

Maybe she should feel bad about involving him in all this, but she didn't. He was right: The worst thing that would happen to him (barring some terrible accident) was that he'd be grounded. And being grounded at his house was like winning the *Price Is Right* Showcase compared to what would happen if Eleanor got caught.

Should she have left a note?

Would her mom call the police? (Was her mom okay? Were they all okay? Eleanor should have checked to see if the little kids were breathing.)

Her uncle probably wouldn't even let Eleanor stay once he found out she'd run away. . . .

God, whenever she started to think this plan through, it all fell apart. But it was already too late to turn back. It felt like the most important thing now was to run, the most important place to be was *away*.

She'd get away, and then she'd figure out what to do next.

Or maybe she wouldn't. . . .

Maybe she'd get away, and then she'd just stop.

Eleanor had never thought about killing herself—ever—but she thought a lot about stopping. Just running until she couldn't run anymore. Jumping from something so high that she'd never hit the bottom.

Was Richie out looking for her now?

Maisie and Ben would tell him about Park, if they hadn't already. Not because they liked Richie, though sometimes it still seemed like they did. Because he had them on leashes. Like the first day Eleanor came to the house, when Maisie was sitting on Richie's lap . . .

Fuck. Just . . . fuck.

She should go back for Maisie.

She should go back for all of them—she should find a way to fit them in her pockets—but she should definitely go back for Maisie. Maisie would run away with Eleanor. She wouldn't think twice. . . .

And then Uncle Geoff would send them both right home.

Her mom would *definitely* call the police if she woke up and Maisie was gone. Bringing Maisie would ruin everything even worse than it was already ruined.

If Eleanor were the hero of some book, like *The Boxcar Children* or something, she'd try. If she were Dicey Tillerman, she'd find a way.

She'd be brave and noble, and she'd find a way.

But she wasn't. Eleanor wasn't any of those things. She was just trying to get through the night.

park

Park walked quietly into his house through the back door. Nobody in his family ever locked anything.

The TV was still on in his parents' bedroom. He went straight to the bathroom and into the shower. He was pretty sure he smelled like every single thing that could get him in trouble.

"Park?" his mom called when he walked out of the bathroom.

"Here," he said. "Just going to bed."

He buried his dirty clothes at the bottom of the hamper and dug all his leftover birthday and Christmas money out of his sock drawer. Sixty dollars. That should be enough for gas . . . probably, he didn't really know.

If they could just get to St. Paul, Eleanor's uncle would help them figure it out. She wasn't sure her uncle would let her stay, but she said he was a decent guy, "and his wife was in the Peace Corps."

Park had already written his parents a note:

Mom and Dad,
I had to help Eleanor. I'll call you tomorrow, and I'll be back in
a day or two. I know I'm in huge trouble, but this was an
emergency, and I had to help.
Park

His mom always kept her keys in the same place—on a little key-shaped plaque in the entryway that said KEYS.

Park was going to take her keys, then sneak back out the kitchen door, the door farthest from his parents' room.

His dad got home around one thirty. Park listened to him move around the kitchen, then the bathroom. He heard the door to his parents' room open, he heard the TV.

Park lay on his bed and closed his eyes. (There was no chance he'd fall asleep.) The picture of Eleanor was still glowing on the inside of his eyelids.

So beautiful. So peaceful . . . No, that wasn't quite right, not peaceful, more like . . . at peace. Like she was more comfortable out of her shirt than in it. Like she was happy inside out.

When he opened his eyes, he saw her the way he'd left her in the RV—tense and resigned, so far gone that light wouldn't even catch in her eyes.

So far gone, she wasn't even thinking about him anymore.

Park waited until it was quiet. Then he waited another twenty minutes. Then he grabbed his backpack and went through the motions he'd planned in his head.

He stopped at the kitchen door. His dad had left his new hunting rifle out on the table. . . . He was probably going to clean it tomorrow morning. For a minute, Park thought about taking the gun—but he couldn't think of when he'd use it. It's not like they were going to run into Richie on the way out of town. Hopefully.

Park opened the door and was about to step out when his dad's voice stopped him.

"Park?"

He could have run for it, but his dad probably would've caught him. His dad was always bragging about being in the best shape of his life.

"Where do you think you're going?" his dad whispered.

"I . . . I have to help Eleanor."

"What does Eleanor need help with at two in the morning?"

"She's running away."

"And you're going with her?"

"No. I was just going to give her a ride to her uncle's house."

"Where does her uncle live?"

"Minnesota."

"Jesus F. Christ, Park," his dad said in his normal voice, "are you serious?"

"Dad," Park stepped toward him, pleading. "She has to go. It's her stepdad. He's . . ."

"Did he touch her? Because if he touched her, we're calling the police."

"He writes her these notes."

"What kind of notes?"

Park rubbed his forehead. He didn't like to think about the notes. "Sick ones."

"Did she talk to her mom?"

"Her mom's . . . not in very good shape. I think he hurts her."

"That little fucker . . ." His dad looked down at the gun, then looked back at Park, rubbing his chin. "So you're going to drive Eleanor to her uncle's house. Will he take her in?"

"She thinks so."

"I gotta tell you, Park, this doesn't sound like much of a plan."

"I know."

His dad sighed and scratched the back of his neck. "But I can't think of a better one."

Park's head jerked up.

"Call me when you get there," his dad said quietly. "It's a straight shot up from Des Moines—do you have a map?"

"I thought I'd get one at a gas station."

"If you get tired, pull into a rest stop. And don't talk to anybody unless you have to. Do you have any money?"

"Sixty dollars."

"Here . . ." His dad walked over to the cookie jar and pulled out a bunch of twenties. "If this doesn't work, with her uncle, don't take Eleanor home. Bring her back here, and we'll figure out what to do next."

"Okay . . . Thanks, Dad."

"Don't thank me yet. I've got one condition."

No more eyeliner, Park thought.

"You're taking the truck," his dad said.

His dad stood on the front steps with his arms folded. Of course he had to watch. Like he was umpiring a goddamn taekwondo bout.

Park closed his eyes. Eleanor was still there. *Eleanor.*

He started the engine and shifted smoothly into reverse, rolled out of the driveway, shifted into first, then pulled forward without a sputter.

Because he knew how to drive a stick. *Jesus.*

52

park

"Okay?"

She nodded and climbed in.

"Stay down," he said.

The first couple hours were a blur.

Park wasn't used to driving the truck, and it died a few times at red lights. Then he got on the interstate heading west instead of east, and it took twenty minutes to turn around again.

Eleanor didn't say anything. Just stared ahead and held on to her seat belt with both hands. He put his hand on her leg, and it was like she didn't notice it was there.

They got off the interstate again somewhere in Iowa to get gas and a map. Park went in. He bought Eleanor a Coke and a sandwich, and when he got back to the truck, she was slumped against the passenger door, asleep.

Good, he tried to tell himself. *She's exhausted.*

He climbed up behind the wheel and took a few rough breaths; then he slammed the sandwich onto the dash. *How can she be asleep?*

If everything went right tonight, Park would be driving home tomorrow morning by himself. He'd probably be allowed to drive now whenever he wanted, but there was nowhere he wanted to go without Eleanor.

How could she sleep through their last hours together?

How could she sleep sitting up like that? . . .

Her hair was down and wild, wine red even in this light, and her mouth was slightly open. Strawberry girl. He tried again to remember what he'd thought the first time he saw her. He tried to remember how this had happened—how she went from someone he'd never met to the only one who mattered.

And he wondered . . . What would happen if he *didn't* take her to her uncle's house? What would happen if he kept driving?

Why couldn't this have waited?

If Eleanor's life had caved in next year, or the year after, she could have run *to* him. Not from, not away.

Jesus. Why couldn't she just wake up?

Park stayed awake for another hour or so, fueled by Coke and hurt feelings. Then the wreck of the night caught up with him. There wasn't a rest stop around, so he pulled off on a county road, onto the gravel that passed as a shoulder.

He unbuckled his seat belt, unbuckled Eleanor's, then pulled her into him, laying his head on hers. She still smelled like last night. Like sweat and sweetness and the Impala. He cried into her hair until he fell asleep.

eleanor

She woke up in Park's arms. It caught her by surprise.

She would've thought it was a dream, but her dreams were always terrifying. (With Nazis and babies crying and teeth rotting out of her mouth.) Eleanor had never dreamed anything as nice as this, as nice as Park, sleepy-soft and warm. . . . Warm through. *Someday,* she thought, *somebody's going to wake up to this every morning.*

Park's face, asleep, was a brand-new kind of beautiful. Sunshine-trapped-in-amber skin. Full, flat mouth. Strong, arched cheekbones. (Eleanor didn't even have cheekbones.)

He caught her by surprise, and before she could help herself, her heart was breaking for him. Like it didn't have anything better to break over . . .

Maybe it didn't.

The sun was just below the horizon, and the inside of the truck was bluey pink. Eleanor kissed Park's new face—just under his eye, not quite on his nose. He stirred, and she felt every part of him shift against her. She ran the end of her nose along his brow and kissed his lashes.

His eyelids fluttered. (Only eyelids do that. And butterflies.) And his arms came to life around her. "Eleanor . . ." He sighed.

She held his beautiful face and kissed him like it was the end of the world.

park

She wouldn't be on the bus with him.

She wouldn't roll her eyes at him in English.

She wouldn't pick a fight with him just because she was bored.

She wouldn't cry in his bedroom about the things he couldn't fix for her.

The whole sky was the color of her skin.

eleanor

There's only one of him, she thought, *and he's right here.*

He knows I'll like a song before I've heard it. He laughs before I even get to the punch line. There's a place on his chest, just below his throat, that makes me want to let him open doors for me.

There's only one of him.

park

His parents never talked about how they met, but when Park was younger, he used to try to imagine it.

He loved how much they loved each other. It was the thing he thought about when he woke up scared in the middle of the night. Not that they loved *him*—they were his parents, they had to love him. *That they loved each other.* They didn't have to do that.

None of his friends' parents were still together, and in every case, that seemed like the number one thing that had gone wrong with his friends' lives.

But Park's parents loved each other. They kissed each other on the mouth, no matter who was watching.

What were the chances you'd ever meet someone like that? he wondered. Someone you could love forever, someone who would forever love you back? And what did you do when that person was born half a world away?

The math seemed impossible. How did his parents get so lucky?

They couldn't have felt lucky at the time. His dad's brother had just died in Vietnam; that's why they sent his dad to Korea. And when his parents got married, his mom had to leave everything and everyone she loved behind.

Park wondered if his dad saw his mom in the street or from the road or working in a restaurant. He wondered how they both knew. . . .

———

This kiss had to last Park forever.

It had to get him home.

He needed to remember it when he woke up scared in the middle of the night.

eleanor

The first time he'd held her hand, it felt so good that it crowded out all the bad things. It felt better than anything had ever hurt.

park

Eleanor's hair caught fire at dawn. Her eyes were dark and shining, and his arms were sure of her.

The first time he touched her hand, he'd known.

eleanor

There's no shame with Park. Nothing is dirty. Because Park is the sun, and that's the best way she could think to explain it.

park

"Eleanor, no, we have to stop."

"No . . ."

"We can't do this. . . ."

"No. Don't stop, Park."

"I don't even know how to . . . I don't have anything."

"It doesn't matter."

"But I don't want you to get—"

"I don't care."

"*I* care. Eleanor—"

"It's our last chance."

"No. No, I can't. . . . I, *no,* I need to believe that it isn't our last chance. . . . Eleanor? Can you hear me? I need you to believe it, too."

53

park

Eleanor got out of the truck, and Park wandered into the cornfield to pee. (Which was embarrassing, but less embarrassing than pissing his pants.)

When he came back, she was sitting on the hood of the truck. She looked beautiful, fierce, leaning forward like a figurehead.

He climbed up and sat next to her. "Hey," he said.

"Hey."

He pushed his shoulder up against hers and nearly wept with relief when she laid her head against him. Weeping again today seemed wholly inevitable.

"Do you really believe that?" she asked.

"What?"

"That . . . we'll have other chances? That we have any chance at all?"

"Yes."

"No matter what happens," she said forcefully, "I'm not coming home."

"I know."

She was quiet.

"No matter what happens," Park said, "I love you."

She put her arms around his waist, and he hugged her shoulders.

"I just can't believe that life would give us to each other," he said, "and then take it back."

"I can," she said. "Life's a bastard."

He held her tighter, and pushed his face into her neck.

"But it's up to us . . ." he said softly. "It's up to us not to lose this."

eleanor

She sat right next to him for the rest of the trip—even though there wasn't a seat belt, and she had to sit with the stick shift between her legs. She figured it was still lots safer than riding in the back of Richie's Isuzu.

They stopped at another truck stop and Park bought her Cherry Coke and beef jerky. He called his parents collect—she still couldn't believe they were okay with this.

"My dad's okay," he said. "I think my mom's freaking out."

"Have they heard from my mom or . . . anybody?"

"No. Or, at least, they didn't mention it."

Park asked her if she wanted to call her uncle. She didn't.

"I smell like Steve's garage," she said. "My uncle's going to think I'm a drug dealer."

Park laughed. "I think you spilled beer on your shirt. Maybe he'll just think you're an alcoholic."

She looked down at her shirt. There was a smear of blood from when she'd cut her hand on her bed—and something crusty on the shoulder, probably snot from all that crying.

"Here," Park said. He was taking off his sweatshirt. Then his

T-shirt. He handed the shirt to her. It was green and said PREFAB SPROUT.

"I can't take this," she said, watching him pull his sweatshirt back on over his bare chest. "It's new." Plus it probably wouldn't fit.

"You can give it back later."

"Close your eyes," she said.

"Of course," Park said softly. He looked away.

There was no one else in the parking lot. Eleanor slouched down and put Park's T-shirt on underneath her own, then pulled the dirty shirt off. That's how she changed in gym class. His shirt was about as tight as her gym suit . . . but it smelled clean, like Park.

"Okay," she said.

He looked back at her, and his smile changed. "Keep it," he said.

When they got to Minneapolis, Park stopped at another gas station to ask for directions.

"Is it easy?" she asked him when he got back in the truck.

"Like Sunday morning," he said. "We're really close."

54

park

He was more nervous about his driving once they got into the city. Driving in St. Paul was nothing like driving in Omaha.

Eleanor was reading the map for him, but she'd never read a map outside of class before—and between the two of them, they kept making wrong turns.

"I'm sorry," Eleanor kept saying.

"It's okay," Park said, glad she was sitting right next to him. "I'm not in any hurry."

She pressed her hand into the top of his leg.

"I've been thinking . . ." she said.

"Yeah?"

"I don't want you to come inside when we get there."

"You mean you want to talk to them by yourself?"

"No . . . Well, yeah. But I mean . . . I don't want you to wait for me."

He tried to look down at her, but he was afraid he'd miss his turn again. "What? No. What if they don't want you to stay?"

"Then they can figure out how to get me home—I'll be their problem. Maybe that'll give me more time to talk to them about everything."

"But . . ." *I'm not ready for you to stop being my problem.*

"It makes more sense, Park. If you leave soon, you can still get home by dark."

"But if I leave soon . . ." His voice dropped. "I leave soon."

"We have to say good-bye anyway," she said. "Does it matter if it's now or a few hours from now or tomorrow morning?"

"Are you kidding?" He looked down at her, hoping he'd miss his turn. "Yes."

eleanor

"It just makes more sense," she said. And then she bit her lip. The only way she was going to get through any of this was by force of will.

The houses were starting to look familiar—big gray and white clapboard houses set far back on their lawns. Eleanor's whole family had come up here for Easter the year after her dad left. Her uncle and his wife were atheists, but it was still a really fun trip.

They didn't have kids of their own—probably by choice, Eleanor thought. Probably because they knew cute kids grow up into ugly, problematic teenagers.

But Uncle Geoff had *invited* her here.

He wanted her to come, at least for a few months. Maybe she didn't have to tell him everything right away; maybe he'd just think she was early.

"Is that it?" Park asked.

He stopped in front of a gray blue house with a willow tree in the front yard.

"Yeah," she said. She recognized the house. She recognized her uncle's Volvo in the driveway.

Park stepped on the gas.

"Where are you going?"

"Just . . . around the block," he said.

park

He drove around the block. For all the good it did him. Then he parked a few houses down from her uncle's, so they could see the house from the car. Eleanor couldn't look away from it.

eleanor

She had to say good-bye to him. Now. And she didn't know how.

park

"You remember my phone number right?"

"867-5309."

"Seriously, Eleanor."

"Seriously, Park. I'm never going to forget your phone number."

"Call me as soon as you can, okay? Tonight. Collect. And give me your uncle's number. Or, if he doesn't want you to call, send the number to me in a letter—in one of the many, many letters you're going to write me."

"He might send me home."

"No." Park let go of the gearshift and took her hand. "You're not going back there. If your uncle sends you home, come to my house. My parents will help us figure it out. My dad already said that they would."

Eleanor's head fell forward.

"He's not going to send you home," Park said. "He's going to help. . . ." She nodded deliberately at the floor. "And he's going to let you accept frequent, private, long-distance phone calls. . . ."

She was still.

"Hey," Park said, trying to lift up her chin. "Eleanor."

eleanor

Stupid Asian kid.

Stupid, beautiful Asian kid.

Thank God she couldn't make her mouth work right now, because if she could, there'd be no end to the melodramatic garbage she'd say to him.

She was pretty sure she'd thank him for saving her life. Not just yesterday, but, like, practically every day since they'd met. Which made her feel like the dumbest, weakest *girl*. If you couldn't save your own life, was it even worth saving?

There's no such thing as handsome princes, she told herself.

There's no such thing as happily ever after.

She looked up at Park. Into his golden green eyes.

You saved my life, she tried to tell him. *Not forever, not for good. Probably just temporarily. But you saved my life, and now I'm yours.* The me that's me right now is yours. *Always.*

park

"I don't know how to say good-bye to you," she said.

He smoothed her hair off her face. He'd never seen her so fair. "Then don't."

"But I have to go. . . ."

"So go," he said with his hands on her cheeks. "But don't say good-bye. It's not good-bye."

She rolled her eyes and shook her head. "That's so lame."

"Seriously? You can't cut me five minutes of slack?"

"That's what people say—'it's not good-bye'—when they're too afraid to face what they're really feeling. I'm not going to see you tomorrow, Park—I don't know *when* I'll see you again. That deserves more than 'it's not good-bye.' "

"I'm not afraid to face what I'm feeling," he said.

"Not you," she said, her voice breaking. "Me."

"You," he said, putting his arms around her and promising himself that it wouldn't be the last time, "are the bravest person I know."

She shook her head again, like she was trying to shake off the tears.

"Just kiss me good-bye," she whispered.

Only for today, he thought. *Not ever.*

eleanor

You think that holding someone hard will bring them closer. You think that you can hold them so hard that you'll still feel them, embossed on you, when you pull away.

Every time Eleanor pulled away from Park, she felt the gasping loss of him.

When she finally got out of the truck, it was because she didn't think she could stand touching and untouching him again. The next time she ripped herself away, she'd lose some skin.

Park started to get out with her, but she stopped him.

"No," she said. "Stay." She looked up anxiously at her uncle's house.

"It's going to be okay," Park said.

She nodded. "Right."

"Because I love you."

She laughed. "Is that why?"

"It is, actually."

"Good-bye," she said. "Good-bye, Park."

"Good-bye, Eleanor. You know, until tonight. When you're going to call me."

"What if they're not home? God, that would be anticlimactic."

"That would be great."

"Dork," she whispered with a leftover smile on her face. She stepped back and closed the door.

I love you, he mouthed. Maybe he was saying it out loud. She couldn't hear him anymore.

55

park

He didn't ride the bus anymore. He didn't have to. His mom gave him the Impala when his dad bought her a new Taurus. . . .

He didn't ride the bus anymore, because he'd have the whole seat to himself.

Not that the Impala wasn't just as ruined with memories.

Some mornings, if Park got to school early, he sat in the parking lot with his head on the steering wheel and let whatever was left of Eleanor wash over him until he ran out of air.

Not that school was any better.

She wasn't at her locker. Or in class. Mr. Stessman said it was pointless to read *Macbeth* out loud without Eleanor. "Fie, my Lord, fie," he lamented.

She didn't stay for dinner. She didn't lean against him when he watched TV.

Park spent most nights lying on his bed because it was the only place she'd never been.

He lay on his bed and never turned on the stereo.

eleanor

She didn't ride the bus anymore. She rode to school with her uncle. He made her go, even though there were only four weeks left, and everybody was already studying for finals.

There weren't any Asian kids at her new school. There weren't even any black kids.

When her uncle went down to Omaha, he said she didn't have to go. He was gone three days, and when he came back, he brought the black trash bag from her bedroom closet. Eleanor already had new clothes. And a new bookcase and a boom box. And a six-pack of blank cassette tapes.

park

Eleanor didn't call that first night.

She hadn't said that she would, now that he thought about it. She hadn't said that she'd write either, but Park thought that went unsaid. He'd thought that was a given.

After Eleanor got out of the truck, Park had waited in front of her uncle's house.

He was supposed to drive away as soon as the door opened, as soon as it was clear that somebody was home. But he couldn't just leave her like that.

He watched the woman who came to the door give Eleanor a big hug, and then he watched the door close behind them. And then he waited, just in case Eleanor changed her mind. Just in case she decided after all that he should come in.

The door stayed closed. Park remembered his promise and drove away. *The sooner I get home,* he thought, *the sooner I'll hear from her again.*

He sent Eleanor a postcard from the first truck stop. WELCOME TO MINNESOTA, LAND OF 10,000 LAKES.

When he got home, his mom ran to the door to hug him.

"All right?" his dad asked.

"Yeah," Park said.

"How was the truck?"

"Fine."

His dad went outside to make sure.

"You," his mom said, "I was so worried about you."

"I'm fine, Mom, just tired."

"How's Eleanor?" she asked. "She okay?"

"I think so, has she called?"

"No. Nobody called."

As soon as his mom let go of him, Park went to his room and wrote Eleanor a letter.

eleanor

When Aunt Susan opened the door, Eleanor was already crying.

"Eleanor," Aunt Susan kept saying. "Oh my goodness, Eleanor. What are you doing here?"

Eleanor tried to tell her that everything was okay. Which wasn't true—she wouldn't be there if everything were okay. But nobody was dead. "Nobody's dead," she said.

"Oh my God. Geoffrey!" Aunt Susan called. "Wait here, sweetheart. Geoff . . ."

Left alone, Eleanor realized that she shouldn't have told Park to leave right away.

She wasn't ready for him to leave.

She opened the front door and ran out to the street. Park was already gone—she looked both ways for him.

When she turned around, her aunt and uncle were standing on the front porch watching her.

Phone calls. Peppermint tea. Her aunt and uncle talking in the kitchen long after she went to bed.

"Sabrina . . ."

"Five of them."

"We've got to get them out of there, Geoffrey. . . ."

"What if she isn't telling the truth?"

Eleanor took Park's photo out of her back pocket and smoothed it out on the bedspread. It didn't look like him. October was already a lifetime away. And this afternoon was another lifetime. The world was spinning so fast, she didn't know where she stood anymore.

Her aunt had lent her some pajamas—they wore about the same size—but Eleanor put Park's shirt back on as soon as she got out of the shower.

It smelled like him. Like his house, like potpourri. Like soap, like boy, like happiness.

She fell forward onto the bed, holding the hole in her stomach.

No one would ever believe her.

She wrote her mom a letter.

She said everything she'd wanted to say in the last six months.

She said she was sorry.

She begged her to think of Ben and Mouse—and Maisie.

She threatened to call the police.

Her aunt Susan gave her a stamp. "They're in the junk drawer, Eleanor, take as many as you need."

park

When he got sick of his bedroom, when there was nothing left in his life that smelled like vanilla—Park walked by Eleanor's house.

Sometimes the truck was there, sometimes it wasn't, sometimes the Rottweiler was asleep on the porch. But the broken toys were gone, and there were never any strawberry blond kids playing in the yard.

Josh said that Eleanor's little brother had stopped coming to school. "Everybody says they're gone. The whole family."

"That great news," their mother said. "Maybe that pretty mom wake up to bad situation, you know? Good for Eleanor."

Park just nodded.

He wondered if his letters even got to wherever she was now.

eleanor

There was a red rotary phone in the spare bedroom. Her bedroom. Whenever it rang, Eleanor felt like picking it up and saying, "What is it, Commissioner Gordon?"

Sometimes, when she was alone in the house, she took the phone over to her bed and listened to the dial tone.

She practiced Park's number, her finger sliding across the dial. Sometimes, after the dial tone stopped, she pretended he was whispering in her ear.

"Have you ever had a boyfriend?" Dani asked. Dani was in theater camp, too. They ate lunch together, sitting on the stage with their legs dangling in the orchestra pit.

"No," Eleanor said.

Park wasn't a boyfriend, he was a champion.

"Have you ever kissed anybody?"

Eleanor shook her head.

He wasn't her boyfriend.

And they weren't going to break up. Or get bored. Or drift apart. (They weren't going to become another stupid high school romance.)

They were just going to stop.

Eleanor had decided back in his dad's truck. She'd decided in Albert Lea, Minnesota. If they weren't going to get married—if it wasn't forever—it was only a matter of time.

They were just going to stop.

Park was never going to love her more than he did on the day they said good-bye.

And she couldn't bear to think of him loving her less.

park

When he got sick of himself, Park went to her old house. Sometimes the truck was there. Sometimes it wasn't. Sometimes, Park stood at the end of the sidewalk and hated everything the house stood for.

56

eleanor

Letters, postcards, packages that rattled like loaded cassette tapes. None of them opened, none of them read.

Dear Park, Eleanor wrote on a clean sheet of stationery.

Dear Park, she tried to explain.

But the explanations fell apart in her hands. Everything true was too hard to write—he was too much to lose. Everything she felt for him was too hot to touch.

I'm sorry, she wrote, then crossed it out.

It's just . . . she tried again.

She threw the half-written letters away. She threw the unopened envelopes in the bottom drawer.

"Dear Park," she whispered, her forehead hanging over the dresser, "just stop."

park

His dad said Park needed a summer job to pay for gas.

Neither of them mentioned that Park never went anywhere. Or that he'd started putting eyeliner on with his thumb. Blacking out his own eyes.

He looked just wrecked enough to get a job at Drastic Plastic. The girl who hired him had two rows of holes in each ear.

His mom stopped bringing in the mail. He knew it was because she hated telling him that nothing had come for him. Park brought in the mail himself now every night when he got home from work. Every night praying for rain.

He had an endless supply and an insatiable appetite for punk music. "I can't hear myself think in here," his dad said, coming into Park's room for the third night in a row to turn down the stereo.

Duh, Eleanor would have said.

Eleanor didn't start school in the fall. Not with Park, anyway.

She didn't celebrate the fact that juniors don't have to take gym. She didn't say, *Unholy union, Batman,* when Steve and Tina eloped over Labor Day.

Park had written her a letter all about it. He'd told her everything that happened, and everything that didn't, every day since she'd left.

He kept writing her letters months after he stopped sending them. On New Year's Day, he wrote that he hoped she'd get everything she ever wished for. Then he tossed the letter into a box under his bed.

57

park

He'd stopped trying to bring her back.

She only came back when she felt like it, anyway, in dreams and lies and broken-down déjà vu.

Like, Park would be driving to work and he'd see a girl with red hair standing on the street, and he'd swear for half an airless moment that it was her.

Or he'd wake up when it was still dark, sure that she was waiting for him outside. Sure that she needed him.

But he couldn't summon her. Sometimes he couldn't even remember what she looked like, even when he was looking at her picture. (Maybe he'd looked at it too much.)

He'd stopped trying to bring her back.

So why did he keep coming here? To this crappy little house . . .

Eleanor wasn't here, she was never really here—and she'd been gone too long. Almost a year now.

Park turned to walk away from the house, but the little brown truck whipped too fast into the driveway, jumping the curb and nearly clipping him. Park stopped on the sidewalk and waited. The driver's-side door swung open.

Maybe, he thought. *Maybe this is why I'm here.*

Eleanor's stepdad—Richie—leaned slowly out of the cab. Park recognized him from the one time he'd seen him before, when Park had brought Eleanor the second issue of *Watchmen,* and her stepdad had answered the door. . . .

The final issue of *Watchmen* came out a few months after Eleanor left. He wondered if she'd read it, and whether she thought Ozymandias was a villain, and what she thought Dr. Manhattan meant when he said, "Nothing ever ends," at the end. Park still wondered what Eleanor thought about everything.

Her stepdad didn't see Park at first. Richie was moving slowly, uncertainly. When he did notice Park, he looked at him like he wasn't sure he was really there. "Who are you?" Richie shouted.

Park didn't answer. Richie turned jaggedly, jerking toward him. "What do you want?" Even from a few feet away, he smelled sour. Like beer, like basements.

Park stood his ground.

I want to kill you, he thought. *And I can,* he realized. *I should.*

Richie wasn't much bigger than Park, and he was drunk and disoriented. Plus, he could never want to hurt Park as much as Park wanted to hurt him.

Unless Richie was armed, unless he got lucky—Park could do this.

Richie shuffled closer. "What do you want?" he shouted again. The force of his own voice knocked him off balance and he tipped forward, falling thickly to the ground. Park had to step back not to catch him.

"Fuck," Richie said, raising himself up on his knees and holding himself not quite steady.

I want to kill you, Park thought.

And I can.

Someone should.

Park looked down at his steel-toe Docs. He'd just bought them at work. (On sale, with his employee discount.) He looked at Richie's head, hanging from his neck like a leather bag.

Park hated him more than he thought it was possible to hate someone. More than he'd ever thought it was possible to feel anything . . .

Almost.

He lifted his boot and kicked the ground in front of Richie's face. Ice and mud and driveway slopped into the older man's open mouth. Richie coughed violently and banked into the ground.

Park waited for him to get up, but Richie just lay there, spitting curses and rubbing salt and gravel into his eyes.

He wasn't dead. But he wasn't getting up.

Park waited.

And then he walked home.

eleanor

Letters, postcards, yellow padded packages that rattled in her hands. None of them opened, none of them read.

It was bad when the letters came every day. It was worse when they stopped.

Sometimes she laid them out on the carpet like tarot cards, like Wonka Bars, and wondered whether it was too late.

58

park

Eleanor didn't go to prom with him.

Cat did.

Cat from work. She was thin and dark, and her eyes were as blue and flat as breath mints. When Park held Cat's hand, it was like holding hands with a mannequin, and it was such a relief that he kissed her. He fell asleep on prom night in his tuxedo pants and a Fugazi T-shirt.

He woke up the next morning when something light fell on his shirt—he opened his eyes. His dad was standing over him.

"Mail call," his dad said, almost gently. Park put his hand to his heart.

Eleanor hadn't written him a letter.

It was a postcard. GREETINGS FROM THE LAND OF 10,000 LAKES it said on the front. Park turned it over and recognized her scratchy handwriting. It filled his head with song lyrics.

He sat up. He smiled. Something heavy and winged took off from his chest.

Eleanor hadn't written him a letter, it was a postcard.

Just three words long.

acknowledgments

I would like to thank some of the people who made this book possible for me—and who made me possible for this book:

First, to Colleen Eickelman, who insisted that I pass the eighth grade.

And to the Bent and Huntley families, who kept me alive with kindness.

To my brother Forest, who promises that he isn't saying things just because I'm his sister.

To Nicola Barr, Sara O'Keefe, and Natalie Braine for being so fierce and so certain, for making the Atlantic Ocean disappear, and, most of all, for looking out for Eleanor.

Thank you, while I'm at it, to everyone at Orion and St. Martin's Press.

Thank you especially to the lovely and insightful Sara Goodman, whom I trusted implicitly as soon as she sat down next to me on the bus.

To my dear friend Christopher Schelling, the best-case scenario.

And finally, I would like to thank Kai, Laddie, and Rosey for their love and their patience. (You're my all-time favorites.)